HIDE

JAKE CROSS

ALSO BY JAKE CROSS

Betrayed

To the family. Always there. And the waistline. Gone for good.

PART I

Fifteen minutes before they tried to kill him, the four men were sitting in a stolen car in a walled car park behind the shops that faced the market square. The only other vehicles present were a minibus with 'Wandering flame' printed on the side and a plain Volkswagen van beside it. Nobody else around. It felt like late at night, even though it was early evening and just starting to get dark. Three of the men lifted heavy satchels from the boot and slung them over their shoulders, and then all four headed for the back wall, where there was an archway and a sign that said 'Barkelow Funicular'. Beyond the wall they could see the promontory on which sat the great castellated manor house, Barkelow Hall, a hundred metres above them.

The archway led into a small courtyard with an illuminated water feature in the centre, a small garden on the right and a row of five shuttered shops on the left, all closed because they were owned by out-of-towners – no need to worry about those people. On the far side was the inclined elevator, a fenced square platform fifteen feet wide that ran up twin tracks cut into the hill.

Sitting in a booth at the bottom was a guy in his late fifties wearing grubby jeans and a woollen coat the same gingery shade as his thick beard. He came out as he saw the four men approaching. Gave a bemused look at the large satchels.

Three of the men were in their late fifties also. The one walking slightly ahead of the others, and who carried no satchel, was the leader. He had the cartoon-like name of Bradan Brogan. He had grey hair that stood up in gelled spikes, a look that was far too young for him and made the top of his head look like a sea mine. Thick crows' feet around his eyes suggested he smiled a lot, or didn't like bright sunlight. In the right light, he was probably handsome.

'Party?' the lift operator said. He eyed all four men warily, as if they wore karategi rather than tuxedoes under waxed jackets.

'Sure thing,' Bradan said. His accent was Irish. 'The show started yet?'

The operator shook his head and turned away. Customer service world champion, this guy. He opened a gate in the lift and stepped back. When his guests were aboard, he entered and moved to a control panel. Its complexity consisted of a single stop/start button and a small lever. 'Hold on,' he said. He took hold of the rail.

The leader also grabbed the rail, as did two others. The fourth, a twenty-year-old called Cathal McGuire, who had a plaster on his face to cover a tattoo just below his left eye, didn't bother. 'Hang on? It's not a rollercoaster, mate,' he said. He folded his arms, making a point, as if to say *Bring it on*.

The operator worked the lever, jabbed the button. A motor whined. The winch made a sound like it was on its last legs. The whole lift vibrated, then jerked as if rammed by a rhino as it started to climb. Each man locked to the rail felt his arm wrench with the violent movement. Cathal stumbled and went on his arse on the steel floor. His comrades laughed at him.

The operator just gave a sly grin, as if to announce *Guess I brought it on.* 'Sorry about that,' he said, but the way he continued to grin said he wasn't sorry at all. 'So, what's in the bags, guys? Not really party uniform, is it?'

'We're camping tonight,' said Bradan, and his team nodded. 'Team building thing. We've known each other ages, but the bosses think we need it. You know how bosses can be.'

The operator nodded. 'And they gave you everything you need, eh? One tin of beans, two toilet rolls, three bottles of vodka.'

Everyone laughed.

'Camping, but with no tent?'

Silence for a moment. Then: 'That's in the car, if you must ask,' said Cathal.

'Couldn't leave the bags in the car?'

'No room.'

'But there was room to bring them here in the car?'

'They went on the roof. Get nicked if we leave them there while we're at the party.'

Bradan wanted to step in here and change the subject, but thankfully the operator just nodded and started fiddling with his wristwatch. Cathal glared at him but said no more. The ensuing silence screamed tension.

As the lift climbed the steep hill, Bradan moved away from his men and stood at the open side and looked out at the lights in nearby towns and villages, nothing more than a sprinkling out there in a sea of obsidian. A far cry from the supernova of cityscapes.

Barkelow itself was spread out before him. Barely 500 metres from end to end, it sat in a valley overlooked by open land across the way, to the west, where three farms sat atop the ridge maybe 400 metres away, and bookended by trees at each end of the road that cut through the village from north to south. Down in the centre of the valley was a market square with shops on one side. There was a forgotten patch of land to his left, where there had once been a housing estate, and to his right the new housing estate. Apart from the housing estate and the few shops, Barkelow had nothing. It was an oasis in a desert, a tiny fragment of civilisation cut off from the remainder.

Perfect.

His men huddled and whispered, and they seemed unaware of the eyes of the lift operator covertly watching them. But Bradan could almost feel them as a physical weight. The man did not trust them, that much was certain. Too many questions, and returned answers that didn't stack up. He hoped it was just a local man's suspicion of strangers.

He heard the operator step up beside him. 'I'm supposed to give you a brief history of the house as we ride up.' He sounded bored. 'The house as you'll see it was designed by the architect James Cooke in 1749, but Barkelow Hall was originally built between 1482 and 1501 by Thomas Lewis, with licence to fortify by the grace of God and... King... of...'

Towards the end he slowed his words, deepened his voice, hung his head, and then stopped, like a robot running out of juice. He reached into his jacket and extracted a leaflet, which he held out for Bradan. 'I could continue, but I'm bored stiff by repetition. The info is all in there, and I'll bless you and yours if you don't tell my guv'nor I'm handing these out instead.'

Bradan took the leaflet with a smile. 'Your history's good for a lift attendant.'

'Thanks,' the operator said. 'But I'm more of a handyman. So, where you guys from?'

'Your history's good for a handyman.'

The handyman shrugged. 'Part of the job. And you pick stuff up over the years. So, where was it you're from?'

And suddenly the boredom was gone from the handyman's

tone. Bradan felt the old fellow was a little *too* interested in where they were from.

Without turning from the rail and the view, Bradan said, 'Originally Ireland, of course. But London for the last half of my life. What about you? You live here all-year round?'

'All my life,' the handyman said. 'I love the country. Couldn't live in a city like you guys. Too many people. There's only about a hundred of us here, although it can get a bit boring at times and the biggest gossip is someone spraining an ankle. The show at Barkelow Hall tonight is a nice bit of action. It's only a local attraction, though, so how did Londoners hear about it?'

He was fishing for details – but why? 'I actually think the country seems great,' Bradan said, changing the subject. 'Your job, too. Outdoors, peaceful, good view, and necessary for getting people up the hill.'

The handyman turned to his control panel and spoke loudly. 'I heard about some roadworks down in London this morning. They closed a couple of major roads. Didn't cause you a problem getting out, did it?'

Nobody spoke. Cathal glared at the man. The others, Bradan's long-time friends Fergal Dempsey and Denis Mulrennan, turned their heads towards the hill. Bradan watched the man as he pretended to fiddle with the control panel. He had no doubt the handyman knew they couldn't answer questions about road closures in London – because they hadn't been there.

They had arrived at the top.

'End of chat, I guess. We'll chat on the way down,' the handyman said as the lift approached a concrete platform at the top. 'Get ready. Hold on tight!' All four guys grabbed the rail this time, but only Cathal used both hands. The lift ground to a quick halt, but softly, clicking into place nice and sweet. The handyman laughed. 'Fooled ya.'

'Comedian,' Cathal said.

The handyman stepped out first. He pointed at the manor house, as if they could miss it. It was about sixty metres away at the end of a wide concrete path between twin high hedges hung with lanterns, and it was illuminated like a rocket launch with ground-based pink spotlights aimed upwards.

'You just wait around here, then?' Bradan said.

The handyman nodded. 'Tedious, like I said.' He then pointed at a button on a post. 'Use this to call me back up when you leave.'

Then he got back in the lift and worked the controls. This time he didn't hold the rail, but shifted his balance just as the lift jerked and he barely rocked as it started its journey down the track. He watched them and they watched him for a few seconds. Then the four men moved along the path, towards the house.

'That arsehole,' Cathal said. 'He suspects something, you know?'

'I know,' Bradan said. 'Don't fret it. Nothing he can do, stuck on that lift. And he'll be out of the way soon.'

'I'll sort him out, don't you worry your little head, Cathy,' Fergal said.

Cathal grunted. He hated being called Cathy, and everyone damn well knew it. 'I know you said we kill only the ones we need to, Bradan, but he's one we need to.'

Everyone was looking at Bradan. Without looking at any of them, he nodded.

2

___

The more peaceful climate of the fifteenth century saw the gentry start to reject the idea of fortified residences and turn towards homes offering more comfort, although the fortress still promoted a sense of bloated status, so many of the first mansions retained the hallmarks of castles. Barkelow Hall, set behind grass lawns, was one such, with turrets on all four corners that stood four metres higher than the rest of the house, almost giving the square building the look of an upside-down brick table.

Most of the other fortifications applied by the original builder had been erased during the building's 18th century makeover, although part of the moat had been retained at the front of the house, like a rectangular pond. Lights under the surface tinted the water whatever colour the owners liked at any time, which was pink tonight to match the spotlights pointing up at the house.

The gatehouse had a bridge in the design of a drawbridge, although it was fixed to the ground and there existed no mechanism for raising it. Six-foot walls ran away from each front corner of the house. Past them were the gardens, which tumbled away in convoluted terraces and terminated at a high wall of trees at the edge of the great hill's eastern side. Out front, though, the lawns were flat and bare, with just the odd water feature or wooden bench. Bradan could see that nobody was around apart from two security guards in high-vis jackets over black suits. They sat behind a cheap foldaway table at the foot of the bridge. On the table was a stack of papers and bottles of bubbly and plastic glasses. Security-cum-receptionists.

'Camping out tonight, fellas?' said one of them as Bradan and his team approached. He nodded at their backpacks.

'All the essentials for a night under the stars,' Bradan said. 'One tin of beans, two toilet rolls, three bottles of vodka.'

The other high-vis guy started pouring four glasses of bubbly. The first, with a decent crack at a genuine smile, held out his hand. 'Just need those invites of yours.'

'Sure thing. Got me one of those special ones that gets me in anywhere,' Bradan said. He pulled his pistol out of his jacket and held it in his palm like an offering. The high-vis guy almost took it, but stopped short, and looked at Bradan with his eyebrows creased in puzzlement. Then both high-vis guys looked at each other, not sure if this was a joke or not. Guests in tuxedoes pulling guns?

Bradan fired. No haste, no doubt in his aim or his weapon. And no overkill. One shot to a forehead, a slight turn left, and another shot in the same zone. The security guards went sprawling over their chairs, landing hard and bloody near the edge of the moat. The weapon was suppressed, but what little sound there was echoed softly off the hall and raced away across the land.

The other three men in suits moved quickly. Fergal handed Bradan his bag and started walking back the way they'd come; Denis rushed across the bridge; Cathal whipped out cable ties and bound the two dead men together at the wrist.

Denis, at the door, opened it and peered in and then gave a thumbs-up and rushed back to help Cathal roll the two security guards into the water. Bradan drained his glass of bubbly and watched the two dead guys sink.

'Should have taken off their jackets,' he said. The lights in the water made their jackets glow even from the bottom. 'Let's get inside.'

He started across the bridge with Denis, but Cathal didn't move.

'You promised me one, Bradan,' Cathal said.

Denis laughed. Without breaking stride or looking back, Bradan pointed at the water. 'They were still alive when you rolled them in. So technically you killed them. And two for the price of one.'

'Let me do the lift man.'

Cathal's comrades stopped and turned to look at him, including Fergal, who had heard despite being some distance away. When Bradan made no immediate response, Fergal cursed and started walking back, annoyed.

On the same page, Denis threw up his hands. 'No way, Bradan. Give him a stray dog or something. He'll arse this up.'

'Better out here than in there,' Bradan told Denis. 'Okay, Cathal, Christmas has come early. But be quick about it, and no games. And this is your one and only.'

Cathal dumped his bag and pocketed his gun and straightened his suit and jogged away, happy as sin. Fergal sneered at him as they passed each other.

'What, I'm not capable?' Fergal moaned as he returned and picked up Cathal's bag.

'Risky letting that fool have his way,' Denis said.

'It'll stop him sulking,' Bradan said. 'I'm still trying to find something that'll work on you two girls. Can we go inside and do some shooting now, please?'

~

Cathal got back to the lift and pressed the CALL LIFT button. Down below, he saw the handyman come out of his booth and look up, and he saw the shoulders drop as the old idiot realised who'd called him. Cathal waved, like a good friend.

The handyman took his time, but finally the lift made a thudding movement that Cathal felt even on the upper platform and started to rise. Cathal looked out over the village as it did so, and at the three farmhouses up on the far hill. He waved at the one on the far right, although he knew he'd see no return wave at this distance.

The lift arrived. The handyman was leaning against the back rail, arms folded, looking annoyed. 'That was quick. Did they kick you out?'

'Nope. Something I need to take care of, that's all.' Cathal stepped onto the lift, and stood in the middle, also with his arms folded. Like a challenge: *try that shit again.*

The guy hit the button. The lift jerked into life. The handyman rocked with it, and remained standing. Cathal tried the same, sure he'd have it this time. He did better, but ended up stumbling like a drunk, and in a way that was worse than falling on his arse.

'It took me a long time in this job to master the balance,' the handyman said. 'Don't be too embarrassed.'

Cathal couldn't tell if there was sarcasm there or not. It didn't matter. The guy had what was coming regardless, even if he now got on his knees and apologised. 'I'm sure you won't be doing this job for much longer,' he said, and smiled at his own joke.

The handyman gave him a look. It said he didn't trust that statement, as if he'd read between the lines. But a moment later he gave Cathal his back. He put his hands on the rail and stared out at nothing. Cathal knew there was no way a guy who suspected anything would turn away from him.

They were halfway down the hill, at its darkest point. Above, no one. Below, no one. Out there in the hills and faraway villages, no one who could see anything at such a distance. It was perfect. He would have called it fate, if he'd believed in such a thing.

He reached into his jacket, where he had a shoulder strap containing his pistol. But what he wanted was the item slotted into a sheath attached to that holster. It was a *kiridashi*, which looked like a knife whose handle had come away from the tang. A birthday present from his father when he was twelve and first showed an interest in hunting small animals. From barfights to alleyway muggings, it had spilled a lot of blood. Over four generations, according to his dad.

He pulled the knife, and held it low down by his side, and stepped towards the unsuspecting handyman.

The gatehouse had been transformed into an entrance hall painted a dull gold colour. Ahead were vast double doors in an archway, beyond which a visitor to a medieval manor would normally find a central courtyard, but here at Barkelow Hall, a cube-like structure, the vast middle space was a ballroom with a brick and timber roof.

In the left wall of the entrance hall, either side of an alcove with a large wooden sculpture of an eagle, was a staircase and a low-ceilinged corridor leading to the many rooms arranged around the ballroom. In the right wall was a reception room that had been turned into a security office, and beside it another tunnel-like corridor. The renovations to the entrance hall were meant to retain an aura of age, but this effect was ruined by a surveillance camera on the wall above the ballroom doors and a large fire evacuation procedure board pinned up next to the security office.

The door to the security room was open and Bradan could see a bank of monitors showing CCTV feed behind a black-suited man facing them across a desk. He looked up at Bradan and his team and then back down at whatever he was doing.

Partway down the corridor on the left were two people staring at a painting. Bradan could hear the low murmur of voices from somewhere around a corner deep down the other corridor. A tourist with a camera around his neck came clumping down the carpeted staircase and pushed open one of the big doors to the ballroom. In the moments it was open, they heard the hubbub of many chatting voices. People everywhere. This first part needed to be done quietly.

'Who are you?' the black-suited man said as Bradan walked into the security office. Bradan said nothing.

Fergal and Denis entered behind him. Fergal shut the door and all three men stood before the security man. He took in their attire, puzzled.

'Are you guys my guys? I didn't know about extra men.'

Bradan said, 'The boss isn't happy.'

The security guy pulled his radio, now suspicious.

Bradan pulled an envelope from inside his jacket, said, 'Call your men. Get them here in this office.'

'What's this about?'

Bradan waved the envelope. 'The boss is unhappy. Call them.'

The black-suited man got on his radio. 'Chaps, Carl here. I need you back in the office in one minute.'

Three voices confirmed. Carl seemed to wait for others. But Bradan said, 'Don't bother waiting for the two out front. Not able to make it. Unless they're zombies.'

The security guy opened his mouth to speak, and Bradan yanked out his pistol and shot him in the forehead. He dropped hard and his head bounced off the stone floor with a thud that made Bradan wince, as if a person with a bullet hole in his face was going to care about a whack to the dome. Denis grabbed the feet and dragged the body through a doorway in the back wall. Blood from the dead man's head wound left a thick trail behind.

'Should have dragged his hands, then his jacket would wipe the blood away,' Fergal said.

'I thought you'd want to lick it up,' Denis called out from the back room, which was a former ladies' room that was now storage for office supplies. He laid the body in a corner and returned with the guy's jacket, which he used to start wiping up the slick mess on the floor. 'Looks like the jacket is getting the blood after all.'

Fergal took a small laptop from where it had been strapped to his back under his jacket and laid it on the desk. Bradan stacked their bags against a wall after extracting a black box the size of an old DVD player, which went on top of a filing cabinet. All three men tossed their waxed jackets in the corner, too.

A minute later there was a knock on the door. Fergal sat behind the desk while Denis disappeared into the storage room. Bradan opened the door and saw a man in a suit standing there. Security guy. Beyond him, another appeared from the stairway. Bradan told the second guy to wait and pointed at the first. 'Joseph Parker, we'll take you first.'

Parker came in, saw Fergal behind the desk and gave a nod of greeting. Bradan pointed to the storage room. 'In there, please.'

In he went, no questions. They heard nothing but the scuffle of feet and heavy breathing, and sixty seconds later Denis poked his head round and gave a thumbs-up. A garrotte dangled from his fist.

Bradan opened the door. The third man called had now arrived. So now they had all six of the security guys Anderson had brought to help him carry off his theatre show against the revolt of local bumpkins.

Guy three was told to wait as number two was shown in, and shown the storage room. This time there was more noise, and a loud smack, and grunting, but soon Denis appeared at the doorway again, wiping blood from his nose. Fergal laughed at him. Denis gave him the finger.

Guy three guy entered with trepidation, not puzzlement, as if he feared he was here for a reprimand. Sensing this, Bradan sat on the edge of the desk and shook his head slowly. 'Mr Strong, that was very naughty of you.'

The guy's mouth moved, but no words came.

'Did you think we would not find out?'

Strong was young, fresh-faced, and didn't look comfortable in a suit. Or in this room. He looked ready to burst into tears. Bradan almost felt sorry for him.

Almost. 'In there, please.'

He went. Fergal followed this time. Bradan heard Denis say, 'I don't need your help, Fergal.'

There was a loud scuffle. Too loud. Fergal said something that sounded like *...help now, don't you?* and Bradan got concerned. It sounded like fresh-faced Strong by name was also strong by nature. He was tempted to help, but instead cracked the main door and peered out to make sure nobody was around to hear the commotion.

Denis appeared thirty seconds later, laughing, and behind him came Fergal holding a hand over his ear. Fergal cursed at him. Denis cursed back. They started arguing. Bradan slapped the table to silence them.

'Stop playing around and get to it,' he said.

Denis sat behind the desk. He took a Post-it note from his

pocket and laid it flat on the wood. Slid it an inch to the left. Slid the laptop two inches closer. He moved the chair into a more comfortable position, and shifted the phone a few centimetres, and then adjusted his chair again.

'You ever get diagnosed with OCD?' Fergal said.

'Missed the appointment because I was checking the windows were locked. Now let the master work, my friend.'

Finally ready, he lifted the phone and jabbed in the number written on the note.

'This is building eighteen,' he said when someone answered. 'We need a twenty-minute window to perform a fire drill. The password is *river.*' He listened for a few moments, thanked whoever he was talking to, and hung up.

Bradan nodded at Fergal, who moved to a fire panel on the wall. He made a pretence of standing before the panel and taking deep breaths, flexing his fingers, and doing the sign of the cross.

'Stop messing about, Fergal,' Bradan said.

'Let the master work.' Fergal broke open the panel with a penknife. He turned a key, pressed a red button marked TEST, and immediately an alarm wailed from numerous sources throughout the building.

'Let's herd some sheep,' Bradan said.

3

____

It *was* like herding sheep, because everyone who entered Barkelow Hall couldn't help but see the fire procedure poster and the large words MEETING POINT scrawled across the illustration of the front lawn. So many of them, upon hearing the alarm and a voice-over instructing them to head for the nearest exit, aimed for the front door. And when they got there, they found the door shut and Bradan standing before it like a sentry.

'Don't be alarmed, it might be a false alarm,' he told the first arrivals, a young couple in jeans and matching blue pullovers. He'd seen a picture of this couple during his research into Barkelow. Couldn't remember the name, but knew they lived at the new housing estate called Woodlands. They ran some internet shoe sales company. 'But you can't get out this way. Make your way towards the ballroom, please.'

Without argument, back they went in a half-walk, half-run. Others came. Some looked annoyed that their night was being messed with, but others seemed to find the episode a welcome piece of fun. He ushered them away. One lady who'd gotten split from her husband, another Woodlands pair, pulled her mobile and tried to call the fire brigade, right in front of Bradan.

'No signal,' he said. 'Fire destroys radio signals, didn't you know? Now get going.'

Next was a roadie for the theatre company putting on tonight's show. He was a big chap, looked like he could handle himself, but he stood before Bradan with fear in his eyes. Maybe he'd been burned as a child. He didn't like the idea of giving up the front entrance, right there, ten feet away, and traipsing back through a building whose flaming roof might come down on his nose.

'I'm supposed to let no one out this way,' Bradan told him. 'I'd have to email my boss to see if it's okay to let you past.'

The guy tried to lunge past, so Bradan pushed him back and pulled his gun just far enough out of his jacket so the guy could see it. 'I got a disciplinary last time.'

The guy fled.

Elsewhere, Denis and Fergal ran about the house like kids playing hide and seek. No calm professionalism for them. They screamed *Evacuate* and *Fire* and *Back terrace, now, run!* Three floors, dozens of rooms, but the people who ran the place had locked up most of the places they didn't want guests sticking their noses into. Six separate staircases meant eventually everyone upstairs ended up downstairs and everyone downstairs in due course got routed where they were supposed to be.

Although the house was big, noise carried well. Bradan could hear voices from within its depths, even over the alarm, as his men rounded everyone up and herded them towards the back. Soon those voices faded, and then there was nothing but the alarm, and then silence after he returned to the security office and shut it off. Beautiful silence. He looked out into the front lawn, just to make sure there was nobody at that evacuation meeting point. There wasn't. So nobody had somehow slipped out of a side door somewhere.

He strolled through the ground floor of the house slowly, peeking down corridors, into alcoves, into rooms, checking for loose souls. Sometimes, he knew, the brain went into panic mode and dumped logic. But he found no blubbering wrecks curled up in corners. Eventually he made his way to the great ballroom. There was a performance stage on one side and on the other a set of tables loaded with party food, but the only people present were Fergal and Denis. They were at the back, before a long series of windows, staring out.

Bradan approached and looked also. He saw people on the lamp-lit stone terrace outside, and loitering on the dim grass tennis court at the bottom of the stone steps. At least sixty people, all now trapped. The court was walled and the gate had been electronically locked by Denis from the security office to prevent people getting into the gardens.

The people hung about in little groups and chatted. Some seemed distressed, but most appeared to be treating the evacuation as nothing more than a mild inconvenience. Then Bradan noticed the roadie from earlier. He was at the gate, trying to bust the lock.

'I found a couple groping each other in a bathroom,' Fergal said with a grin. He pointed at them through the window.

Bradan didn't look. He pulled his radio and dialled Cathal's channel. 'House secure. Cathal, put that guy's spleen down and secure the lift and come back now.'

He didn't wait for an answer. The doorway onto the terrace was blocked by a fat guest who'd escaped with his buffet plate. Bradan bumped him out of the way when he opened the door, then all three men started ushering people off the terrace, down the steps and onto the tennis court. Everyone went willingly. They broke into their groups. Of the sixty or so, a handful were non-locals who'd heard about the show and popped along. Bradan also saw the show's producer and his wife, and the three actors who performed in every play the theatre company hosted, and a few more hired hands. The actors, two men and a woman, were down there now, surrounded by people, and dressed in garb from ancient Greece. Nobody seemed to mind the interruption, because the show wasn't due to start for another hour and clearly there was no real fire.

Bradan stood at the top of the steps, lit by lamps arranged around the three walls behind him, and watched the people watching him. Those who weren't looking at him were looking at mobile phones. One lady even had a tablet on a strap on her wrist, like a giant cartoon watch. He gave a nod and his two men yanked their guns, and the screaming started. A bullet sent into the night air calmed things.

Fergal started counting people. Bradan addressed them. 'You won't get a phone signal, ladies and gentlemen, and not because we're in a remote location. eBay phone jammers, two hundred quid each, post and packing included. I'll sell them on later if you promise to give me good seller feedback. There is no land-line coverage, either. You're all trapped here. This is one of those hostage situations you've seen in films. You're the hostages, and we're the kidnappers. But don't get your hopes up because of how those films end. There will be no SAS team rappelling from helicopters to save you, and there's no lone wolf hero out there coming to save you. In this production, the scriptwriter – me – doesn't have to worry about PC endings, so heroes get shot in the face.'

The landline part was bullshit, but here in the manor there were three phones and they'd already destroyed each one.

Fergal whispered in Bradan's ear: 'Fifty-one ticket holders, but I count forty-seven. We've got four non-shows. Let's hope

Paul can control his team at the houses. And I told you it was too cheesy to do that movie analogy.'

'I don't see anyone rolling their eyes at–'

Just then there was a commotion amongst the people at the back. People turned to see. There was a guy climbing the gate. Not the roadie, but some guy in a white shirt.

The people parted as Bradan walked amongst them, towards the guy. He grabbed a foot and yanked the guy off. The guy landed hard, but got up unhurt. He was an out-of-towner.

'Needed a piss,' he slurred, clearly drunk. And then he laughed.

'No,' Bradan said, 'you were going to climb the gate and come around and take me and my men out and save everyone. I said no lone wolf would come to the rescue, and here you're trying to embarrass me. I also made a promise about heroes, didn't I?'

And he raised his gun and fired. As promised: right in the face. People screamed and backed away, against the other walls. But nobody else tried anything. Successful example made.

Bradan made his way back into the ballroom and shut the door for some quiet. He called Cathal, but again got no answer. Where the hell was he? His job had been to kill the handyman and then lock the lift at the top of the hill and come back, and that shouldn't have taken this long. Not even for a dickhead. Bradan called Paul Ó Caiside, but Paul hadn't heard from Cathal.

Denis entered the ballroom, eyebrows raised. 'Cathal?'

Bradan shook his head. 'Get Fergal to get those people back in here. And then go check on that little shit for me.'

Denis jogged to the lift, but found it gone. He stood at the edge of the platform and peered down, and there it was at the bottom. No one aboard, and no one in the handyman's booth, either. He looked to the right, over at the housing estate, Woodlands, whose streets were empty. Down and ahead, at the car park and the market square, and between them the curve of shops that looked like giant smiling lips. To the left, at the large patch of wasteland that nobody had touched in the years since the demolition of the housing estate that had once stood there. And further ahead, at the three farms up on the rise. Nowhere did he see human movement, which was according to plan.

But where the hell was Cathal? Fergal had been instructed to kill the guy right here at the top and carry him into the undergrowth, but of course Cathal had snatched away that task and been given no instructions. So he had probably stepped onto the lift and formulated a plan while it was riding down, and then suddenly found himself at the bottom with a body. Bradan should have thought about that. He should have instructed Cathal on what exactly to do.

Had Cathal decided to carry the body somewhere remote? Cautious, but wasting time.

He pulled his radio. Channel two. 'Cathal?'

No answer again. Dropped radio? Busted in the attack?

He knew he would have to go down. There was a thin set of steps alongside the track, but he didn't fancy them in the dark and with the wind blowing, especially if they were slick with the morning's rain.

Denis scrutinised the post with the call button. There was a button below that one under a glass cover, and he pushed it, and from far below heard the lift whir into action. He felt the vibration of its violent start even way up here. So, a button for automatically calling the lift.

When it arrived, he jumped on and set it going down. He

looked around the floor for evidence of a fight. Nothing. No blood. It was as if both men had simply vanished.

He leaned against the rail and stared out over the dark land, and breathed slowly, and tried not to think about the fact that this delay was playing with their timetable, and just beyond the halfway mark he heard a heavy snap from beneath the lift.

He went to the back and looked, sure that a log had fallen into the tracks somehow and been broken.

Blacker than the darkness surrounding it, the shape that emerged from under the lift wasn't a log. He stopped the lift and climbed the fence and dropped onto the steep track, which also had steps. Grabbing the winch cable to avoid slipping, he climbed towards the object that had passed under the lift.

He plucked a pen from his pocket and broke it apart and pulled the spring into a long wire, and fed one end through a hole in the tang of Cathal's weird knife. He wrapped both ends of the wire ends around a finger to create a garrotte and pulled.

With a sickly squeal of bone the weapon slipped out of Cathal's forehead.

Careful not to touch the weapon's tang, he slipped it into his pocket. Quickly he climbed back aboard the lift and pulled his radio and turned away from Cathal's battered body, whose back was twisted unnaturally where the spine had snapped as he was rolled and dragged by the heavy lift. Denis pressed the button to move the lift back up the slope, and tried not to listen out for more snapping bone noises as it again rode over Cathal's corpse.

'Bradan,' he said into the radio.

'You found him,' Bradan came back. Not a question, because he'd read the dullness in Denis's tone.

'Dead with his own knife sticking out of his head.'

He heard a wheeze of exasperation. 'Please tell me that handyman is lying dead next to him.'

'No, Bradan, he isn't. He's gone. I'm barely surprised. The

anger was pulsating out of that kid so bad, he might as well have carried a sign saying *I'm going to kill you.*'

After a pause, Bradan said, 'Now I feel silly. I stood in front of all those hostages and told them there was no lone wolf hero running about. So where the hell is this handyman?'

Denis looked out at the village. And beyond, at the world. 'He could be anywhere. Running like a madman for the nearest cop shop. And if he gets there it's game over.'

'Warn our people, especially Jack and George, because he might go their way. But we don't want them panicking, so make out our lone wolf is a... a homeless guy sleeping rough that we could do with capturing. Avoid any hint that he's comfortable with sticking knives in heads.'

'And if they find him?'

'We've got enough hostages already.'

4

Emil Torrance didn't know how they'd found him, but they had, and it was time to run again.

He'd always known that creating a new life somewhere would make it harder to uproot if they came for him, and he was angry that they'd waited until he was settled and happy. But what other choice had he had? Live on the move, never making friends, never really feeling at home? And he had to focus on the positive, which was that at least he had the option of running. A quarter century of peaceful stability had eroded caution and he'd long stopped looking over his shoulder. They could have killed him before he knew it.

He heard the first creak from the ground under his weight and stopped.

He shifted direction and continued crawling forward on his belly, stopping every few seconds to kick his legs and try to raise some of the grass he'd flattened. He did not want to leave a visible trail.

He turned onto his back and stared up at the promontory that seemed to loom over him. And froze as he saw a tiny dot of a man up on the platform at the top, exposed in the lights from the manor house. Another one of the four men he had escorted up the hill earlier. One man looking for the missing other one. He waited for the guy to point, waited for a tiny shout of *There he is*. But then he heard the faint rumble of the lift climbing the hill. The man had called it. Emil knew he didn't have long. The dead man was wearing black and hidden in the dark, but his body would surely be spotted by someone riding the lift down. Then a general alarm would go out. And Emil had no idea how many of the enemy were scattered around Barkelow.

Despite his urgency, Emil couldn't risk moving again while his enemy held elevated ground. He waited until the lift had started to ride down with its passenger, and once it sank out of sight beyond the tall grass, he crawled on. He found the marker he'd left, just a twig sticking out of the ground, and dug his hands in the earth, and crawled backwards and dragged a soil-covered wooden board with him, to expose the jet-black hole it had covered. He stuck an arm into the hole and turned on the small torch he had on his house keys.

The beam lit up the metal ladder he had placed here many years ago. It was hooked over the edge of the hole, but the bottom swung free where last time it had been planted in the earth. So the ground had shifted and sunken somewhat since he had last been here.

His visits had always been after dark, when the world around was silent and empty. Crawling like an insect, because the last thing he wanted was a local seeing him and wondering and, after he'd gone, venturing out here and falling into one of the old cellars from the long-gone houses. Or worse – finding the item he'd hidden.

The beam of the torch now found that item, right where he'd left it. Wrapped in plastic and sitting in a small tin bath. His satchel.

It was packed with everything he'd need if ever the day came when he had to abandon his life. Over the years, he'd periodically visited this old cellar to clean the gun, to change the clothing. He'd put a lot of weight on over the years and had even had to get fresh fake passports with a photo that resembled the new, older Emil. Every time, he came and repacked it and hoped he'd never need it. Now he needed it.

He moved quickly down the ladder, which swung and creaked under his weight but held. He splashed through water from that morning's rain that filled holes and hollows on the ground. He tore open the plastic wrapper and opened the satchel to check the gun. At first, years back, when the threat had been forefront in his mind, he'd maintained this weapon once a month, but complacency had bred laziness and he hadn't checked it in half a year. Thankfully, it was still in good condition. He slung the satchel on his back and climbed the ladder. He slid the board back in place and crawled back the way he had come.

At the edge of the waste ground, he paused, looking for life. Nothing. Ahead was a small car park for the shops and beyond it the fenced back gardens of the establishments. An alleyway led between the back fences of the gardens and the wall of the big car park for Barkelow Hall. He entered the alleyway at a run, went past the first alleyway branching off to his left, and took the second. Here, shrouded in darkness, he sat on cobblestones wet from prior rain and took what he felt was his first breath in the last half an hour.

Beyond the end of the alley he could see the market square and the fields beyond. That was where he needed to be. In the country, away from roads, he could trek to another village, steal a car, and be gone forever. Time was pressing and the urge to bolt was almost undeniable.

Almost. Because first he needed to say goodbye to his son.

Emil was going to have to flee this place forever, and although he knew Pete would not leave with him, he needed to try to convince him. And if his son refused, then Emil at least needed to say goodbye. He tried not to think about the latter, though. Tried not to think that today might be the last time he ever saw him. He would worry about it when they were face to face.

He pulled his mobile, but the call to Pete's phone failed. Not even straight to voicemail – nothing. Not Pete's phone, then. His own. Maybe Pete's as well. Maybe all of them. Jammed, possibly. A village the size of Barkelow could be covered by two or three high-powered jammers, effectively cutting off everyone from the outside world. If that were the case, then this was a serious mission that Cavil had mounted to get his man. A lot of people involved. Emil knew he had to get moving, because Cavil's people might search every portion of the village. The longer he sat here, the harder escape would become, especially once word got out that the guy ordered to kill him had failed in the most miserable way.

His only choice was a bad one. The people hunting him would surely know where he lived, if their research had been good enough to find him all the way out here, but he had to go home. Home was where he would find Pete.

Standing at the end of the alley, he looked left and right, and the hairs on the back of his neck prickled. To the right, the green light in the upstairs window of Bob Jonas's shop was on. Bob never turned that light on, preferring the soft glow of firelight in the last few years since his eyes had deteriorated. A light on at night should be no big deal, but it reeked of wrongness. It said something untoward had happened in that shop. It made Emil wonder how many guys Cavil had sent after him. Surely more than the four who had faced Emil on the funicular. What else had these people been up to? Interrogating the residents for information on Emil?

He heard a whiney engine. It sounded like a quad bike. Sometimes the sound of quads and motorbikes carried across the land, when yobbos from other villages raced them in the fields. But this one was closer, slightly north, maybe from Woodlands, the housing zone. And that was where he was headed. Was the rider one of the enemy?

There was a quad parked outside Mrs Clocker's old bookshop, down to his right, building on the end. Clocker's bedroom light was on. That was normal, the quad wasn't.

Mrs Clocker was a nice lady, but a busybody, always sticking her nose into people's business. If the quad rider was a guy hunting Emil and had gone in there to ask her about him, she would spill the beans. He could be in there still, hurting her. But Emil didn't know for sure and couldn't risk going inside.

He rushed across the road, through the market square with its empty stalls, and across the road on the other side. From the field he would better see movement in the shops, and could move north unseen until he got close to Woodlands.

He tossed his satchel over the stone wall. He was lifting his leg to follow it into the field when a shout filled the air:

'Hey.'

He turned to see a young woman over by the shops, standing outside Mrs Clocker's bookshop, smoking a cigarette. Mrs Clocker had a daughter off at college, and this must be her. He'd last seen her eight or nine months ago during a visit. Since then she'd lost weight and chopped her hair and dyed it blonde, if this was her.

She came racing over. He had no time to waste, but figured she might have seen something that could help him. So he waited. She stopped in the middle of the road. She was wearing a boiler suit, which he found strange. He noted her hair was more towards white than blonde.

'Who are you, then?' she said. 'Going over the wall for piss?'

This close, ten or so metres, he could see he'd had it wrong. Not the Clocker daughter. Much younger, just a teenager. A friend of hers, or a niece or something? She had a strange foreign accent, as if a mix of more than one.

He heard another quad and cast his eyes to the left. He saw the vehicle exit the car park of the abandoned old hotel halfway up the north road, no lights on. The rider seemed to drop something as he exited onto the road and skidded to a halt to retrieve it. Emil had only seconds if he was to move now, because at that distance, with no other movements on the road, he'd be spotted easily.

He ran at the girl, saying, 'Quick, we have to hide.'

Amazingly, she was smiling, which was not what he had expected from a female being rushed at by a strange man in the dark. He grabbed her arm and yanked her. They ran through the market square, over the road, and into the open doorway of Mrs Clocker's shop. Emil shut the door and moved to the window.

'Leave the light off,' he said to the girl, who backed away through the dark room with its bookcases down each wall.

At the window, he put his head between two vases and peered out. He realised he hadn't retrieved his satchel after tossing it over the wall. At least it wouldn't be seen from the road. But he needed it back.

'What is out there?' the girl said in that jerky English of hers, no emotion. No fear. He wasn't worrying her, which was good.

'Nothing. Just stay inside here. You never saw me.'

'Someone chase you?'

The quad got closer. And then it raced past, far side of the market square. He saw the rider, saw what the guy was wearing, and his alarm bell started ringing.

'You been naughty boy?' the girl said.

Emil turned, fast, whipping his hand, releasing the vase even before he really knew where he was throwing it. The shot went wide, missing her head by a good three feet, but it made her jerk, and for a second the pistol she held pointed at him wavered, and he used that second to launch himself at her. He thrust a palm over her face, forcing her head back, and rammed his other fist hard into her solar plexus. Down she went with a grunt.

He knew he should have taken her gun, but it was too late. He yanked open the door and was running out before he'd realised it. He should also have bolted for the field again, and gotten his satchel, with his own well-oiled gun inside, but again it was too late. Behind him he heard her shouting, cursing him. He ducked down the first alley he came to and turned left at the end wall. Seconds later he was out of the alley and in the long grass that led all the way to the sloping lane between the main road and Woodlands.

He crawled halfway and lay still. He knew he'd left a trail of flattened grass, but from the road he knew he wouldn't be seen, especially at night. So he lay and thought.

How many people were after him? The quad rider had been wearing a boiler suit, just like the girl in the shop, which meant they were working together. So, six at least. But why had she been in the shop? Why were some of his pursuers wearing tuxedoes and others boiler suits?

He needed answers, but he also needed to escape. He would get neither if he stayed here. Only capture and a long prison sentence. Or a bullet, to return an old favour.

So, on he crawled, and that was when he found a murdered friend.

~

Joseph Tepper was a good mate, or had been. He lived on Emil's street, and they'd shared many beers in their sun-washed back gardens. Emil had built Tepper a shed, and Tepper had put a booming stereo system in Pete's car. Now Tepper was dead two feet away.

Emil had spotted the car in the grass, away to his right and a few metres from the road leading into Woodlands, and crawled towards it. His low angle hadn't allowed him to see inside until he was right there, but splashes of blood on the near-side rear window had prepared him for bad news. Emil opened the driver's door carefully, and hoped the interior light didn't alert anyone.

Tepper had been lying across both front seats. His face was half-gone and there was a clear bullet hole in the back of his head. He was dressed in his work outfit, which was the giveaway. He must have been driving out to work when the people here for Emil had accosted him. They'd killed him and run his car off the road and into the grass.

Now, Emil knelt by the driver's door, just two feet from Tepper's body, and considered the problem this murder posed. It had changed things, but to what degree? Emil stood and reached over the body, to take one of Tepper's hands. No cuts on the fingers. No nails pulled. No broken bones. Maybe they had pulled teeth, or beaten him about the face, but the bullet had erased any evidence of such activity.

But even if Cavil's people had grabbed and interrogated the first lone resident they came across, what could Tepper have told them? What could any of Emil's friends and neighbours have divulged about him? In a tiny community such as Barkelow, everyone knew everything, but everything about Emil was a lie. Cavil knew only of the man who'd existed all those years ago, and that man resembled no one in Barkelow.

Except that the four men at the lift had tried to kill him. They had known exactly who he was and where he was.

He felt a painful knot in his stomach. If Tepper's interrogators had been skilled enough to ask the right questions and read between the lines of the answers, then they might know everything about Emil. Including that he had a son.

Emil took deep breaths and beat back dark thoughts of armed men storming his house, and hurting Pete in order to learn Emil's whereabouts. He couldn't assume anything yet, until he knew for sure. He had no idea how many hunters there were, where they were, what they already knew. They might not know Pete existed, if Tepper had sent them directly to Barkelow Hall, or they might have captured or killed him. They might not know where Emil lived, or his house might be full of the bastards. Hell, Tepper might not have even been questioned, but killed to prevent him raising an alarm.

Emil needed answers and there were none here, next to a dead man in a dark field.

5

———

Emil crawled on, soon reaching the road leading into Woodlands. He poked his head out of the grass and surveyed the housing estate, up the hill to his right.

It lay in a sloping field of stunted grass fifty metres from the main road, like an incongruous skin graft. A shiny new stretch of tarmac leading off the main road ran past the houses on the right and continued up the hill another fifty metres before terminating at a chain-link fence. Just like that. Like a limb ending in a stump. There was nothing beyond the fence but scrubland that rose even steeper, and then the top of the hill, along which was a thick line of trees.

The estate was composed of three rows of beige brick houses separated by two streets that ran off the new road at right angles, like rungs on a ladder. Eleven houses to a row. Row two stood higher than its predecessor, sloping gardens helping to create the elevation, and row three was higher than row two. From a distance the three lines of roofs looked like a short set of giant stairs.

Emil scooted across the road, into the grass on the other side, and rushed into the shadows of the back garden fences of the first row of houses. He worked his way along to the third house, clambered over the fence, and walked across a dark garden, to the path between the two houses.

Across the street was his own house. The living room light was on, but the curtains were closed. His official address was Oak Lane, this road, but Ash Lane, on the other side of the row, was where Pete usually parked his car so he could use the back entrance. So Emil didn't know if the car was present or not. Despite being so close to home, Emil paused at the back end of the path, unwilling to risk exposure just yet. The estate seemed too quiet. He called his landline number, and Pete's mobile again, but both failed.

He jerked behind the house as a young man with a burger in his hand came out the side door of the same building. Emil didn't get a look at his face, but the boiler suit he wore was answer enough. Not the homeowner, but another of Cavil's team, which made seven enemies, minimum. The guy went out into the street and Emil heard an engine start, and saw a head-light splash across the tarmac. Moments later, a quad bike roared past and away to the left. Emil hurried down the path and carefully looked out into the street. He saw the quad take the turn and vanish. Seconds later, he heard it whiz by his position, but on the far side of the houses across the street.

The silent street unnerved him. It was early evening, but everyone knew everyone and there was always a conversation going on by someone's car or over a garden fence, or someone walking a dog. But the street was desolate, and that was just wrong. He knew that more than thirty of the housing estate's residents hadn't attended the theatre show at Barkelow Hall. So where were they?

Emil darted out of sight as the quad returned, having completed a circuit of the two streets.

He opened the side door of the house, the one the guy had

used, and got inside just as the quad zipped by. He was in a porch with a glass door that allowed him to see a living room devoid of people. The light was on, but the TV was off. He knew the owner was a single lady who'd lost her husband four years ago and didn't socialise much. She owned a business in London that she oversaw from home. He wanted to shout for her, but knew there could be other bad guys inside. Instead he paused and listened. No radio or second TV, no running shower, no sounds of a boiling kettle or footsteps, and no voices. The house was silent. She could be at the Barkelow Hall theatre show, of course, but she hadn't ridden his lift so he doubted it.

He went inside. The kitchen was dark. He climbed an open staircase onto a landing with every door wide open. Empty bathroom, empty bedrooms, all lights off. But in the illuminated main bedroom, the wardrobe had several items of women's clothing crumpled on the floor, still on their hangers, and a wet towel was nearby, and there were spots of water leading from the bathroom. He pictured a guy dragging a woman out of the bathroom in just a towel. Grabbing something from the wardrobe for her and knocking other items off the rail.

At the window, he watched his house, but saw no movement, heard no sound. But that provided no clue to anything. The house could be empty, or loaded with baddies quietly awaiting his return.

The quad reappeared, another circuit done. Maybe the young man was patrolling, looking for people, or he was riding for fun. He was drinking from a can, which he launched away as he passed Emil's position. It landed in Emil's front garden. He was very nonchalant, this fool. And that was a big clue.

Twenty seconds until the quad returned.

Emil rushed downstairs and outside, and across the road. Ten seconds. He heard the quad on Ash Lane. The sloping gardens of the middle row of houses began atop four-foot stone walls with a gate and a short flight of steps. Emil leaped right onto the top of the wall and bolted across his own lawn, with a slight pause to snatch up the drinks can the rider had tossed. The quad was off to his right, its engine roar softening as the rider no doubt slowed to take the turn onto the main road. Three seconds until he turned onto Oak Lane.

Avoiding the front door, which was often left locked, Emil darted down the path between the houses. He threw open the side door and ducked inside just as the quad blew past.

He froze in the porch, listening. No sounds. The TV was off, and Pete usually played music if he was in his room. Every coat they owned was hanging up beside the door, which might mean something or nothing. And the house just *felt* empty. A quick search proved this to be correct. Nothing seemed stolen or broken. But there were faint muddy footprints everywhere and drawers were open. Some bastard had definitely been inside, searching the place. That made him angry.

In the kitchen was a cork noticeboard and amongst the bills and notes was a single red pushpin with nothing attached. When Emil took down a note, he took out the pin. Pete never did. So Pete had recently taken something from the board by ripping it off the pin. And Emil knew what it was. Every Barkelow resident had been sent an invite to the theatre show at Barkelow Hall tonight – Emil's was still on the board, alone. Pete had said he wasn't interested – not his thing, some travelling theatre show that performed moralistic messages with historical settings – but maybe he'd changed his mind when he saw the neighbours getting dressed up and heading out.

So Pete had gone to the show. Emil had been manning the lift, but he'd swapped places with Alan for twenty minutes while he attended to a problem in the gardens, and that must have been when Pete arrived. But why hadn't Pete told his dad he was going there?

Emil slumped into his favourite armchair, now very worried. His earlier assumptions had been way off the mark, but it was now all starting to make sense. The presence of the quad rider, roaring around the estate conspicuously, had proved that Cavil's team weren't waiting to ambush Emil upon his return home. The white-haired girl at the shop hadn't recognised him, and if the four men at the lift had known who he was, they would have taken him immediately – their attacks upon him had probably been because all residents needed to be captured. Nobody in the village would have been of any help, pulled fingernails or not, because he had smothered his past from them. It all suggested his old enemy, Cavil, didn't know Emil's new name or current appearance. But he knew Emil was a master at hiding his identity. So Cavil had had to construct a clever plan to find his nemesis.

All phone lines had been jammed to cut the village off. Everyone at the housing estate and the shops had been captured. And gunmen had entered Barkelow Hall, no doubt to seize that place, too. With all the townsfolk together, Cavil could easily eliminate people by age, sex, and then clever questioning, until that special one remained. But that seemed like massive overkill.

Outside, the noise of the quad grew. Emil went to the window and through a chink in the curtains watched the man in the boiler suit cruise by. For the first time, Emil noticed a helmet hanging off the handlebars. The kid took it off at one point, but not because of a sudden desire to ride safely. He swiped it at the door mirror of a parked car as he flashed by, then hung it back on the handlebars.

Patrolling or riding for fun, Emil remembered thinking. But now he reassessed that theory. Cavil knew how the Emil of old would react if innocent people were in danger, especially loved ones. And by taking the entire population, he was guaranteed to capture those Emil cared about most. The whole village had been turned into a giant trap designed purely to snare Emil. To make sure Emil didn't flee into the shadows for another quarter of a century.

But for it to work, first Emil had to be made aware of the danger to those he cherished. So, quad guy was not patrolling the streets, and he wasn't riding for fun.

He was the messenger.

~

Emil was finalising the details of a plan – involving tea and sugar – when immediate action was somewhat forced upon him.

The next time the quad raced along Oak Lane, it did not pass by. This time it stopped. Emil peeked through the gap in the curtains. The quad was in the street, over to his right, and the boiler suited guy was standing in front of it, his backside bright white in the headlight. He was holding a radio and smoking. His back was to Emil as he stared at the last house on the first row. It belonged to Harry Boyners, who lived alone. Harry's skylight was open. The man's attic had been transformed into a shrine to ancient Egypt, and according to local rumour he spent all his time in there, reading up on old pharaohs and kings. Dressed as one, some said.

As Emil watched, the young man rushed up to the front door of the house and vanished inside.

Movement at the skylight caught Emil's eye. Shocked, he watched Harry appear. First a head, then the arms. Harry started to climb out, onto the roof. He wasn't dressed as an Egyptian pharaoh.

That explained the boiler suited guy's haste: he knew Harry was home, somehow, even though all the house lights were off.

Harry must have heard him come inside and decided to escape onto the roof.

The young man returned, rushed partway down the garden, and turned and looked, as if he knew Harry was escaping through the roof. Emil heard the young man shout. His accent was Irish, like the others. 'Nowhere to go, friend.'

Harry scuttled across the roof, back and forth, as if seeking a magical ladder to escape down. But he was stuck.

'Don't make me come up there,' the young man called up, laughing. He took a last drag on his smoke and tossed it. 'Jump down, now.'

Harry stared at him, and stood tall. 'Who the hell are you people? Terrorists?'

'I have now hypnotised you,' the young man called up. 'If I tell you to bark like a dog, you will bark. So jump now or you will collapse and fall. Jump on three, or I will say the word FALL, and you will tumble down and break your bones. One...'

Harry started to panic.

'Two...'

Harry stopped at the edge again, hurling abuse at the man below, and demanding to know what they'd done with everyone. There it was, then. Proof that the residents, Emil's friends and neighbours, had been taken hostage.

'Three. FALL.'

In awe, Emil watched as Harry's legs gave out and he toppled forward, off the roof, landing hard on his lawn with a sickening thump and the loud snap of a major bone breaking. The next sound was the young man's laughter.

With growing anger, Emil watched the young man take Harry by the legs and drag him inside the house. His old friend was clearly dead.

Two thoughts came to Emil right then. First: he knew how

the young man had apparently hypnotised Harry, and if he was right, it would be something he could use to gain an advantage.

And second: no way men from Cavil's organisation would be permitted to kill innocents, not in such a cruel way, and certainly not with such enjoyment. This method was a far cry from the execution of Joseph Tepper, dead in a car outside the estate. That meant this was not an official mission. No mission would last over a quarter of a century, no matter how obsessed its leader. Cavil was going it alone, aided by a privately hired team. That calmed Emil somewhat. Cavil might have the skills and contacts to have found him way out here in a rural village all these years later, but at least his clout had limits. Cavil did not have the backing of the government, even if the bastard still worked for them.

But there was bad news: if Cavil had bought help from outside his organisation, it meant he had not sent these people to capture Emil.

He had sent them to kill him.

6

―――――

When the quad rider woke, his eyes fluttered, then blinked, then flashed all around, taking in his new surroundings. Emil let him get his bearings, let him realise he was tied up and flat on a carpet in a living room. Then he stepped into view, carrying a carving knife. He knelt next to the young man, who was on his right side, hands tied behind his back, a short length of washing line securing them to his feet, which were up by his arse. He couldn't move an inch and quickly realised it.

Emil put the blade of the knife to the man's right eye, hooked a piece of flesh and pulled the lid slightly away from the eyeball. He held it there.

'Name.'

'Glendon,' the young man croaked.

'Okay, Glendon. Maybe Cavil told you I'm old now, or maybe you just fancy your own skills. If you believe you can take me, even in your condition, you need to do it right now, because I'm going to kill you.'

Terror locked the young man in place. One second he had been on the street, having stopped his quad because a teapot had suddenly appeared in the road, and the next he was here, no idea that Emil had rushed up behind him and cracked him with his own discarded drinks can, now filled with sugar for weight.

'Where's Cavil?'

The guy looked blank. Shook his head. Didn't know what he was talking about.

Emil flicked his wrist, and the blade sliced through the eyelid. Blood started pouring onto the carpet, around Glendon's head. He screamed.

'Maybe you don't know anything about me. But Cavil does. He knows that a bad guy left visible in the streets will get my attention. You are his messenger, even if you don't know it. Your message is information. Enough to get me to take the next step towards him, which is probably where a trap will be sprung. I know that, but I have no choice. He's got my son, even though he doesn't know it.'

'We're not here for you,' Glendon croaked. 'Don't know you.'

Emil felt the shock like an electric pulse. In that single visible eye, behind the terror, he read the truth. This boy did not have a clue what Emil was talking about. These people were not here for him. He had gotten it wrong.

Emil went into the kitchen and filled a glass with water. He found a sausage roll in the fridge, then returned to his captive.

He bit into the food and spoke around a mouthful. 'I've been at work all day. A busy day, getting ready for the theatre show. I didn't eat or drink, so I must be dehydrated, no energy, and not thinking straight. My theory that Cavil must have kidnapped everyone in the town to make sure he got me in his net? Stupid. There's probably about twenty men of the correct age in this town. My skin is darker and leathery, and I'm fatter than I was back then. Even my eyes have lost a bit of their colour. But my DNA, my fingerprints, they haven't changed. Cavil could have sent a couple of bogus police officers into the village with those new-fangled handheld fingerprint scanners, pretending they needed to mass-screen people because of some crime in a nearby village. He would have found me quickly and quietly.'

Emil drank three quarters of the water in one go. 'And my idea that Cavil had kidnapped everyone in order to make sure I didn't flee the town? Even more stupid. He would only do that if I had already gone into hiding, and that would mean he knew Emil Torrance was the man he wanted. But I was at Barkelow Hall all day, riding the lift and helping those theatre people with their equipment. The kidnappings started long before I killed that boy on the lift and escaped.'

Emil finished the last of the food and water. 'That's better. I feel sharper already. Oh, and if Cavil really had planted you as bait to bring me out of hiding, he would have put you under intense surveillance and put a sniper bullet in my head the moment I exposed myself. I tried to fit my logic around the facts, because I was so determined that this was all about the past. But it's not. This is not about me, and it doesn't involve my old enemy.'

Glendon's single visible eye crunched shut as Emil knelt before him and put the point of his knife close to it. Emil opened it with two fingers.

'Good-looking young guy like you probably has a girlfriend. Maybe a dog. Some close friends. A dealer for sure, given the reek of marijuana coming off you. The odds are that one or both of your parents are still alive, maybe some grandparents. Put all those people in your mind. If you want to see them again, all you have to do is talk to me.'

The guy just looked at him. Fear, a lot of it. Too much, maybe, to allow him to answer, or even think of the right answer. A young guy, not much experience. Emil stepped back, to give the guy room to breathe, let his mind orient.

'Only one of your team is going home today, Glendon. That's you, if you do exactly as I say. Do that and you'll live. It might be a lonely existence with no friends, but I'll suffer the same fate if your people kill all mine. If I'm all alone here in this village, who will bake all the cake shop cakes? You?'

Some life, some understanding was filtering into those terrified eyes now, as if Emil had suddenly started talking in a language the guy understood.

'This house has a cellar with a lock. If I like the answers you give to the questions I'm going to ask you, I'll put you in the cellar until all this is over. That's a promise. What I also promise is that I'll bury you there if you don't co-operate. No one will find you for a long time. Even when your bones are eventually discovered, this is the historic Peak District. They'll assume you were some medieval pauper and you'll be interred in a glass case in a museum. So let's not waste each other's time. Nod or shake your head right now to show whether or not you're going to play ball.'

The guy nodded.

'On another day, Glendon, I might have just fled, even knowing this isn't about me, about Cavil. Better safe than sorry. Unfortunately for you, I'm now part of this. Because you people have my son, and I want him back. So now you have a story to tell. How you got here, and why all my friends and neighbours are missing from their homes. Start right at the beginning.'

7

The first pair, young brothers called Nolan, arrived at the centre farmhouse, something that looked like it belonged in a cartoon. A red brick building with a smoking chimney and a white picket fence. Their quad bike – no headlight – pulled up beside a tiny brick structure that looked like an outside toilet. They got off and checked their pistols, and that was when the toilet flushed. They froze as a fat, bearded guy came out, earphones blasting classical music and his eyes cast downwards as he fiddled to close the fly on his trousers. They were just feet away, unmissable, but without looking up he turned away and kicked the door shut.

The two gunmen looked at each other and grinned. Dalaigh, who was only eighteen, put the barrel of his pistol against the back of the farmer's head, only to have a lazy hand fly up and swat it as if the farmer thought an insect had landed in his hair. But the shape and feel obviously blared in his mind as wrong. He turned to see two guns aimed at him by guys whose bright green eyes and sharp chins pegged them as brothers. His eyes went from one weapon to the other. Up jumped his hands. And down fell his trousers.

Farm 1 secure.

It went a little less easy for group two, who were 150 metres north along the ridge. There was no sign of life at the decrepit farmhouse they arrived at, except for a big Alsatian chained to a loose tractor wheel out front. Already bouncing around as if insane, it went into overdrive as the intruders pulled up behind a battered caravan some thirty metres out. There were no lights on in the building, but they held back, waiting for someone to investigate the dog's distress, or the noise of the quad. No one did.

These two weren't men, although you wouldn't know it because they wore biker helmets as well as boiler suits. They were mother and daughter. Capucine, only seventeen but already a double murderer, started to walk slowly towards the animal, shushing it, hands held out as if for a hug, but her mother, Maryse, pulled her pistol and fired. The bullet missed and pinged off the metal tractor wheel with a spark. The dog went berserk again. Capucine sneered at her mother.

A spotlight above the front door came on, bathing the dog in bright white. Both women ducked behind the caravan a moment before the door slammed open. They listened as a woman screamed at the dog. Then they heard slapping noises and tortured yelping.

Capucine marched out from behind the caravan to see the owner beating the dog with a rolling pin. It was cowering against the tractor wheel. The woman saw the intruder on her land, the boiler suit and helmet and the gun, and screamed a man's name and turned and ran for the door.

Capucine ran after her, past the dog, which tried to nip her thighs. The door slammed in her face. There was a peephole in the old wood, so she put two bullets ten inches below it. Behind her: the soft phut of a silenced pistol. She turned to see the dog dead on its side and her mother striding past it. She slapped her mother's arm in anger.

Together they pushed at the door, but there was a heavy weight behind it, which slid along the floor under their force. They stepped inside to a smell of age and the sound of church music from a nearby room, and a man's voice calling out a woman's name.

Capucine pointed at another door, meaning her mother should go take care of the husband. Then she bent over the woman lying behind the front door. The old lady was silent and bleeding everywhere, two holes in her chest, but her eyes blinked up at Capucine with life. Not dead then.

Her hands still clutched the rolling pin. Capucine took it and raised it and watched the lady's eyes follow it, then brought it down hard. Seconds later, *phut phut* and a heavy thump from another room.

Farm 2 secure.

Group three, all the way south, were riding a beeline straight for the farmhouse when the driver suddenly veered with a yelp of pain.

'Aggh, what the hell?' he moaned. His accent was Irish, his voice thick and slow to match his body, like a cartoon giant.

'Keep the bloody quad st– agggh!'

That was when the passenger, a fifty-something guy called Paul Ó Caiside, made his own yelp of pain as something stung his hand.

'Someone's shooting!' said a younger Luke Ó Ríagáin as he regained control of the quad and brought it to a skidding stop behind a Land Rover parked out front of the wooden farmhouse, a converted barn.

'Who?'

Then a shout from the farmhouse: 'Get the hell off my land, ya thieving bastards!'

Holding his neck where he'd been shot, Luke peeked over the bonnet of the Land Rover, then ducked sharply back down.

'Rifle,' he said. 'First-floor window.'

'Just an air rifle,' Paul said, fingering the red welt on his hand. 'Stop panicking.'

'Stick your head up, then.'

Something pinged off the bonnet of the Land Rover.

'I'm calling the cops right now!'

Both men looked at each other. The plan had been to take the owners quietly, no fuss, no violence, before anyone could grab a weapon. End of plan. As if reading each other's mind, both men stood and aimed their pistols at the darkened upper window, firing three shots each. The guy there ducked out of sight and their bullets blasted nothing but wood and glass.

Both men charged for the front door. The farmer reappeared like a pop-up duck in a shooting alley, managed to get off one more pellet that went nowhere, then fell away again half a second before bullets tore through the window once more.

Luke, younger, taller, fitter despite his bulk, got there first and opened the door with one hard kick. He vanished inside. Paul stopped at the doorway and turned, surveying the land to make sure no one was around. He knew the gunshots could have carried far across the land, despite the weapons' suppressors.

'Come here, you dick,' he heard Luke shout from within.

Thumping: feet on stairs, maybe.

'Now where you going, you dick?'

A crash: maybe a door succumbing to another heavy boot. Maybe the farmer toppling a wardrobe in front of a door.

'Get the hell off my land, ya thieving bastards.'

More noise: wood breaking, and glass smashing.

He heard Luke yell, 'What's with the shooting at people? We could have been pizza delivery guys.'

Another crash. Paul turned his gun on the doorway now, not knowing what to expect.

Luke again: 'Hey, what's that? Hey, don't be stupid. Put it down. You want to kill us all?'

'Get the hell out of my house. Thieving bastards.'

Crash. Bang. Meow. Some cat with a stamped-on tail, maybe. Paul thought, *Jesus, this is like a scene from a slapstick cartoon.*

Luke's voice went higher, now a little panicked: 'Put it down, now. Don't be– hey, hey, hey, stop!'

'Nah ya goddamned scared, eh?'

And then: a banshee-like wail. And silence.

'What's happening?' Paul called inside. He jerked as a cat came past his legs like a cannonball and vanished into the night. He panic-fired but got only the doorstep. Thought himself damned lucky he hadn't put a bullet in his own leg.

From deep within: 'It's real. *Jayzuz.* Who the hell has real grenades lying around the house? Anyway, Farm 3 secure.'

Glendon lay his head back on the carpet, eyes closed, as if awaiting judgement on his story. The blood from his gashed lid had slowed. Emil reached down to wipe the blood away. Glendon blinked rapidly, then both eyes focused on him.

Emil said, 'The farmhouses have a good view of everything. Your plan makes sense. Visitors from nearby villages sometimes come here across the fields. The land is too rugged to the east. But what about the main road? You would have to secure that.'

North end, the road passed through a gatehouse in some ancient defensive wall now mostly lost to nature. So this route was easy to block.

George Whelan, driving a Transit van with some bullshit painter's business decal on the side, crashed into the archway at an angle so his vehicle blocked the single lane road passing through. Brick dust sprinkled off as the entire old structure vibrated. A few minutes earlier he had placed a diversion sign and some traffic cones in the road at the last turn-off, a small roundabout just off the A6020 north of Ashford-in-the-Water. But he had blocked the road here as well just in case some ignorant soul cut past the diversion.

And here came an ignorant soul. George, who was wearing a paint-splattered boiler suit, stood in the road with his mobile phone to his ear, pretending to make a call about the crash. The headlights of the new arrival washed over him and glinted off rainwater that had collected in dips and cracks.

A head poked out of the driver's window. Some self-important twat in a shirt and tie. 'What's going on?' the executive said, checking his watch. 'I need through. I live here.'

George cursed under his breath. The only thing worse than an ignorant soul was a Barkelow resident headed home. 'Can't move it, mate,' he said. His Irish accent was thick, but here he adopted a Brummie twang. 'Fumes in the cab.'

The executive checked his watch again, maybe in case it had been wrong the first time. 'I need through. Can't you just reverse it away?'

'Fumes, mate.'

The executive huffed, but started to turn his car around. George was surprised a Barkelow resident had been shut down so easily, but there it was. Chuffed with his performance, he pulled his radio and announced: 'North road secure.'

At the south end it went down a little the same. Here the road passed through a tunnel bored through a thick wood, like a path cut by a meteor, before dropping down steeply into Barkelow. A young man called Jack Keegan set his 'road closed' sign at the far end of the tunnel, then took a chainsaw to a tree and sliced it so it fell across the road.

The road had been clear behind him, and it only took a minute to cut down the tree, but when he finished and turned the chainsaw off, its growl was replaced by another, and he turned to see three guys on motorbikes waiting at his 'road closed' sign. All in black and set against the dark sky beyond, they looked like ghostly apparitions sitting astride snarling beasts. They just stared at him.

He thought this was going to be a problem. Bikes could get around the fallen tree easily by riding into the wood. And if he was going to stop these guys getting into Barkelow, it wouldn't be with his gun, because that was in his car and the bikes were between him and the vehicle. He thought he might have to use the chainsaw to chop some flesh, like someone out of a slasher movie. He even imagined himself with the weapon raised above his head and silhouetted against a giant movie moon. But then the bikers turned and roared off. Just like that. Sensed their own impending doom, maybe. Or they were guys out for a ride rather than guys with a destination in mind, and were happy enough to take a detour out amongst the winding roads. Saved themselves some death, either way.

Jack raised his chainsaw in one hand like a victorious knight wielding a sword.

Radio. 'South road secure.'

Tale told, this time Glendon knew better than to close his eyes. He just watched Emil and waited. Emil grabbed him by the hair and lifted him into a kneeling position, and adopted the same stance so their faces were level. Now gravity painted a slow line of blood down Glendon's nose, past his mouth, onto his chin.

'So the perimeter is secure,' Emil said. He wiped the blood with a thumb before it could drip off Glendon's chin. 'No one in or out. Lockdown. Very good. But empty roads and remote farmhouses owned by a handful of old folks is the easy part. Now tell me how you took my village and my people.'

The guy in charge of stage two was Paul Ó Caiside. He left his farmhouse and got on his quad and was pulling away, the wheels kicking up waves of loose dirt, when he saw his partner in the mirrors and skidded a half-turn and yelled, 'What the hell are you doing?'

Luke Ó Ríagáin was coming out of the house with the dead male owner over his shoulder, like a fireman rescuing someone. He paused and shrugged, as if he didn't understand the question.

'And what the hell are you going to do with that?' Paul said, jabbing a finger at the item Luke held in his free hand. Luke dropped the guy on the ground with a thud. He waved the old grenade that the farmer had threatened them with.

'Disposing of the bodies, Paul. You think I'm digging a great hole, especially in this cold, then think again.'

Paul couldn't believe his ears. The guy wanted to blow the bodies up? These damned young fools that the boss had hired.

'You'll make enough noise to wake everyone within ten miles. Leave them to rot. We'll be long gone by the time anyone finds them. Don't mess about. Put him back. Besides, that thing's probably deactivated.'

Luke rapped a knuckle on the grenade and cocked an ear, as if expecting to hear something that would confirm it was live. 'I just carried him out. I'm not going all the way back in. Anyway, I don't want to be in the house with them.'

'What are you worried about? Zombies?' Paul sighed. This hulking imbecile didn't look like he was on the verge of being convinced anytime soon, and Paul didn't have the time to sit around and argue. 'Look, if you have to drag him out here, then bury him. Both of them. But hurry the hell up and get back into position.'

'His wife's gigantic. Bet she hasn't left that bed in ten years. He probably built this house around her. It'll take all day to bury her. What's your problem with this?' He waved the grenade.

And of all the damned young fools the boss had hired, this guy was the worst of all. No brain, and the dangerous inquisitiveness of a two-year-old. He was in his twenties, a big guy with thick lips and wide cheekbones that gave him a constant mean look. But now he pouted like a child. Paul left him like that after a final order to leave the damned grenade alone and bury the bodies.

But once the quad was over the hill and gone, Luke hauled the dead guy onto his shoulder and carried him around to the back of the farmhouse, where there was a small barn with logs stacked up one side. He thought that would be a good place to bomb the bodies. He tossed the guy by the logs and turned to go fetch the whale of a wife, and that was when he spotted something that made him smile. Something better than an old grenade. It was large and yellow and looked like a trailer, but Luke had seen one of these before, and knew exactly what it was.

A hundred and fifty metres south of Luke, Dalaigh Nolan was at the front bedroom window, watching his brother down below as he loaded the quad bike in preparation for joining the others in the village centre.

His sniper rifle was on the deep windowsill. He looked through the scope, into the village a couple of hundred metres away. Mostly dark, except for the housing estate and the spot-lighted manor house high on the promontory. He wished he could have been part of the crew that was going to capture the villagers, rather than stuck out here alone in a strange, cold building.

He turned his radio to channel thirteen, which was Capucine's. He spoke her name and soon heard her warped but sexy French accent come back.

'Nothing's up,' he answered. 'Just bored and wanted to hear your sweet voice.' He lifted his rifle and started walking for the door.

She said, 'Oh, we have time for this? You in position? Has brother left yet?'

'He'll be gone in a minute, babe. And what do you mean by *in position*? I gotta walk all over this house constantly to watch all four sides, over and over like some old guy with Alzheimer's looking for his keys. Listen, why don't you send your mother into the village instead? You stay at the farmhouse.'

'And why will I do that?'

'Because it's then just me and you out here. Alone.'

Capucine laughed. 'With hundreds of metres between us. Not far enough to please me. And too far for you to do anything.'

'Now, don't be like that. And anyway, I could be there and back in no time. Just say the word. It won't take long.'

She laughed. 'Won't take long? Impressive.'

He realised his error and also laughed. In the back bedroom, he looked through the rifle's scope, away across the black western landscape. Just fields out there, and a few spiderweb roads connecting shards of civilisation with other fragments. If the police ever got wind of tonight's fun-filled events and planned a surprise attack, then this was the way they'd come. Dalaigh imagined armed black shapes oozing across the dark fields like alien invaders, and being picked off one by one by his magnificence.

'Gone quiet? Aww, embarrass, eh?' Capucine said over the radio. 'Just remember you have no chance anyway. I got boyfriend, remember, and love him very much.'

Just then Kane came into the room. 'I'm off, bro. Off to kick butt. Take care. Don't be touching none of that vodka. I'll bring you some rare wine.'

Dalaigh gave him a thumbs-up with one hand and the bird with the other. Kane threw the gestures right back, then left. Dalaigh clipped the radio to his collar and put it on open transmission, so he wouldn't need his hands or the transmit button. He picked up his rifle. 'No offence, Cap, but your boyfriend's a dickhead.'

Capucine hissed like a cat. 'A what? Maybe I tell him you say that.'

'A dickhead. Means he has a penis for a head. How about I arm wrestle him? Winner gets you.' He started towards the door.

'He will kill you. Kill you at anything you challenge him to. Are others in position?'

'What the hell–'

Capucine heard his exclamation. '*What is it? What happened?*'

'Back in a sec,' Dalaigh said. He'd just stepped out of the bedroom, which was right at the top of the stairs, above which was a window facing south, and despite the dark a tiny movement outside the farmhouse a hundred and fifty or so metres away had caught his eye. Through the scope, he saw Luke Ó Ríagáin standing by a large yellow mechanical contraption shaped like a swan. The big brute was stripping a body of its clothing. What the hell? He flicked his radio to channel eight. 'Sex outdoors, Luke?'

Luke stopped stripping the body. He pulled his radio and looked at it, then at Dalaigh's farmhouse. Dalaigh could see him clearly, even the puzzled look on his face, but Luke had no scope and could see nothing but a tiny building.

Luke put his radio to his face. 'Getting rid of the bodies. You should, too.'

'My guy's not dead, Luke, because my education involved books instead of gory video games. And if the police catch us, it won't be because of a dead farmer, so it's a waste of–'

And then he realised what he was seeing. The machine, with a long chute like a swan's neck.

'Is that a wood chipper, Luke?' He laughed. 'You've got a body next to a wood chipper, and I've got a funny feeling.'

Luke looked annoyed. 'You laugh like you think this won't work. There'll be nothing left, Dalaigh. Nothing. Police'll get no DNA off these bodies.'

'That's not the funny part, Luke. It's you thinking a wood chipper will destroy bone and gristle, but not clothing.'

Luke looked at the chipper, then at the naked body. And back at the chipper. And seeing this baffled cartoon character animation, Dalaigh laughed again.

A hundred and fifty metres south again, Capucine put her radio down and finished her tea in one gulp. Above her, she could hear the groan of floorboards as her mother dutifully patrolled. Like Dalaigh and Luke, her mother was supposed to go from room to room in an endless loop, checking the view from the windows. Checking for problems at the neighbouring farmhouse. Checking for a problem down in the village. Checking for a battalion of SAS storming towards them across the fields from the west.

She didn't envy them. She had a much better job to do, when the main event went down.

And it was time. She shouted up to her mother: 'I'm going, *Maman*. See you in bit.'

She went out of the kitchen door and into the chill wind. She got eight steps towards her quad before her mother yanked the door open.

'Be careful, Cap,' Maryse said.

Capucine turned and faced her. They had similar noses, and of course they wore identical dark blue boiler suits, but that was where their likeness ended. Capucine was pale and had white hair cut in a bob, while her mother had a healthy brown tint to her skin and curly brown locks.

Capucine had not expected her mother to break protocol, and that she did tugged at her heart. But she liked playing the role of independent young woman, so gave her mother a sneer, to show she hated being treated like a child. Unfazed by it, or maybe seeing right through it, Maryse grabbed her and hugged her and ruffled her hair, and laughed as Capucine made a childish noise of disgust.

'I gotta skipping, *Maman*.'

'Oh, you and your English slang. You think there comes a time, just because a child grows up, that a mother stops thinking she's cute and fun to be around?'

'There comes time when parents get annoying.'

Meant to sting, but Maryse only laughed. 'Ever wondered how many times you would have choked to death on a bottle top or walked into traffic if not for me?'

Her mother often played this game – reminding Capucine of all she had done for her daughter over the last seventeen years. She had never managed to work out if her mother wanted thanks, or just to wind her up. Capucine thought of two responses, but both tasted of cheese in her throat, and she voiced neither. Maryse put a hand on her daughter's shoulder.

'Be careful out there, Cap, because there's danger.'

Capucine patted the pocket that held her pistol. 'Unless I decide suicide, I am fine. I am only danger out there, *Maman.*'

Glendon Ahearne was already at the meeting point, the car park out front of an abandoned hotel on the north road. He watched Capucine's quad zip over the fields and enter the main road through a break in a low stone wall running its entire length. He shook his head as she looked left and right before crossing into the car park, like a kid who'd just been taught 'Stop, Look and Listen'. Beyond her, he saw another dark dot zipping through the fields towards the hotel. He heard the second quad's engine even over the much closer roar of Capucine's.

Capucine drew alongside his quad and nodded at him. He nodded back. These two weren't great fans of each other. Capucine thought Glendon was boring. Glendon thought Capucine had an attitude with the whole world.

Side by side on their quads, far away from the only street lamp that cast anything approximating light across the car park, they waited for the others. Kane Nolan pulled up thirty seconds later. He barely got as far as turning off his engine when Capucine said to him, 'Tell your dirty brother to stop try it on with me.'

'Tell your mum to stop biting my balls so hard when she's blowing me,' Kane told her.

They bickered for a few seconds, but stopped when they heard another quad approaching. Paul Ó Caiside, their annoying, ancient boss. He came from the south, having used some other exit from the fields, and turned into the car park.

'Everything okay?' he said.

Capucine, Kane and Glendon nodded.

'Good, then we're ready to rock and... what the hell?' Paul pointed at Capucine's quad. Attached to the front bull bars was her assault rifle, just as planned. But very much against the plan was the missing canvas sack it was supposed to be wrapped in. Instead, the AK-47 was displayed for the world to see. Paul's was the only one wrapped, in fact.

'Why aren't these guns covered? Do you brainless idiots want to get arrested before we've even started?'

The brainless idiots started to object:

'No one can make phone call.'

'There's seventy-five million AKs in the world, so half these country yokels probably have one.'

'My sack got ripped.'

Paul realised it was too late to do anything about the show of weaponry. 'Any more mess-ups? The farmhouse owners – all breathing, right? Teeth and fingers and things all where they should be?'

The boss's orders – don't kill or torture anyone. Paul thought of Luke back at the farmhouse, with the dead farmer and his dead wife. He tried to keep the guilt out of his face.

Kane and Glendon nodded. Capucine gave a grin and a thumbs-up.

Paul pulled his radio. 'In position, Helen?'

He got an affirmative reply. Helen had been the first of the team to get into position, having trekked east through rugged, empty land to take her spot. Her job was a lonely one, but if anyone was good at living inside their own head, it was her.

Capucine said, 'See, we not all idiots.'

Paul said, 'You're all idiots if you think that.' He called the boss next. Told him they were ready for stage two. Good, came the reply. And: keep an eye on those youngsters. Paul was roughly the boss's age and they went back a long way. Which meant he wasn't happy about this babysitting job. He should have been with his old friends at the manor house, but he'd been swapped for that volatile fool Cathal, just so the boss could keep him in check. And away from Capucine, who was the TN to his T.

Paul told the boss he would watch the young idiots, and said it loud enough for the young idiots to hear. Call done, he gave a signal and his people tore out of there, whooping with glee. He shook his head and followed.

On the main road, the three young idiots went south, towards the market square, but Paul turned north, up the hill. He rode to the tree-enshrouded gatehouse at the top and parked inside its gloomy archway, glad to see that George had blocked the other end with his van. George, at least, was someone with a cool head.

George was in the road beyond the van, just standing there. As he was supposed to. He gave a thumbs-up.

'Any problems?' Paul called out. His voice sounded tinny as it bounced off the stone walls.

His answer was another thumbs-up. Paul returned the gesture and did a three-point turn and headed south, past the hotel on his left, and past the housing estate, and past the market square, where his crew of three were hiding, and up the south hill to check on Jack Keegan's roadblock.

Jack's car was in the trees near his roadblock and he was sitting cross-legged on the bonnet, eating something. Paul rode his quad over the fallen tree and flung his arms out in annoyance.

'See how easy that was? That the biggest tree you could find?'

Through a mouthful of whatever, Jack said, 'How many tourists ride quad bikes? Get lost. Go find someone to shoot.'

Just then: headlights. Twin balls of light at the end of the dark tunnel through the trees, like brilliant stars glimpsed through a telescope. Some guy or gal headed for Barkelow, or just plain lost way out here in the boonies. Either way, it was some dick who'd ignored the diversion sign way back. Paul told Jack to sort it. Jack told him to get lost again.

Paul gave him the finger. 'The boss doesn't like attitude, you know. This'll be the last mission you lot come on.' He had to suppress a grin at that, knowing what he knew.

Now Jack gave him the finger. 'It's a young man's world. You're living in the past, old man. Now piss off and let me do my job.'

Paul pointed at the approaching headlights. 'Then do it, and don't mess it up.'

Turning away strangers should be no problem, but he worried what Jack might do if the headlights belonged to a Barkelow resident returning home. Someone who insisted on getting through. The plan was to delay as long as possible, and capture if things turned bad. George could handle such a problem professionally, but this brash idiot Jack? Paul considered staying to help, to minimise the bloodshed, but knew the timetable wouldn't allow it. Reluctantly, he three-pointed again and rode away.

So, stage two.

The shops by the market square, all grey stone and slate roofs and oak doors and bay windows, were dark and dead. The owners were probably at the theatre show at Barkelow Hall. They were old folk who'd lived in the village for years, whose lives were simple and quiet and calm – what else would they have to do round here of an evening? But assumption was risky, so, earlier, Glendon had arrived on his loud quad, parked up and smashed a bottle and started whistling – just the sort of hullabaloo that would annoy old people and bring them to their windows to look and tut. But no wrinkled faces had appeared at any windows. He had then cut the phones lines and gotten out of there.

But assumption was risky.

Paul pulled up on the far side of the market square. The others were across the way, parked in an alleyway cut into the long, curved building housing the shops, barely visible in the darkening world. Capucine's apparently fashionable white hair was all he could really make out. But he could see the dark outlines of the others, all tense with energy and anticipation. He gave a signal for it to begin, and it was like unlocking the door of a lion's cage.

Out they came, fast, splitting up. Capucine ran to one end of the row, where there was a bookshop. She started to pick the lock. Kane took the other end and did the same. Glendon picked an establishment in the middle.

Capucine was in. Two seconds later, Kane pushed open his door and vanished inside. Glendon, bloody dope-head amateur, took another thirty seconds.

Paul was nervous: they had pistols, and combining such a thing with a brash young mind was akin to mixing hazardous chemicals. He waited for gunshots and screams.

Although last in, Glendon was first out. He gave a hand signal to say the place was empty and rushed to the next door. This time, probably because he felt certain no one was home, he just booted the door open. Paul slapped his own thigh in anger and wished the door had opened on a cantankerous old man in a rocking chair, with a shotgun.

Kane was out next. He gave the *all-clear* signal and darted to the next shop and started on the lock.

No sign of Capucine. Ninety seconds later, Kane and Glendon returned at the same time and gave the signal as one, like synchronised robbers. They rushed down to Capucine's end of the row. Glendon went to the final unexplored establishment, while Kane stood at the bookshop's open door and called inside for Capucine. She appeared a few seconds later, wiping her hands on a piece of fabric.

There was a shout. Glendon, from inside the shop. The shout drew Capucine and Kane inside. Paul jumped off his quad and rushed across the road.

A wall-mounted sign said the shop was called *Anne's Tiques*, but Paul thought it should have been named *Anne's Useless Shit*. A wall of gimmicky illuminated clocks cast a rainbow of low light across a maze of short display cabinets brimming with all manner of tacky trinkets that naïve tourists would probably go crazy for. It looked more like a storeroom than a shop. He knocked over at least two knee-high displays as he rushed for an open door in the back wall. He could hear voices coming from upstairs.

In a study at the front of the upper floor, his people were crowded around a guy on a reclining chair near a roaring log fire that provided the only illumination. Paul slapped a light switch and the room lit up green. The guy in the chair was old, easily in his eighties, and dressed in stripy pyjamas. Breathing funny. Looking funny. Clawing at his face with one hand. No sign of any *tiques*-owning Anne.

'Heart attack,' Kane said. 'What do we do?'

'It wouldn't be fair to tie him up, would it?' Glendon said.

'Put him out of misery,' Capucine said.

The guy was looking at them with contradictions in his eyes:

fear, yet relief also. Armed intruders in his house, but at a time when he needed help.

Paul barged Glendon aside and grabbed the man's arm. 'Help me,' Paul said. They all grabbed a limb each and swung the guy off the chair.

'No way we can get him to a hospital,' Glendon said.

'Can't bring a bloody ambulance here,' Kane said.

'Put out of misery is the way,' Capucine said.

They were gravitating towards the exit, but Paul yanked on the old guy's arm and got them moving the other way. Towards a smaller door in one wall. Paul freed a hand to pull it open, exposing a small utility cupboard with cleaning gear on the shelves and scattered on the floor.

'Really?' Glendon said.

'We came to incapacitate them,' Paul barked.

Capucine said, 'This not out of misery, this more misery,' but she was grinning.

They dropped the old guy on the floor and used their hands and feet to thrust him into the cupboard, his body forcing a path through the clutter. The space was small and Paul had to fold up the guy's legs to get the door shut. The last thing he saw before it slammed was the old guy's eyes, loaded with fear and incomprehension. Paul turned the key to lock it.

'Could have put the light on for him,' Glendon said.

'Maybe make him a pot of tea, also?' Paul said. He rolled up his sleeve to expose a hairy forearm written on in pen. There was a list of names, and beside that a to-do list with the first four items scored out:

~~Farm 1~~
~~Farm 2~~
~~Farm 3~~
~~Check on George & Jack~~
Shops (remem phones!)

Housing estate (remem phones!)

He drew a line through the penultimate entry. The others sniggered. Kane said, 'Write *fart* and strike that, too. I just did one.'

Paul ignored the jibe. 'Order, not chaos, my immature friends. That's the key to success. Now, get your AKs into position and then let's go. Timetable.'

And finally: the housing estate.

Glendon looked into the trees and saw portions of a ruined gatehouse in the wall that had long ago surrounded Barkelow. He knew the ruin, like the gatehouse at the top of the north road, had been rebuilt and weathered to look like the original constructions – but he didn't get why. Why rebuild a ruin to look like a ruin?

He turned his attention back to the junction box set just beside the end of the road. Ninety seconds later he shut the box's door and pulled his radio, and told Paul it was done. Phone lines to the housing estate cut – none of these bastards will be calling anyone.

He rode his quad back down the hill and stopped a short way past the estate. Right in the middle of the road: his job now was to prevent anyone entering or exiting.

Except his own people, of course. They rode up the hill and passed him without nod or word and halted their quads alongside the housing estate.

Right then a hatchback car turned out of the highest street, Ash Lane, and came down the hill towards them, headlights bright.

It passed the parked quads, but stopped before Glendon, who was blocking its path and waving it down. The driver's side window buzzed down, but Glendon marched round to the passenger side because he didn't want the driver to get a good look at him. Down came that window, too. The driver, a middle-aged man in a construction uniform, said, 'What's up? You people don't live here. You lost?'

Bending to peer through the window, Glendon faked an English accent and said, 'We're here for the theatre show tonight. You not going, then?'

'Nah, mate. I was supposed to, but I just got called into work. Are you lot part of the show?'

Glendon caught sight of one of his colleagues rushing past the back window. Capucine appeared by the driver's door. Before Glendon could wonder what she was up to, she thrust a pistol into the back of Construction's head and pulled the trigger. Glendon darted aside just in time. Blood and brain matter sprayed out of the passenger window and he caught it only on the shoulder. God knew how close the bullet had come to his flesh.

'Shit, Capucine, shit!' he moaned.

From thirty feet away, by the quads, Paul bellowed: 'What the hell? Why? What possible reason?'

Capucine said, 'Now there only seventeen left. And can not drag him along while we get others.'

Paul cursed. 'Now you'd better hide that car.'

She opened the door and released the handbrake and jumped onto the doorsill. The car rolled down the hill and she rode it like a windsurfer, and when it had achieved enough momentum she twisted the steering wheel. The car bumped off the road and into the longer grass on the other side of the road from the housing estate. It ground to a standstill ten feet in. Capucine pushed the dead owner into a lying position and shut the door and looked smug with herself.

'That's not hidden,' Paul called over.

'He look parked in the dark,' Capucine yelled back.

She walked back onto the road. Glendon was using a spit-covered hand to try to wipe the mess off his shoulder. Paul and Kane approached.

'Don't bother, it just look like paint,' she told Glendon. 'I too got some on me. That is why we wear this outfit, remember.'

'I've got a guy's splattered brain five inches from my face and I should just leave it there?' Glendon said.

She grinned. 'I would be more worry he has bad nasal infection and his snot all over you.'

Glendon grimaced at the mess on his shoulder, as if considering this. It made Capucine laugh.

Paul said, 'You children stop farting about. From now on we leave everyone's blood and snot right where it is, eh? Remember your training.'

A bad move, putting that back in their minds, he quickly realised. Three weeks ago in a desolate inner-city slum in Belfast, he had watched these idiots practice their house storming technique. Armed, kicking in doors, dragging out mannequins, all in preparation for this day. But they had laughed and joked and treated it like a game. Same in the fields another day, when they'd been let loose with pistols and long-range rifles to hone their skills. All fun and games to them. He feared they'd fail to take this seriously.

Paul pulled his mobile and called his mother, just to test the signal jammers. No connection. Time to do this.

If their intel was right, then of the eighty-two people who lived here in Woodlands, all but thirty-six had tickets to tonight's party. Research and surveillance had determined that seven of those thirty-six were away on holiday, another seven were working late in other towns and cities, and a pair of young couples into swinging had gone to attend some other social engagement.

So there should be only eighteen poor souls here to capture. The construction guy, though, had been one of the ticket holders, which was proof that plans could change. There could be more non-shows. Paul rolled up the sleeve of his boiler suit.

'Hey, you didn't write down my fart,' Kane said. Glendon and Capucine laughed.

'Shut up,' Paul snapped. 'I'm making sure we do this right.' He checked the list of names written on his arm. 'Right, first is number two, Oak Lane. Joshua King and Lana King, and they've got a dog. But we're going to have to change things a little. Some of the people who should be out won't be. So after we've gone through this list, we're going to need to check all the other houses to make sure– hey, wait, you dicks.'

Kane and Capucine had already started running across the grass, towards the fenced rear gardens of the houses on the lowest row. They stopped at the back of number two.

'No one in or out,' Paul said to Glendon, then left him in the road and darted over to the fence. He saw Capucine and Kane shaking their fists at each other. Rock, Paper, Scissors. Capucine won. She whooped – quietly, at least. But both seemed as giddy as kids about to join a birthday party.

'Jesus Christ,' Paul said. 'We do this my way. Or the highway and no pay. And Kane goes first on this one.'

Finally he got the pair to calm down and follow his instructions. They hauled themselves over the wooden panel fence and scurried across the garden. Kane tried to lockpick the back door, but found it already unlocked. He rushed in, followed by Capucine. Paul waited at the corner of the house, peeking out and into the street to make sure nobody in a house across the way was noseying through a window.

Capucine was back in two minutes. 'Done,' she said. She had blood on her knuckles.

'Christ, you people. Where's Nolan?'

'He wants to steal.'

'Christ, you people.' Paul went inside. In the kitchen, the cellar door was open and rummaging noises came from its depths. Paul called down.

'What are you doing? We're not here to rob.'

Kane's voice came back: 'Old folks have wine. Domaine wines sell for thousands of pounds.'

'Get out of there.' Paul slammed the cellar door, just to be childish. Ignoring Kane's yelp of shock, he moved on.

In the bedroom, he found the King couple. On the floor, gagged, bound with cable ties, a neat job. But beaten about the face. Had retired old cronies really needed subduing in such a fashion? The room stank of dog shit and there the dog sat in a cage in the corner, just watching him, seemingly not giving a hoot that its owners had been victimised. At least no one had killed the dog. Small graces.

Back outside, he found Kane and Capucine sitting at a plastic garden table, chatting as if they lived here and were just enjoying the cool evening. Kane was moaning about a lack of booty in the cellar. 'You all think this is nice and fun, don't you?' Paul said, looking at them both in turn.

Kane got up and grabbed Paul's forearm and looked at it.

'Number five next. Sandra Jackson. Single.'

On they moved without waiting for him. He bit back the temptation to shoot both of them in the back and followed.

8

'Are you going to kill me?' Glendon said, once his story was told. 'You could untie me. I'm not going to try anything against you. Look, I'm only eighteen, and I've got my whole life ahead of me. You're right, I've got a girlfriend, and my parents love me and...'

He stopped, probably aware of the iron indifference in the eyes staring back at him. Now Emil knew what had happened to his friend, Joseph Tepper, and it was worse than he had imagined. Tepper wasn't killed during tough interrogation, or even to keep his silence. He was dead because these people were soulless and mindless. He wanted to make the man cowering before him suffer, and to know why, but there was no time.

Emil said, 'Village and perimeter, locked up. And you have everyone who's attending the show at the manor house tonight. Almost ninety people taken with ease. Very good. We're nearly done here. Keep those loved ones in your mind during the next question, because the truth will help you reunite with them. This is the most important question. This is the one that could save you. So here goes. You're not here for me. So why are you here?'

~

'Ladies and gentlemen, please relax and allow me to explain why we're here.'

The villagers at the manor house were watching Bradan intently. They were captives, but their eyes said they yearned to know why. So it was time to tell them.

He took to the stage where these people had come to watch a show, and put his own on.

'You should know that we're extending your night out by a few hours, that is all. In no more than four hours' time, you will all be freed. You can go home, have a drink, have sex, sleep, and wake tomorrow with more to gossip about than the weather or next week's fete. That's the nice outcome, of course. The nice outcome will only come to be if a certain man or woman gives us what we want.'

He gave a nod to Fergal, who moved amongst the people, handing out two little sheets from a Post-it notepad and a pen to each person. When it was done, Bradan addressed them again.

'On one sheet of paper, write your name. Do that now. Stick the sheet to your forehead.'

He waited while this happened. Fergal laughed at the arrangement of terrified people with squares of yellow stuck to their heads. Bradan was not smiling. He had a show to put on.

'Last Saturday evening, just a few miles from here, a young girl was robbed at knifepoint. She was cut, badly, and her money and mobile phone were taken. It was dark, and the assault happened so quickly that she did not know if her attacker was male or female, or even how old. Her uncle swore revenge. The police had no clues, but her clever uncle managed to track the vicious thief here, to Barkelow. I am that uncle, and I am here for justice.'

Murmurs travelled around the room. Bradan did not interrupt. As he suspected, the townsfolk were eager to see this play out and quickly quieted themselves, and his show continued.

'That vicious attacker is here, in this room. Right now his heart is beating wildly. Five minutes from now it will not beat at all. But I will give that man a chance to do some good with his remaining moments. If he stands and comes to me within the next thirty seconds, he will be the only man destined for a bullet. If I have to step down and approach him, I will kill him and one other.' Seeing Fergal trying not to laugh, Bradan threw his hands wide, head back. 'Stand now, and save an innocent soul.'

Fergal nearly lost it, but nobody noticed. And nobody got up. Heads turned and eyes scanned the crowd. Most of these people had known each other for years, and Bradan could see the shock on their faces. For just a moment, their predicament was overwhelmed by the idea that one of their own could have committed the crime Bradan talked of.

'I feared as much,' he said. 'Now you will write on the other sheet of paper the name of the person you think most likely to have committed this crime. Someone who was out of the village last Saturday evening, man or woman. Do that now.'

Now, heads didn't move, but eyes roamed as people scrutinised their neighbours without appearing to do so, thinking, wondering about that guy or this girl, because they had gone out of town last Saturday. And pens reluctantly went to paper. Names went down: those who might have talked of money problems; those who had become flush recently; those who may have acted shifty on Sunday or were generally considered a bit weird. Perhaps even the odd chap who'd pissed some neighbour off recently. Fergal went around when it was done and collected them all. He got down on one knee, head bowed, to pass them to Bradan, who had to bite back his own laughter.

He flicked through the notes, then let them scatter by his

feet. 'I believe we have our criminal. Thirteen different people have named you, *Mr Bailey.*' As he spoke the name, he flicked his eyes onto the man in question. A gasp went up from the crowd, and all heads turned towards Mr Bailey, a gangly man in his late thirties in a creased shirt and trousers that looked as if he'd last worn them years ago and had dragged them out of a dusty closet just for tonight.

Bailey's reaction created more gasps. His skin flushed instantly red, and he lurched to his feet. 'You bloody arseholes,' he yelled, jabbing his finger. 'Piss on you all, blaming me. What the hell?'

He stopped, as did everyone else, when Bradan and Fergal burst out laughing.

'That was so brilliant,' Bradan said afterwards. 'Nice to know your fellow people think so highly of you, eh, Mr Bailey?'

They were all staring in shock. Bradan pointed and all eyes followed his finger. He was indicating a grey-haired tall man in a grey suit who sat with an elegant woman about his age, early sixties. They looked shocked.

'Just a joke, I'm afraid. You can all relax. Far as I know, none of you is a secret serial killer or paedophile. We're here for money, that's all. That man there is Alfred Washington, founder of Wandering Flame, the reason you're all here tonight. A small theatre company, for sure, but what you might not know is that Mr Washington inherited money. Lots of it. You're all captives because of Mr Washington, so it's only fair that he pays for your release. Five hundred thousand pounds, payable by bank transfer tonight. Once he's paid, you will all be released.'

Everyone was glaring at him, dumbfounded, and clearly unsure of his sincerity.

'No joke this time, people. Now, poor old Alfred is not alone in paying. You will all pay. I am going to take you each aside for a chat about finances. Do not be afraid. We're not taking you out to put bullets in your head.'

He closed his eyes and swept a hand, and blindly picked someone with a pointing finger. An old lady sitting with her husband, holding hands. They looked terrified, as if selected for death. 'You two first. Come with me. The rest of you, go have a chat with Alfred.'

Now that they knew this was only a robbery, people started firing questions at Bradan, as if believing the threat of violence was gone. He ignored them all. He strode off the stage and towards the old couple, who found Denis looming over them. Bradan swept an arm, indicating a room nearby.

'Please, let's go talk about money,' he said to the woman, with a smile. Fergal got them to their feet, and all four headed towards a side room.

Behind them, Alfred was crowded by people eager to convince him that money was no big deal. Never was when it was someone else's. Bradan grinned as he heard the man denying he'd inherited riches, to vocal disdain.

Bradan's mind was in turmoil, though. Cathal. Dead. So now they were a man down, and running around out there was someone who knew there were people here with a lethal agenda. Someone who might or might not have lethal skills himself.

Bradan tried to think positively. He had decided not to warn his team that there was a dangerous enemy out there, because they were young and brash and might start shooting anyone they saw, or might go off plan to hunt him. That meant the guy was running free, but it didn't matter. Even if the town handyman was some ex-army hardnut who knew bad things were going on here in his small village, there was nothing he could do about it. He could not phone out, and he could not escape because Bradan's team had the place locked down. The man would have to hide, and a hidden man would be no further threat.

~

Of his own will, Glendon lay back down on the bloody carpet, and closed his eyes. His mouth moved silently, as if reciting a prayer. His demeanour said, *There's no more to tell. Now I await my fate.*

Emil leaned over him. When Glendon's eyes felt the ceiling light had been blocked, they flipped open and his whole body tensed. He wasn't yet ready to impotently succumb to that fate.

'We're nearly done here, Glendon. There's just one more thing I need from you.'

~

Glendon's voice came over Helen's radio.

She was lying on cold stone atop the gatehouse in the trees above Woodlands, sighting down the scope of her F2 rifle at the housing estate. She had been given this job because she was a good shot with a sniper rifle – better than Dalaigh, despite his claims otherwise – and never got bored. Boredom barely seemed possible in one who had lived a solitary lifestyle for ten years, since a house fire had badly disfigured her face at age fifteen.

'You there, Helen?' said a crackly voice. The display on her radio said 'CHANNEL 6', so it was Glendon, down there on his quad bike. The idiot was supposed to be hiding as he waited for the emergence of people that their net had missed, but she had listened to his damned quad bike as he raced around like a kid on a track.

She picked up the radio without taking her eyes from the scope. 'What's the latest?' she said.

'You have to see what I just found, Helen. I'm coming to you.'

'No, Glendon, you stay there, that was the plan. And stop pissing about on that quad. The sound carries for miles. Where are you? I can't see you.'

'In one of the houses. This you have to see. I'll bring it to you.'

'You can't leave the streets. And I have to stay here.' She was curious, though. 'Just tell me.'

He couldn't, he claimed. Couldn't describe it. You gotta see this.

She wanted to say no, but the intrigue was itchy and needed a scratch. All the houses had been searched, so it was unlikely any of the residents had been missed. And it would take her just moments to glance away from the scope, at whatever Glendon wanted to show her. If a loose straggler appeared while he was absent, she could incapacitate with a leg shot and Glendon could ride down and pick them up.

That decided it. 'Be quick, Glendon. If anyone gets away while you're playing around, we're in trouble. Hurry up.'

She put the radio down and waited, watching. She looked at the three farmhouses on the far hill and hoped none of her comrades saw Glendon ride to her.

Three minutes later she heard Glendon's quad, then saw it exit Oak Lane and turn up the hill. He was wearing his helmet for once. He raced up the street, coming her way. She tracked him with the rifle until he reached the fence at the end, got off and started to climb the fence, at which point she turned her attention back to the houses. She could hear him stomping through the undergrowth below her.

Thirty seconds later she heard his footsteps on the stone steps inside the gatehouse. Heard him force open the old door and emerge onto the roof.

She tapped a point beside her, eye locked on the scope and

its magnified world. 'Put it right here. Whatever magical item you gotta show me. This better make me orgasm. It better not be something stupid, Glendon.'

Glendon didn't move. She turned her head. And that was when he booted her in the face.

9

____

The room Bradan took the old couple to was a small library that was undergoing renovations. Sheets hung across the bookcases and the plastic that had been protecting the floor was rolled into a tube by one wall. There was a painter's desk, bare, brand new: so work hadn't quite started yet.

Dead centre, an armchair faced two wooden chairs and a coffee table. There was no other furniture. The old couple were told to sit in the wooden chairs. They were ten inches apart, but the old guy shifted them closer together and helped his wife to sit. Both were shaking with fear when Bradan sat in the armchair and stared at them. He placed his radio and a mobile phone on the coffee table. The phone had been taken off the old lady as they entered the room. They avoided his glare.

Fergal came in with a decanter of a golden spirit and slapped it onto the glass table with a trio of tiny china teacups. Bradan picked one up and sneered at it.

'What's this doing for my image, Fergal?'

'All I could find.' He shrugged and left.

'Ruffian,' Bradan said after he'd gone. 'Surprised he didn't bring us lemonade. Drink?'

The man said nothing, but the old lady, wiping tears from her eyes, nodded. Bradan poured, and the lady took hers eagerly. The old guy shook his head at the proffered cup, then took it six seconds later when Bradan refused to put it down. The men sipped. The woman gulped hers in one and didn't seem phased, as if her tongue and throat were used to such fiery liquid.

'We haven't got money,' she said, suddenly full of Dutch courage. 'So you need to pick on someone else.'

Bradan said, 'Have you got a cleansing wipe?'

She looked at him, puzzled. Then she pulled a sachet from her handbag. Bradan tore it open, then pulled out his gun. After ejecting the magazine and a single round in the chamber, he put the weapon and the sachet on the table, right in front of the old guy.

'Alan, clean it for me, please.'

Alan didn't really want to touch it, but he obeyed. He cleaned the gun almost at arm's length, as if it were toxic. 'What do you want, sir? I don't think it's money,' he said. 'And my wife doesn't need to be here. Let her go sit in another room. I can answer all your questions. Please.'

There was a clock on the wall. Bradan glanced: just past nine o'clock. He put his finger to his lips. 'Quiet for now. It's almost time.'

He pushed the old lady's mobile phone towards her. 'Almost time,' he repeated.

The man had taken the pistol from her pocket, but it was the knife Helen stared at, the one he claimed he'd hurt Glendon with. She was tied with her hands and feet behind her, and her face still hurt from his boot, so she wasn't about to doubt his threat.

'Nice trick earlier,' he said. 'Glendon shouts *fall*, and you shoot my friend, up on the roof. Had me fooled for all of two seconds. His name was Harry. He was a nice man and didn't deserve what you did, just for a joke.'

He had removed his helmet. She was surprised to see he was old, surely close to sixty, but he had skills. She found herself wanting to ask him about his past. She figured he must have been an army guy when he was younger.

'I'll tell you whatever you want to know,' she pleaded. 'Don't kill me. I have a child.'

'So do I. And I'll do anything to keep him safe, so please remember that. I don't need you to tell me anything. Your friend was most helpful in that department. I know everything.'

He used the blade of his knife to pull up the sleeve of the boiler suit he had taken from Glendon, which was short on his legs and tight in the torso. She saw marks on his arm. Ink. She realised he had written a list of names and numbers on his skin. The entire team, and their radio channel numbers. Skills for sure.

'I know there are fourteen of you, as you can see. I know that four are at the manor house, although they are now three because one of them couldn't control his hormones. There are five covering the perimeter, three of them in the farmhouses to the west and two blocking the road to the north and south. Then there's you, here to watch over the village. A very good vantage point, by the way. Four others had the job of capturing all my friends at the housing estate, and two of those are now roaming around the village, looking for stragglers your net missed, while another is watching over the captured residents, who are all my close friends. Number four is incapacitated in a house down there, half-naked because I have his outfit. This is his blood.'

He pointed the tip of the blade at a spot of red on his shoulder.

'Fourteen people, and only one of them is going home. That's you, if you do exactly as I say. Do that and you'll live. You might end up lonely with all your friends gone, but hey, so will I if I allow you people to kill everyone here. Can you imagine me living here all alone? Who's going to sell the bookshop books? You?'

Helen looked at him. At the knife. At the radio he now thrust close to her mouth. Her radio.

'What I want from you is simple. The guy barring the north road is called George Whelan, and he's the one I'm going to take down next. George is on channel seven. You're going to call him and say what I tell you to say. If you try a code word, a funny pause, any kind of Irish slang, anything that I think might be a warning, I'll kill you. They won't find you here for years. An archaeological treasure trove, this area. They'll think they've found the old bones of some woman from the Middle Ages and you'll be interred in a glass case in a museum. Understand?'

She nodded frantically.

'Then get your best acting voice on. I need an award-winning performance of joy and excitement. Picture yourself as a child with the best toy you ever got for Christmas. This is what you're going to do...'

At seventeen minutes past nine, Denis came into the library with his laptop. Bradan sat up straight.

'Pick up your phone,' he told the old lady. He then picked his gun from the table, where her husband had put it following a good clean. He slotted in the magazine and chambered the loose round.

Denis sat on the floor, with the laptop on his knees, and tapped a few keys. His finger then hovered above a final key. 'What if someone's got a hidden phone and they just happen to try calling the police once I do this?' he said.

Bradan shrugged. 'That would be bad luck of the first order, and probably God's way of telling us we're destined to fail. But we'll never know until you hit that key.'

Denis made a big show of it, riding his finger high and then making an explosion sound as he jabbed a key. 'There. Jammers deactivated,' he said. 'You have two minutes.'

Bradan lifted the old lady's phone and dialled a number, then handed it to her. In his other hand he held a slip of paper. He lifted his gun and pointed it at her husband's head.

'Read it word for word, please,' Bradan told her. 'I don't want to have to clean this gun again.'

'Did you do that clean-my-gun daftness again?' Denis shook his head. To the old couple, he said, 'He thinks it scares people.'

The phone started ringing on speaker. The old lady looked at the screen, and the name displayed there painted shock on her face. 'You want me to... call...' Her face grew angry. 'You're just thieves. I'm not making this call. Sara has nothing to do with this foolishness.'

Her husband put a hand on her arm and tried to shush her. Clearly he hadn't expected his wife to speak in such a way to this man.

But Bradan just smiled at her. 'Actually, Mrs Everton, your daughter has everything to do with this.'

10

At the northern gatehouse, George watched the executive come back again.

He'd been gone a long time. Maybe he'd got lost, or he'd been sat stewing about the roadblock, or he'd tried the southern entrance and been barred by Jack. This time the car screeched to a halt and the executive got out and slapped his own bonnet. 'I don't care about your problems. I live here and I'm going home. Move that damned van.'

He started waving a fist, only it wasn't the fist he was waving at all. It was a mobile phone.

Despite knowing his line wasn't going to work, George said, 'Fumes, mate' anyway.

The executive started jabbing numbers and hurling threats. Apparently his cousin was a policeman, and he was going to come up here, and George was going to spend the night in a cell and get his van taken to a scrapyard.

Or not. George took two steps towards him, so the distance was something he was comfortable with. A distance he was sure could guarantee a hole in a face every time. And then he yanked his pistol and put a hole in the executive's face. Down he went in front of his own car, lit by the headlights.

'Fumes, mate.'

George jumped and nearly put a bullet in his own foot when the passenger door burst open and something flew out. Something? A woman. Some woman in a long skirt with a slit and a short purple jacket over a white business blouse, and a pretty face. He saw all of this in the two seconds it took her to dart into the woods, screaming. Christ, the guy had had a passenger all along, someone George had failed to see sitting there behind the windscreen.

He went in pursuit.

George made the mistake of trying to have fun with the woman. He had no intention of killing her, but he didn't mind if she died of fright. He caught up to her, but made no attempt to actually grab her. His fingers scraping across her collar and a breathy threat did the trick nicely.

'Come to daddy, little whore.'

He grunted in fake annoyance at his near-miss, and then fell back ten feet. Wailing still, the woman stumbled over a root and fell hard. To continue the game, he put his foot under a tree root that wasn't there and also fell.

'Daddy wants fun, baby.'

Despite her panic and her haste, or because of it, she took a long time to get up and get stumbling away, so George had to fake another trip in order to let her put some distance between them.

'Daddy's coming again.'

She screamed at him to get lost. Twenty seconds later, after twice pretending to get his arms tangled up in branches, George stopped laughing as he realised he was getting far away from his van, and he wasn't supposed to leave it. So he increased his pace, meaning to end this now.

Despite her runaway fear, the woman managed to kick off her shoes in mid-stride so she could run better. Suddenly, he found that he had to run at full pelt just to keep pace with her, fifteen feet back. Where did a woman who made a living working in an office get such stamina? He almost asked her to please slow down.

Just as he was about to give up, knowing he couldn't continue to move away from his van, she stopped. Dead. He drew up five feet from her, panting but trying to hide it. She was flicking her head between him and the land ahead, which fell away steeply.

'Nowhere to run,' he said, grinning at her. 'So, you gonna come to daddy or what?'

She chose the 'or what' option, which was to launch herself into the abyss. George rushed to the edge, full of guilt. He did not hurt women. It had all been a joke. His plan had been to tie her up out here so she wouldn't cause a problem, that was all.

'Hey, just kidding,' he called after her as she barrelled down the steep slope, and then, 'Slow down' when he saw that her momentum was getting too much for her. Her legs pistoned as she built speed, too much speed. A trip was inevitable.

'Watch out,' he yelled when it happened. He watched her tumble down the steep slope like a ball, legs and arms flailing, totally out of control. A collision was inevitable.

'Watch the tree,' he yelled, again too late. He watched her hit a dead stop against a thick trunk, head-first. After that she lay still, half-hidden in the undergrowth. He suspected she was playing possum in the hope he'd leave, so he kicked at the undergrowth to give the impression he was coming down for daddy fun. But she didn't get up and flee again. And then he saw, even in the dark, a great dark patch on the trunk of the tree. Blood.

George made his way down the slope slowly, on his butt,

until he was close enough to see the woman's face in there amongst the undergrowth. Her head was caved in. No longer pretty. Blood was all over her. Dead or not, she was going to cause no further problem for the mission.

'Sorry,' he said to her. 'It was a joke. I don't hurt women.'

He looked into the sky beyond the black spiderweb of branches and repeated that word: *sorry*. He felt daft doing so, because he didn't believe in God. But, just in case, he wanted her to know he was not that kind of man. Just in case.

Then he looked at the ground. Because maybe she was a bad woman and not destined for a trip to Heaven.

So he said 'Sorry' to the ground as well. Just in case.

Ten minutes later, George's radio barked. 'George, are you there?'

It was channel eleven, Helen's. But he knew her voice anyway. He calmed his heavy breathing before answering.

'What's up, Helen?'

She said Glendon had something to show him. Something amazing that he needed to see. Glendon was going to come and show him.

'Glendon can't leave the housing estate, Helen, you know that.'

But he needed to see this. Glendon had showed her, and it was quite amazing. She would watch the estate with her gun while Glendon rode to George. George just had to see this thing.

He tried to say no, but not because Glendon would be leaving his post. Because George was not at his. He was still in the woods, no longer wondering if he was lost but now damn sure of it. Worried that a direct route ahead in any direction might take him the wrong way, he had been criss-crossing and backtracking, like a bird trapped in a room. His ankles hurt from whacking protruding roots and stones and he was soaked by rain dripping from trees that had retained the morning rain. Great bloody fun. And if the boss found out he'd left the road, there would be hell to pay.

Then he had an idea: if Glendon came on his quad, George could use the noise to make his way back to the road. He'd claim he'd rushed into the trees for a piss if Glendon got to the van before him.

'Come on, then. Tell Glendon to come up on his quad. Show me this great whatever-it-is.'

Five minutes later he heard the engine coming, got a bearing on it, and started running. And it bloody worked. He found the road in no time.

But as he got to the edge of the trees, he saw the quad emerge from the battlement and circle to park at the back of his crashed van. Glendon got off, his back towards George, helmet still in place. He looked at the executive's abandoned car and the dead guy in front of it, washed in headlights, and George cursed. He'd forgotten about the car and the body. Should have gotten back here earlier to get rid of them. The boss didn't want unnecessary kills and if Glendon told him about this one, there would be trouble. Helen might have let it go, but Glendon was a brown-nose and sure to rat him out. Why the hell hadn't George asked Helen to come instead?

Glendon went to the van and tried to open the back door. And that was when suspicion sparked in George's mind. Glendon tried to yank the handle down, but the team knew it was faulty and had to be lifted upwards first.

Then he saw the pistol in Glendon's hand.

Something was wrong.

Hiding behind a tree, he got on his radio and dialled it to channel six, Glendon's. 'Glendon?'

He heard nothing from across the road, where the figure was standing looking puzzled now he knew the van was empty. George tried Helen's channel too, and heard his own tinny voice from the figure's location as he spoke her name.

He pulled his pistol, and started to inch forward, seeking a good distance to fire from. Not one comfortable enough to put a hole in a face, but just to guarantee a hit somewhere. Because something was badly wrong here. Glendon's outfit, but not Glendon. Helen's radio, but for damn certain not Helen.

He saw the figure lift the radio, and realised what was about to happen. Too late he tried to turn the volume down on his own device. The man in the helmet whistled into the radio, loud, and the noise shrieked from George's handset, and the man heard it and turned, and dived aside just as George fired, and his shot was good because a window in the van burst right where the imposter's head had been.

One-handed, George twisted his dial to channel one, the boss's, ready to scream that their mission had been compromised, and that was when a bullet blew fragments out of a branch hanging low by his head, and he staggered back and slipped and fell, and the radio flew from his hands.

George landed hard on his arse just as his floored enemy rolled into a sitting position, too. Thirty feet apart, facing each other, they fired together. Another good shot, as he saw the guy's helmet jerk, but it must have been a glancing strike because the bullet put a hole in the van, behind and to one side of him. But the impact caused the imposter's bullet to ignite a spark on the tarmac between them.

George steadied his aim, but the gun started to drop. He couldn't stop it. It dragged his arm down as if it weighed fifty kilograms. Beyond, he watched the helmeted enemy get to his feet and approach. George tried to hold his gun with both hands, but his other arm wouldn't move. Then he seemed to feel immense weight on his head, and shoulders, as if pressed upon from above. Both arms sagged. The gun fell from useless fingers. His head lolled forward. And that was when he saw a big red stain on his stomach. The pain announced itself a moment afterwards. *Shit. Bullet ricocheted off the road. Damn fluke.*

George toppled backwards. He heard but didn't feel his head smack the road. He saw the helmeted man float into his vision and block the moonlight, alien-like in George's clouding vision.

'Who are you?' George managed to whisper as the guy grabbed his legs and started to drag him. Towards the woods, George thought. Where his body wouldn't be found. Maybe next to the tumbling woman. His woozy brain had enough power to try another tactic: 'I'm a father. Three babies.'

'Then you know what fathers will do to keep them safe,' was the last thing George ever heard.

Emil hid the body in the back of the van, then put the other body beside it. Some innocent guy who'd turned up at the wrong time. He then got in the dead guy's car. The keys were in the ignition. He started it up, reversed, then powered it forward, hard into the back of the van, shunting the vehicle forward and sideways so it created an even better blockage of the battlement archway. A roadblock nobody was going to shift without heavy machinery. Then he got on the quad bike and hid that in the trees. It was too noisy for what he needed to do.

Emil had killed Glendon and Helen after using them in his little gotta-see-this trick, and he had planned the same for the guy called George. But George was dead, and a dead guy was not going to be able to put on a happy voice and claim he had something cool to show someone. So now Emil's plan had to change.

He climbed past the van and rushed through the battlement,

stopping in the darkness at the other end, where he'd hidden Helen's powerful rifle. He set the bipod on a rock by the roadside and lay behind the weapon, which was aimed down into Barkelow.

He knew sniper rifles quite well, although it had been many years since he'd held one. This was the FR F2, a weapon used by the Irish military. 7.62 x 51-millimetre rounds in a ten-round magazine. The Leopold scope had a series of dots running vertically through the bottom half, marked in increments of fifty metres up to 800, and each dot had a horizontal line running through it that was marked in increments of 5 mph. Simple, but effective. Pick your distance, shift left or right depending on wind speed, and place the correct dot on your target and fire. There was also a switch for jumping to night vision. These were serious people with a serious agenda.

The village was opened up below him. His home for so many years now. He knew its history and he knew its foibles, its nooks and crannies, its people. A stranger could drive through and notice nothing untoward: just another Peak District village sitting silent in the night. Emil had wandered at night a hundred times, just to think, to clear his head, and he was accustomed to the feel of the inert air, the silence, but he was connected to this place on some kind of unexplainable mental wavelength, and right now he felt the difference. Like the almost palpable energy in a room that someone has died in. It felt wrong, hollow. He could sense badness where none belonged. More important, that connection felt like something vital to his well-being, like a dialysis machine for a patient with a faulty kidney. He did not want to leave this place. He was not going to leave. He had run once before, and he was damned well not going to run again.

The scope moved. Portions of the village were thrust at him in zoom. On the left of the north road, a hundred metres away, the old hotel, a three-storey stone building that had once been a house, then a factory. The hotel had closed in the eighties and was now a shell with a rotten roof and boarded-up windows. It sat alone and desolate like a child on a naughty step. Local authorities wanted it torn down, but the residents had vetoed their attempts, like a person who preferred a rotting tooth over an appearance-changing gap. Well, that old hotel was once more a major feature of the village, at least for tonight.

The scope shifted. Beyond the old hotel was Woodlands, the housing estate. Barkelow had thrived as a farming community a hundred years ago, and then as a tourist spot because of Barkelow Hall, but that had changed a generation back. Barkelow Hall had been taken over by new owners, and they had fixed the rotten portions, and rejuvenated the remaining battlements and sections of a wall that had long ago ringed the village. But any chance of prosperity for the village had then been struck down: the family had wanted peace and quiet, not flocks of people traipsing through their home, and they had closed the manor house to the public.

Barkelow had felt the effect like an earthquake. Tourism had dried up and locals who'd relied upon it had shifted out in droves. Those who remained to run their quaint little stores survived only because they already had savings or pensions. Fearing the village would implode, planners had erected Woodlands to draw in rich retirees and childless couples with out-of-town employment. Emil had entered their world during that bleak time and taken a handyman job for the reclusive manor house owners, which had guaranteed him one of the new homes. At one point over three hundred people had lived in the village, but that number had withered to forty-nine during the dark days. Today just shy of a hundred souls called Barkelow home, which was a number everyone felt comfortable with. A healthy number. The village had found a nice balance, and Emil was damned if these invaders were going to upset that.

The scope moved again, south, but still on the eastern side of the village, and onto the promontory bearing Barkelow Hall, which sat a little higher than his position, roughly 300 metres away. Barkelow Hall: death of the village, and rebirth of it too: glorious tourist cash had returned after the hall had once again changed hands and reopened to the public.

They were in there, the bad guys, holding hostages. Holding his son. He wished the house were made of glass, so he could rend open heads right from this spot.

The rifle scope moved further south, onto the wasteland. Another casualty of Barkelow's demise, like the old hotel. There had once been a much larger housing estate there, and a row of shops on the roadside, but the tourism decline had forced the owners to sell up, move on. Emil had heard rumours of a private theme park planned for the abandoned site, and a cricket ground, and a hypermarket, but instead it had been left to ruin. Today it was considered a danger spot, because while the foundations of the buildings had been torn up, their vast cellars had been left alone, and nobody knew where these great pits lurked. Nobody dared come in with a digger, or even go walking there in case weak land above a cavity fell away. Emil's emergency satchel had spent years in one of those cellars, although now sat out in a field. He wondered if he might ever need it. Hopefully, after today, he could dispose of it. Barkelow was his home. He would only abandon it if he had zero choice. He still had a chance to put things right. But he would have to get that satchel at some point in case a resident found it and saw grumpy old handyman Torrance's face on three passports with different names. Not to mention the gun.

The scope moved on. At his height, dead ahead at the other end of the valley, top of the south road, he saw the hole in the trees where the road vanished into blackness. Once there had been a plan for a suspension bridge to cross from here to there because the locals didn't like the summer traffic. They would have less liked the idea of vehicles passing over their heads, of drivers tossing rubbish below, of perched birds raining shit on their heads. Also, it would have allowed people to bypass the village without spending money. The plan hadn't gained any ground, of course.

He cut the reminiscing. In those trees was another bad guy.

And back again, now west of the main road. The scope climbed the hill, to the trio of farmhouses atop the ridge. The scope was eighteen times magnification, but the furthest farmhouse was close to 500 metres away. Too far to make anything out in the windows. As he'd said to Glendon, it made sense to put snipers in those three properties. Sitting on the ridge like that with a bad guy in each, they created a powerful defensive wall against an approach from the west. The coarse land to the east made infiltration by the police tricky, at least by vehicle, and a sniper in the gatehouse on that ridge would see them coming. That left only the main road, easily cut off by a man at each end. Plus, all these elevated positions, in a ring around Barkelow, allowed eyes to watch over all movement in the village. Emil had to commend the invaders' tactics: six people, and Barkelow could be locked down.

Those six were now four, though, and about to decrease again.

11

Emil ignored the furthest two farmhouses and watched the nearest, just 170 metres away to his immediate right. All the distances were in his head, which would make shots easier. The woman inside would be at the back bedroom so she could watch the village, according to Glendon, but the window was dark and even with the scope he could see nothing beyond the glass. It didn't mean she wasn't there, though. Her name was Maryse and she had a daughter also here, who Emil had already met by the shops.

He left the battlement and moved west, off the road and over the stone wall and into thick grass. He crawled 100 metres through this unkempt land until he reached the post-and-rail fence surrounding the Harris farm. Here he put his eye to the scope. The Harris' dog, chained as always to the tractor wheel, was lying dead and bloody. The back door was ajar. Still no movement at any of the darkened windows. Maybe the woman inside was taking a shit.

Emil crawled through the fence and got up and ran across the grass. He knew he was more exposed at speed, but crawling would have left him out in the open for too long. He reached the nearest outhouse in seconds and ducked behind it, panting from his exertions. Another reminder that he was too old for this lark.

He went to the back door of the farmhouse and opened it slowly. He could hear dance music from a room within, and that, more than Glendon's tale or the dead dog, told him bad shit had happened in here. No way the Harris couple ever listened to the devil's music, as they called anything that wasn't suitable for a quiet afternoon.

He heard a voice. Female. Coming closer. He didn't catch the exact words, because of the accent and a wall in the way, but he thought the woman was giving an all-clear at this farmhouse. This could be tricky, if those securing the farmhouses had to report in by radio every so often.

And then the living room door opened and there she was, frozen. Just a black shape in the doorway, but the thick hair said it was a woman. Maryse. Thirty-eight. Former bank clerk turned terrorist. His shock was less than hers, because the last thing she had expected was a man with a gun at the kitchen door.

He had a pistol in his hand, as did she. But that extra shock of hers stayed her hand a little too long. Two black figures in a black room, drawing like wild west gunslingers. Two loud bangs that sounded like one because they came close together. Beside Emil, the kitchen window sprinkled into a thousand pieces all over the worktop and the sink, and the bullet that caused it went out and away. Ten feet ahead of him, the black shape crumpled to the ground, and the bullet that caused it stayed right there.

He didn't want to use the light, but found himself needing to see her face. The face of another kill. He flicked the light on and off quickly, using that half-second to imprint the face he saw in his mind. She was handsome, apart from the death grimace. Then the darkness overwhelmed her again and he tried to shut her from his mind. He wished he hadn't looked.

~

Paul Ó Caiside finished his cigar and tried channel eleven again, but got the same result. Nothing from Helen up on the eastern ridge. So he tossed the butt and dialled seven. Nothing. Six: zilch. Static all the way. He hoped it wasn't because the bastards were ignoring him. On channel eight he got a reply, finally, from Luke.

'What's going on around there, Luke? Anything? You heard from Helen, Glendon or George? They're not answering the radios.'

Luke said he hadn't heard from them.

Paul was parked behind a bus shelter on the western side of the road where it split to curve around the market square. He turned and stared out, focusing on the three small farmhouses he could see a few hundred metres away. He looked for movement, but his automatic rifle did not have a scope and it was too dark.

He tried Glendon again. Helen again. George again. Six people, and he'd only had replies from Luke and Maryse and Dalaigh in the farmhouses. Not a peep from three of the four he was supposed to use for the damn mission in barely half an hour's time.

He called Jack at the south end of the road, but he also hadn't heard from the missing three. Why would he? 'The rule was not to talk to each other unless we have to. Just you guys running this show, that was the rule. I'm to do my job not worrying about them doing theirs.'

Paul got angry. 'Well I need them. If they don't do theirs, the whole thing falls apart.'

'Well, the rule was I take care of my job, and I'm doing mine,' was all Jack said.

Paul checked his watch. There was time. He rushed across the market square and opened the door of the bookshop. There was Capucine, sitting in the dark at a table like a customer, only she had her AK-47 on the table rather than a book. And she was fiddling with a necklace that she hadn't had last time he'd seen her.

'What?' she said.

Paul frowned. He really hated young people. Always full of attitude, always emotional. He told her to stay ready.

'Are I not I sitting where supposed to, with a gun?'

Capucine's shop was on the north corner of the semi-circle. Other end was Kane's. He rushed there. Kane was straightening pictures on the walls. Using the barrel of his AK-47. In the dark. These people!

'What?' Kane said.

'Jesus Christ,' Paul barked, and rushed back to the bus shelter, where he yanked his radio and tried the missing three people again. Hello white noise.

That was it. He was not supposed to call Bradan until the target arrived, but the plan was going askew. So he called, and he got straight to the point. Three fools not responding.

Bradan didn't sound that surprised. More like angry. 'Check on them,' Bradan said. 'Make it quick, because time is running down. Be back in position in twenty-five.'

'It's these young idiots you hired,' Paul said. He was ready for a long rant, and for Bradan to tell him he'd been right, well done, we won't hire green blood next time. But Bradan cut him off:

'We were the same young idiots once, Paul. And our bosses gave us the leeway to grow. Check on them. Back in position in twenty-five.'

Bradan killed the call. Paul swore and ran across the road again.

'What now?' Capucine barked. She was at a mirror on the wall, admiring her new necklace.

'Helen's not answering the radio. Go check on her. That's an order from Bradan. Up on the ridge. You, he said.'

He slammed the door on her before she could object.

'Glendon's not answering his damned radio,' he told Kane thirty seconds later. 'Bradan says you need to go check. He's watching the housing estate in case we missed anyone.'

'And what are you going to do?'

'George isn't answering, either. I'm going to check on him. This has come from Bradan. You know, the boss, the guy paying you, the guy you swore loyalty to. He wants you to check on Glendon, so get going.'

Again, he slammed the door before he could get backchat.

He retook his position at the bus stop. He watched Capucine leave the shop and hop on her quad and head north. Kane did the same a minute later. *Good. At least these fools could still follow simple instructions.*

He called Maryse, Dalaigh and Luke again, asking each simply: 'You okay?'

Luke said, 'Aye, *mein führer.*'

Dalaigh said, 'I don't need babysitting, Paul.'

Maryse said: nothing. He repeated his question, got the same nothing, and grew more concerned. Now Maryse was silent as well. Were his people fleeing? Spontaneously combusting? Had old Mrs Harris at the farmhouse hidden in the pantry and jumped Maryse with a knitting needle?

Emil found Mrs Harris lying dead in the kitchen pantry, her skirt up over her hips. Nothing sexual, just a result of being dragged by her feet. Nothing of note in the living room, except that a money jar's contents had been scattered across a coffee table. But the Harrises could have done that. Maybe they'd been counting the money when the invaders burst in.

Mr Harris was on the stairs, lying flat on his face, two bullet holes in his back and one in his neck. There was a bloodstain on a higher stair, as if he'd been shot there and had slipped down.

In the back bedroom, he found a sniper rifle laid on a fallen wardrobe so the user could sit and aim it out of the window. An F2, same as the one he carried. That window faced west, away from the village, so the gunman could pick off approaching cops. He had a quick look through the scope. Saw the dirt road that led to the house, but no police. Thankfully.

He picked up the rifle and carried it into the small bedroom on the south side of the house, opened the window wide and through the scope scanned the Hunter farmhouse 150 metres away. He didn't see any movement. And time was of the essence, so there could be none wasted on waiting.

Downstairs, clipped to the dead sniper's waist, was a radio. He took it, and then found a small vanity mirror in the bathroom. In the south bedroom once more, he aimed the rifle at the upstairs windows of the Hunter farmhouse. There were two, and it took him half a second to flick between them. One was a window at the top of the stairs, one a bedroom. The bedroom was the most likely location of the sniper, but he couldn't afford to ignore the landing window.

He checked his arm, where he had written down fourteen names and fourteen numbers: radio channel locations for each of the fourteen terrorists, courtesy of Glendon. He dialled channel three. Dalaigh Nolan, eighteen years old. Eighteen. The kid had hardly lived. But Emil reminded himself that life was about choices, and these people had to suffer the consequences of bad ones.

He scraped his thumb over the microphone as he spoke, in order to mask his voice.

'Problem,' he said in his best girl's voice. Then he tossed down the vanity mirror he held in his other hand, and made sure the radio was close enough to catch the sound.

Two seconds later a young man's voice came back at him. 'Maryse? There's a problem? What just smashed?'

Dalaigh knew this was Maryse's radio then. Maybe each had a signature, or the number of an incoming transmission flashed up. He was sure that could prove to be advantageous.

Emil ticked the barrel of the F2 from landing window to bedroom window and back again, like a metronome.

'Maryse? Did something just smash? What's the problem?'

Emil ignored the questions. The metronome ticked back and forth, quickly. Too quickly, in the end. He started to flick back and forth without really looking, and when he caught movement at the bedroom window, he automatically tracked away from it before realising. He flicked back fast, but the guy was good. The window floated into the scope, but Dalaigh wasn't just already there, he was already there and watching through his own scope, rifle aimed at Emil's window. Emil fired too quickly, weapon still travelling, and he watched the window burst inward. But the gunman didn't move. A miss. A direct hit into the glassy aura around the young sniper.

Emil froze, dead on now, and fired again, and the rifle exploded in his hands. But as he fell back, pain blooming, weapon dropping from his grip, he knew that was not the case. His enemy had been given a half-second's reprieve that he shouldn't have had, and he had used it well, perfectly; had employed that half-second in the only way possible in order to save his own life. A quarter of a second to realise he was seeing a foe rather than the friend he expected, and the other quarter second to pull the trigger.

Kane rode around the housing estate, but there was no sign of Glendon on the streets. He killed the engine on each road, listening for the sounds of breaking, or laughing, whatever. Maybe even the screams of a young woman Glendon might have found hiding. Nothing.

He did another loop and stopped halfway along Oak Lane, and his eyes fell on the road as he tried to think, and because his brain wasn't focusing on it, the mark on the tarmac didn't register at first.

Then it did. He jerked as if exiting a trance, leaped off the quad and lifted his assault rifle and pointed it this way and that. Nobody around. He went to the mark and knelt by it and touched it with his finger, and knew then it was what he'd feared it was.

Blood.

Not good. The villagers had been taken with unbelievable ease, none of them hurt, and this blood was fresh. He knew it was Glendon's. If he tasted it and it got him high, he'd know for sure it was the dope-smoking gobshite's life fluid.

Maybe Glendon had tumbled off his quad and gone to find a first-aid kit, or just to lie down. So Kane rushed towards the nearest house on the right side of the road. He ran from room to room, calling Glendon's name. When he was sure the guy wasn't sleeping in a corner somewhere, he went next door. He quickly checked the nearest four houses on the right, but came up short on dope-heads and fine wines. He rushed across the road to continue his search.

In the first house that side, his hopes soared. Here, the cellar trapdoor was under a rug, as if to pretend it wasn't there. He kicked the carpet away and yanked it open. The strip light above him illuminated only wooden steps with no risers, but suddenly he felt apprehensive and had no clue why. He descended into a room with wet stone walls and junk under canvas sheets. His arms broke out in goosebumps as gloominess closed around him. Before, he'd entered the cellars like a kid in a toy shop, darting here and there, delving into black corners for hidden gems, feeling walls for secret cupboards. But now he didn't want to press deeper into the underground. No Glendon, no blatantly visible wines, and he damned well wasn't going to look under the sheets, so he turned to leave.

And that was when he saw his friend lying behind the staircase.

He froze. Then he burst for the steps, jumping the first three with an irrational fear that a hand would snake through and grab his ankle. He slammed the trapdoor and put the rug back and stood on it. When his mind threw up a vision of a hand bursting through and dragging him down, he leaped away like a burned cat and overturned the kitchen table onto the rug. Mere seconds later, he was in the street, taking deep breaths. The big open universe above him managed to dampen anxiety created by that claustrophobic little underground hole and rational thought returned. He realised two things: zombies didn't exist, and he needed to tell Paul that goddamn Glendon's dead. He pulled his radio and used those exact words.

'What do you mean goddamn Glendon's dead?' Paul barked. 'Where is he?'

'Down in a cellar. Dead.'

'Jesus Christ. How did he die?'

Kane hadn't checked. Hadn't seen the point. Still didn't. *You want me to go back there and kneel next to him and check for a stab wound or whatever? Are you kidding?* That was what he wanted to say, but what came out was, 'Strangled.'

'Someone strangled him? An escaped resident?'

But then Kane wondered. Might Glendon have not been dead? No, he was dead, Kane convinced himself. Of course he was, the way he'd been all crumpled up behind the stairs. 'Don't know. Didn't see anyone around. But he's definitely dead.' *I hope, for my sake.*

'Get back into position,' Paul ordered him, and Kane relaxed. For a moment there, he had feared Paul would instruct him to bury the body.

Just sixty seconds after Kane's call, Capucine contacted Paul with no better news. She had just found Helen, atop the old battlement. Dead. Capucine stood over the woman as she made the call, but was staring out over the village, marvelling at the dotting of lights. So much more beautiful than the cityscapes she was used to. She was thinking about moving out into the country after all this was done.

'Jesus Christ. How did she die? Strangled?'

Strange guess, she thought. 'No, bleed out. Stabbed in neck, I say.'

'Who the hell is killing our people?'

'Eh?' That perked her up. 'People? Who else dead?'

'No one,' Paul said. 'Get back into position.'

Capucine rode back to the bookshop. Upstairs, in the gloomy main bedroom, she saw that the old woman had moved. She was on the floor, not the bed. Capucine went over and rolled her from her front to her back. The woman looked asleep, even with her hands tied behind her back and her feet bound, but Capucine slapped her.

'Don't play game,' she said.

The old woman looked up at her in fear.

'But maybe this was not escape attempt,' Capucine said. 'Maybe you just want to get closer to lover. Okay.'

That morning when their crew had slipped through the village, mingling with tourists, pretending to be sightseers while they scoped out the places they would take that evening, Capucine had entered the bookshop and engaged the woman in chatter, and had learned that Mrs Clocker was a widow whose weeks-dead husband had insisted on his deathbed that she wait at least a year before she sought love again.

Hadn't happened, because that evening when Capucine had broken into the shop, she had found the lady cuddling on the bed with a man. Capucine knew full well that love couldn't be denied. So now she grabbed the old lady's feet and dragged her across the room and into the bathroom.

Here lay her lover. Capucine had planned on tying them both up, but the guy had tried to stop her and his reward had been a slit throat. He lay dead in his own dried blood. Capucine had to yank hard to unstick him from the linoleum. She rolled him on top of the old woman. He was bigger, and now her own weight and his were trapping her arms under her back. There would be no shaking him off. Capucine moved his head so it lay against his lover's neck.

'There you go,' she said. The bathroom had no window, so the meagre light from the bedroom was cut away when she shut the door on them, leaving both in the pitch black.

Downstairs, she retook her seat behind the table bearing her assault rifle, facing the window, and while she waited tried on some more of the old lady's jewellery. And thought about what Paul had said. *People dead. Plural.*

~

Forty seconds after his chat with Capucine, Paul yanked open the back doors of George's van and saw his corpse. With some unknown guy lying dead right beside him. What the hell?

He called Bradan and relayed the news. Glendon, Helen and George, all dead, all killed. What if it was the same guy?

'It is,' Bradan said. 'He got Cathal as well.'

Paul had to lean against the side of the van. 'What? Who is this guy? A ninja here, in this tiny village?'

'The world has a whole bunch of lethal people and they have to live somewhere,' Bradan said. 'Don't worry about him. He's not part of this. Probably just got lucky. Heck, might not be the same guy at all.'

'Well that's worse,' Paul snorted. 'What do we do?'

'We do what we came here to do. Look, hide George's body if it's on show to the world then get back into position. There's only a few minutes to go. We can worry about this guy later.'

Paul hung up. Time was ticking and he didn't want to waste any hiding bodies. So he locked the van and got on his quad, and made some more radio calls as he rode back towards the market square.

Maryse was still quiet.

Luke said, 'Stop with the interruptions while I'm thinking.'

Dalaigh said: nothing.

Holy shit, so now Dalaigh was silent, too. Dropping like flies. Had the missing people decided to abandon the mission? Or had this mysterious ninja taken Dalaigh, too? That seemed unlikely: Dalaigh could see anyone approach from his position and never missed with that rifle of his.

13

———

Dalaigh knew he'd gotten the guy, and with a high-powered rifle, and on any other day he would have thought that was that. Whoever that bastard was, he was toast. But the guy had gotten him, too, and that should have been that – but wasn't. And if Dalaigh could survive, so could his enemy.

He'd felt the blow like a hammer to his chest. There was no time to even try to break his fall. As if he'd been fired downwards, he felt the thud and hit the carpet a fraction of a second later.

Now, he got to his knees and grabbed a chair from the vanity desk and slid it before the window and sat on it and grabbed his rifle before his strength could evaporate and make all of that impossible. Bent double to keep his head below the window, he checked out the wound to his chest with a shaking hand. Christ, his whole body was vibrating.

The hole was right where the heart should be. One of his ex-girlfriends had said he had a heart of stone, but of course that couldn't biologically be true. But the bullet had gone right in where the heart should have been, and he wasn't dead.

He needed two hands to lift the rifle and lay the barrel on

the window frame. He managed to get his shivering hands to hold the weapon still enough so he could put his eye to the scope. He found the house across the way, and then the window where his enemy had been, but could barely keep it steady in the crosshairs. No movement. Even if there had been, there was no way he'd get off another good shot. The guy would have to be much closer.

Instinctively, he aimed the scope down, which took a mighty effort to sit up even straighter in order to move the rifle into the desired angle. And there his enemy was, at the side of the house, having exited through the back door. Dalaigh aimed and fired, but the wavering barrel meant a gigantic miss. The guy probably didn't even hear the bullet whack anything nearby, because he started running towards Dalaigh's position, clearly not as badly hurt.

It was guesswork, sort of. The target was dancing about in the scope, and Dalaigh had to fire almost blind, because there was no way to get a bead. And blood loss was making his shivering worse. He could feel wetness now on his legs and in his groin. For the first time in his life, he hoped he'd just pissed himself. But nope, it was his life fluid cascading down from his chest. No heart shot, but something in there had torn asunder. A damn bag of blood, given how soaked he was.

The guy, just a black shape in the black night, slipped closer. Dalaigh fired, and fired, and fired, and then realised, if his count was right, that he had just two shots left, and that was when he paused. He'd wanted the guy closer, right? Let him come.

A noise nearby, somewhere near the roof. The black shape was pointing at him as it ran. No, not pointing. Firing. A handgun. Too far away, though. Dalaigh worked out a distance at which he thought he could take the guy without the guy having a decent shot in return, and he waited with his head now resting on the gun like a pillow.

More thwacks upon the house as bullets went wild. He tensed, in case a lucky shot got his face. No shot got his face. The guy came on, nothing out there to hide behind and seemingly no care, as if he knew exactly how badly he'd injured Dalaigh.

And then the guy was in range. With a monumental effort, Dalaigh raised his head and put his eye to the scope, and found the target bigger, surely now unmissable, but he didn't pull the trigger. If he missed, he would have one bullet and no way to reach the spares in the other bedroom. It made him wait, and he knew he'd waited too long when the guy stopped and aimed, and let his head flop to one side and heard the bullet smack a wall behind him as it travelled through the space where his face had been half a second before. When he tried to aim again, the guy was too close. To get the downward angle, Dalaigh would have to stand. He tried, but it felt as if his butt had been welded to the chair.

One bullet. He swept the rifle onto the floor and let himself fall off the chair, right next to it. He struggled into a lying position with his feet pointed towards the open door and his head propped up against the wall. Next he dragged the rifle onto his chest and got the bipod straddling his ankles. It had taken all but an ounce of his strength, but it was perfect. A neat line from eye to barrel to the doorway. But he would have to take the man as he climbed the stairs, otherwise he'd have no target higher than a shin.

Below, he heard the sound of the man entering the house. Dalaigh wanted to shout to him, but couldn't afford the energy. He had just enough left to pull the trigger.

Emil kicked open the back door and rushed in. He knew he was doing so blindly, and if there had been a second enemy present, someone downstairs, he would have had no defence. But there was no second enemy and he moved through the kitchen and towards the stairs and up. There was a half-landing near the top, with the final three steps jutting at a right angle and facing the room he needed, so Emil knelt when he got there and crawled and slowly lifted his eyes above the level of the top stair with his pistol aimed before him. He watched the top of his enemy's head come into view, and then the face, and then the rest of him, and then Emil stood up and, still aiming, walked into the room.

The blood and the closed eyes told the tale. Dalaigh was dead in a pool of his own blood. No trick, because closed eyes was a big risk. But he kept his gun on the young man and stepped out of the rifle's line and kicked it when he got close. He checked the guy's pulse. Gone.

Emil's F2 was damaged, so he took Dalaigh's. In the other bedroom he found a spare magazine. The bedroom was Don Hunter's private boudoir. It had a double bed, big mirrors and leather restraints on the walls, and a sex swing hanging from the ceiling. Don was middle-aged and had lost his wife years ago. Most people thought he still found it hard to try to move on and secure another relationship. Emil knew better. Don liked the kind of relationship that cost money and lasted one night. It gave him an idea and he quickly searched the bedside cabinet.

As he was leaving through the kitchen, he heard moaning. In the pantry he found Don, bound and gagged. He'd probably been tied up this way for fun a dozen times, but he wasn't enjoying it on this occasion. The relief in Don's eyes when Emil turned on the light was massive. Emil ripped off the large plaster over Don's mouth. He'd been careful to set his rifle out of Don's sight.

'Thank God,' Don moaned. 'Get me out of here. Two men with guns kidnapped me, Em.'

'I know,' Emil wheezed, shaking like a leaf. 'There's gunmen everywhere. We're going to die.' He made no move to untie Don.

Don started to struggle. 'I can't get these off, Em. I'm tied.'

Emil shook his head wildly and stammered over his next words. 'I can't, Don. It's safest to stay here. I'm going to hide upstairs. Stay here.'

Don's eyes found the fear again, and a dose of anger. 'Don't piss about, Em. Untie me. We have to phone the police. We'll get a couple of my guns and make a break for the next village.'

'They've cut the phones lines. We can't run about, making noise, in case they find us. We have to hide. The police will find us. I don't want to die, Don.'

Don started to struggle against his binds, but his kidnappers had done a thorough job. And he was tied in a way that wouldn't cause any kind of permanent injury. 'Em, I can't be left like this. We have to go fetch help.'

Emil put fake panic into his tone. 'Just stay quiet, or they'll find us. They'll shoot us. I don't want to get hurt, Don. Please be quiet.'

'Em, you cowardly little wimp. Let me out or–'

Emil shut the door.

14

———

Capucine had the patience for the job. Usually. Not right now.

She was worried about her mother. The boss had suspected a problem with Helen and her dead body proved there was a big one. Someone was out there and he wasn't on their side. He had killed Helen. Why had they sent Capucine? Clearly, she was no one's first choice. So the better choices had been sent, too, and that meant a check on others in the crew.

Sitting in the dark bookshop again, she called Kane. 'Ó Caiside act funny around you, Kane?'

'He asked me to go check on Glendon. Glendon's dead, Cap. He was dead in a house. Did you know?'

'I suspect. Helen dead, too.'

'What?'

'I think Ó Caiside suspect it. Someone is out there, killing us.'

'Don't be stupid, Cap. You mean one of the townsfolk we missed? Don't be stupid.'

'Perhaps, yes, I am being stupid.'

'If you're worrying in the dark, I'm only fifteen seconds down the road.'

She killed the call.

She took her pistol and went outside into the cold air. Suddenly this quaint little village had an eerie feel. The quiet wasn't peaceful any longer. She looked out to the west and saw the three farmhouses in a line above her position. All three were dark, as planned, but even that darkness reeked of negativity now. She got her quad.

The engine noise was loud and surely would alert any enemy they had out there. She drove past the market square and the road and aimed through a gateless gateway in the low stone wall, and into the field. Towards her mother's farmhouse.

She parked at the fence surrounding the property and trekked the remainder. No rush. The longer she took, the longer her mother was still alive. Until she got there and found the worst, her mother was fine.

The back door was closed, which she thought was a good sign. Maybe not. She opened it, and saw her mother immediately. Lying there in the kitchen, blood everywhere like a sheet she had been laid on. Even so, Capucine did not believe it.

'Mother?' she said quietly. No answer. She stepped inside slowly, into the dark. The dark would hide the worst of it. The dark would hide the killer, if he was here. If Capucine died now, fallen beside her mother, then there would be no more pain.

It was real. Even in the dark, Capucine could see the ragged bullet hole in her mother's neck. Her feet squelched in the blood.

She knelt beside her, head bowed, ready to be sacrificed. No killer came. The pain remained.

So be it. The pain would continue, and Capucine would continue. Besides, she had her Cathal.

She lifted her mother. Slim, like the daughter, she rose into her arms easily. Capucine carried her upstairs, kicked open a bedroom door. No killer lurking. Pain everywhere.

She laid her mother on the bed, and pulled the quilt over her. Over her body and neck, leaving just the face exposed. She wiped that face clean, straightened the hair, and then finally brought light into the world using the bedside lamp. She looked at that face, just once, just to imprint a final memory of her mother in her head. One second. Then the light went off again. She pulled her pistol, suddenly worried now about that killer. The pain was gone. The pain was a grain of sand washed under a tsunami on a beach. How could she have been so stupid earlier, bowed over her mother and totally defenceless? How could she risk a killer whisking her from the world she shared with her Cathal?

Pistol aimed at the door, she pulled her radio. 'Ó Caiside. My mother is dead. Did you know?'

'Shit. No.' Shock, but not a trace of sympathy. 'She let her guard down. Just like Cathal did.'

She killed the call. Made another. 'Bradan. Where is my Cathal? Is he dead?'

Silence.

It was as good as a direct yes.

She had expected something to tumble loose inside her and drop her dead on the carpet. But the shock was manageable. 'Who kill him?'

Bradan said, 'The handyman got him. Cathal went to kill him and got killed himself. It was his own fault.'

'Where is this man?'

Now Bradan seemed angry, any trace of sympathy gone: 'Capucine, keep your mind clear. You can have revenge later. The mission comes first. Understand?'

Silence.

It was as good as a direct yes. She hoped.

~

The final farmhouse showed no signs of life. But many of death.

Through the F2's scope he saw the Deavers' wood chipper and all around it were the Deavers. Their blood, anyway. It was sprayed as if the machine had had a massive red oil leak.

Mr Deaver had been a human rights lawyer in his younger years, and Mrs Deaver had organised the Barkelow Trolley Dash back when they'd had a monthly festivities day, although a Netflix and pizza addiction had put her own dashing days long behind her. Worse, they had been one of the first couples to show him and his son friendship when they first arrived in the village. Emil had helped them paint their interior walls. Mrs Deaver – Lucy – had rescued him from the woods one night nine years ago when he'd gotten drunk on his birthday and had gone wandering. He still remembered sitting against a tree, half-freezing to death, and watching her torchlight come towards him. And now they were nothing but a coating of red in the dirt. He decided, right then, that their killer, one Luke Ó Ríagáin, was going to suffer.

His haste threw caution to the wind. He ran across the grass with his rifle, no care that he might stand out, not even fearing a bullet to strike him down.

He reached the building and slipped down the side, and didn't even duck below the side window as he went past. He stepped out from around the corner–

–and ducked back as Luke exited.

The guy was big, his muscles straining at the boiler suit he wore. He had a big face that immediately made Emil think he was dumb. He carried a cardboard box in his hands. Emil couldn't see what was in it, but it looked heavy.

Luke went to the wood chipper and tore off the curtain over the hopper, exposing the lethal teeth beyond. He dumped the contents of the box onto the tray. Emil slung his rifle across his back and raised his handgun. No good at this distance of about twenty metres. But then he wasn't going to shoot this guy in the back anyway. He had not killed any of the others with any kind of malicious intent, but malicious intent was thudding away at his brain right now.

He closed in on the man, wide steps, slow, watching where he placed each foot so he wouldn't catch something that made a noise, then faster when Luke fired up the chipper. By now Emil was close enough to see what lay on the tray. Detritus. Junk. A metal teapot, and a wooden sculpture, and all sorts of other items from the house. The big lug was chipping any old crap he could find, like a playful child.

He stopped six feet away, and aimed the gun at the man's knee. Then his arse. Then his shoulder. He didn't know where he wanted to shoot him. Just somewhere that wouldn't cause instant death. Luke was oblivious as he plucked up a broom handle where it leaned against the chipper and started to push items towards the spinning teeth. It ate greedily and noisily.

Emil wanted to use the chipper. He thought about pushing the guy forward, trying to get him inside it. Too risky. In the end, there was risk with anything, and he did not have time to spare.

So he blew out the left knee. Luke screamed and dropped, cracking his head hard on the edge of the steel tray, and out he went.

When he came to a few minutes later, his legs and hands were tied, and Emil was kneeling beside him. At first Luke just stared up at him.

'The Deaver couple were nice people,' Emil said. 'That was very naughty, Luke.'

'Who you?' Luke said, and then he blinked hard, fast, and that was when the pain came back. He started screaming again.

'Me good guy,' Emil said, smacking his own chest with a fist,

Tarzan-style. He slipped a clear plastic bag over Luke's head and pulled the string tight. Luke immediately tried to draw a big breath.

Emil stood and watched Luke die. Watched him try to use his useless arms to tear away the bag, but he couldn't get them free from behind his back. Watched him roll over and scrape his face against the ground to tear the bag, but that didn't work, either. And just before the eyes started to close, all breath gone, life slipping away, Emil leaned close and smacked Luke's chest the same way, and in the same deep voice said, 'You... go... in... chipper.'

When Luke's final breath was a moment in history, Emil entered the farmhouse. In the back bedroom, he found an F2 propped on a chest of drawers on its side, barrel aimed out the window and across the village. He put his eye to the scope. At just less than 200 metres, fifty metres below his level, the scope put everything in clear form, even in the dim light from the few street lamps.

He saw, just north of the market square, a car parked in the road. Sideways on, blocking the way past. He saw a man with an assault rifle – an AK-47 according to Glendon – and a pistol crouched behind the bus shelter. The guy had a thick beard like Emil's own and looked to be about Emil's age. So that would be Paul Ó Caiside. Channel ten.

He saw the window in the northern shop bust outwards as a chair hit it. A guy reached out and pulled the chair back in. In his other hand was an AK-47 – planted in the shop earlier, according to Glendon. This guy looked a little like Dalaigh, from the centre farmhouse. His brother, then. Kane. Channel twelve.

The shop at the other end was where the brash young girl, Capucine, should be housed, but Emil could see nothing beyond the window. She was channel thirteen.

And finally, here came channel nine's owner, Jack Keegan,

riding a quad bike down the south road. He stopped short of the market square, pulling in behind a tree on the far side of the road. He was carrying an assault rifle – cheaply acquired AK-47s all round for the players performing in this endgame, according to Glendon.

Luke's radio garbled: 'Affirm if in position.'

Emil lifted the radio and in a deep voice said, 'Affirm.' He didn't know if that would work, didn't care.

'Target en route,' the voice said. 'Five minutes. Let's do this.'

Capucine entered the old hotel on the north road and went to the dining room. It was barred by a pair of thick wooden double doors. She yanked the metal bar from between the handles and pushed it open.

Immediately the townsfolk stopped talking. They stared at her. They were lying on their backs and fronts or sitting up if they'd managed to manoeuvre into that position, all with their ankles tie-wrapped and their wrists similarly bound behind their backs. Upon seeing her, standing there with an assault rifle in one hand and a large knife in the other, they tried to shrink back, moaning. She liked it.

She chose a young woman with buns on the side of her head, like Princess Leia from *Star Wars*. She hauled the woman to her feet by one of those buns and dragged her, hopping, across the room. Old dining tables and chairs, broken and discoloured, were stacked against one side, and she thrust the woman down into a sitting position against a table on its side, so she sat as if with her back to a wall. The bun had come loose. Her make-up had run from tears. A guy somewhere behind her started shouting for Capucine to leave her alone.

Perfect. Princess Leia had a loved one. Capucine eyed the

young man, who'd gotten to his feet, and stormed towards him. Those nearby vacated his area as if he were explosive. No messing, no threats: Capucine whipped out her knife and slid the blade quickly across his forehead, opening a cut that immediately painted his face red. He screamed and thrashed his arms, desperate to put his immobile hands on his wound. She tripped him to the floor so he wouldn't stumble about, then returned to the young woman. Behind her, everyone was amazingly silent, except one. The last guy to make a noise she didn't like, and look what had happened to him.

Capucine knelt and put the blade against Princess Leia's forehead. Pushed it hard, so there could be no mistake in the woman's mind that any movement from her and the knife would open a nasty gash.

'I will do all of you same way,' she shouted, for the room. 'You will floating in blood in this room in five minutes unless get what I want. And what I want is man who is handyman at shitty manor house.'

15

—————

Bradan took his position on the roof of the manor house, leaning in a crenel, elbows on the stone like a man enjoying the view. In the next gap was Denis, sitting there with his back against the drop, laptop on his knees, rifle leaning nearby.

So, it had all come down to this. Two months of planning. Six different trips here with one or two of his people so they could get a feel for the village. He had eaten in the coffee shops, visited the manor house, chatted to the locals, just playing the part of a regular tourist. That was the great thing about such places: strangers were not frowned upon, and foreign accents expected. You could stand around and point and whisper and plan an invasion, and it just looked like you were doing the tourist thing. Denis had irked the locals because he didn't talk to them, or even make eye contact. Said he didn't want to get cosy with people he might end up hurting. Bradan had not agreed. He was no malicious bastard, but for some reason he found it thrilling to put smiles on faces he knew would look at him in terror in days to come.

His radio buzzed. Fergal said, 'Anderson has agreed to pay.'

Bradan laughed. Five hundred thousand pounds would be a bonus, but the mechanics of getting to it were not a priority. They were not here for money. If it had been about money, he could have sneaked into the village and taken Anderson alone. For that, you didn't need a big team and you didn't need to capture a whole village.

His radio buzzed again. Jack Keegan: 'Target's coming.'

It was time. 'Radio blackout,' he told Denis, who worked his laptop.

Capucine parked outside the house. She looked up and down the street, just to make sure. It was empty and silent and glowed orange in the streetlights. A place she could enjoy living. Or maybe not anymore. Maybe that house right there, for her and Cathal, with her mother living a couple of doors away. Never to be, though. Because of the handyman.

She went to the house she needed. The side door was unlocked. Inside, she found a quaint hallway lined with pictures. Black and white, depicting summer scenes and winter countrysides.

The living room was basic. The furniture, strangely, was newer than the electronic equipment. A VHS video recorder was hooked up to a box-like TV that seemed twenty years old. The stereo had a turntable. There was a black cabinet with books and bottles of spirits mixed together, as if the owner didn't know the difference. There was a stack of DVDs, but no DVD player.

The kitchen was a mess. Untidy, but clean. There was a downstairs bathroom with a brand-new toilet whose lid was still wrapped shut in cellophane.

Nothing personal, though. No photo albums, no box of paperwork.

Bedrooms. The main bedroom was clearly that of a single man. Clothing hung wrinkled in the wardrobe, and haphazardly in drawers, and there was a chair stacked with folded trousers. A tiny portable TV older than she was sat on a slab of wood at the bottom of the bed, its cable trailing under the mattress and to a plug socket by the headboard. The other bedroom was more modern, with a flash stereo and a PlayStation like Cathal's and clothing for a more fashion-conscious man. A younger man.

Intriguing.

She searched the rest of the house, seeking a clue where the handyman might hide, but there was nothing of help. Not even a photograph, so she still didn't know the face of her enemy. Or the young man who lived with him.

She went out into the back garden. A grass lawn, a border of flowers mixed with weeds, and an old shed. Unlocked. She took a garden fork and returned to the house. Started in the kitchen. Living room. Bedrooms to finish. Afterwards, her shoulders ached, and the skin on her palms was rubbed red. Her clothing was sweat-drenched, heart thudding, but she felt better. The house now looked like a bomb site. No way penance enough for her mother and Cathal, but she felt better.

Before she left, she went to the noticeboard in the kitchen. Pinned there was an invite for the show tonight at the manor house. So, the handyman hadn't gone to the show. She took it down and turned it over, and there found a Post-it note attached. On this someone had scribbled:

SEE YOU THERE, POPS.

Pops. Her English was not brilliant, but this was a word she knew. Pops was slang for father. So, just as she had suspected upon seeing the smaller bedroom, the young man who also lived here was the handyman's son.

And he *was* at the manor house.

16

Aglow of white light from the trees up at the south. Headlights. They exited the trees, and Emil watched a white van come down the road. It passed Jack Keegan, and took the curve around the market square, and then it stopped by the bus shelter, between it and the shops on the other side of the square. The driver had obviously seen and become agitated by the vehicular roadblock some metres ahead. Emil took a half-second to flick the scope slightly downwards: there was his satchel, in the field.

And then it began. Jack was first. Fifty metres behind the van, he leaned out from behind his tree and started shooting, and Emil caught the gunfire a second later as the sound carried to him. He flicked his scope to the shops, where bright starbursts of light appeared in the broken window. Kane firing away. Closer, Paul was sticking his gun out from behind the stone bus shelter, also firing, but doing so blind because of the chance of bullets from Kane coming his way. Sparks danced all over the van as it rocked to the thuds of bullets. Three seconds, then it was over. The firing stopped. Everything was silent. The van's tyres were gone, wheels busted, but the metal sides were intact.

Bulletproof. Even the windows had held. But the van was going nowhere.

Then, shouting. Paul, from behind the bus shelter: 'Your van is disabled and you're covered by numerous armed men. Open the doors. Open the doors now.'

Nothing. Paul stood up, rifle aimed. Jack started moving closer. Beyond the van, Kane was framed in the busted shop window, also aiming.

'Look around,' Paul shouted. 'You're covered. Come out, or we kill everyone. You have no radio or mobile phone signals, no way to call for help. Out, out, out.'

The passenger door opened. Emil let it get far enough so that he could see the locking mechanism, and a woman in a uniform sitting in the seat, and then he let out his breath and the minute movement of the scope ceased, and he fired.

Nobody heard the gunshot at this distance, but Paul heard the ping the bullet made off the metal. He spun, looking out, towards the farmhouse. Emil had planned to take Kane first, but he couldn't resist when he saw Paul's face in a mask of anger, and the man's mouth form the word LUKE.

'Not quite,' Emil said, and fired. Nose shot. Paul's face turned to red mist and his body jerked backwards, gun flying. Even before he hit the stone bus shelter and dropped to the ground, Emil was moving the scope. It alighted on Jack, whose forward movement down the road had suddenly stopped. He aimed his rifle, but swept it left and right, clearly unsure where the shot had come from. He even aimed behind himself, fearful like some kid on a ghost train who doesn't know where the ghosts will pop up.

'Use your brain, Jack,' Emil said.

And then he did. Slowly he turned his head towards the west. The farmhouses. Of course: where else did you find a nice, elevated position to fire from? Hadn't they chosen such a location for that reason?

'That's it, smile for the lens,' Emil said, staring right into Jack's eyes. He squeezed the trigger, and Jack hit the tarmac minus a face.

The scope swept left, the ground rushing past like the view through a moving car window. In the dark north shop, Kane was ducked below the sill, just his eyes and rifle visible. No top of his head because he wore a woollen hat. Kane couldn't see his dead pals because Jack was too far to his left and Paul was on the other side of the van.

Emil put the crosshairs at the top of the hat, where there was a loose portion that didn't touch the head. The hat flew off. Kane jerked, and stood up, angry, just as Paul had been. He jabbed a finger hard and repeated against his chin, as if to say, *it's me, it's me.*

But that wasn't the message Emil chose to see. 'You want it in the chin, Kane? Whatever you say.'

The next bullet was again dead on. Kane fell back into the darkness and was gone.

By now the van was trying to move. The door banged shut, then again, but it wouldn't close properly. Emil's first bullet had busted the locking mechanism.

Emil stood up. It was time to go collect the package that these bastards had come all this way for.

'You're not really here for money, are you?'

Fergal, sitting on the stage, playing a game on his phone, looked up, scanned the faces, and saw who everyone was looking at.

A young man in jeans and a T-shirt. Wavy blond hair, early twenties but lots of teenage spots. And he didn't look that scared.

'What do you think you know?' Fergal said.

'I think, with the Irish accents, you're terrorists. Provisional IRA.'

'Real IRA,' Fergal snapped, jumping off the stage. People moaned, thinking violence was coming. But Fergal approached the boy without his weapon, and with his hands in his trouser pockets. He stopped before the young man, but looked at everyone. 'That's right, you should all be scared. No, we're not here for money. This is all part of the war. You're prisoners of war. What do you make of that?'

The young man said, 'Isn't your war in Ireland? Fighting the British Army for independence? Why are you in the Peak District?'

'We didn't move the goalposts, young man. Your government did when they took something from us. And we came to get it back. So now death is at your doorstep, and maybe you care a bit more now. We came here the same way your soldiers came into our country. You know what it's like.'

'So what did they take from you? A bomb?'

Fergal laughed. 'You think we came all this way to steal back a bomb? You can have all the bombs you want. They're easy to build. We came for... something else.'

The young man shrugged. 'Sounds like things aren't exactly going according to plan out there.'

They had all heard the faint sounds of gunfire.

'That's just war, kid. Don't you go getting your hopes of rescue up. Everything's going according to plan.'

'I think the plan's gone to shit,' Denis said.

Through the rifle scope, Bradan saw Jack, dead in the road. He saw the bus stop and an arm poking out from behind it. He scanned left and right, but saw no other people. He was the wrong side to see into any of the shop windows. 'Open the radios,' he said.

Denis objected: the guards in the van were still alive, trying to call for help right now.

Denis was right. Bradan continued to watch, and then saw it – but too late.

A shift of green from the edge of the hill. Like a portion of the grass moving. And as he watched, a man tossed aside that grass, and Bradan realised it was a blanket. A man who had been creeping close under a green blanket, invisible in the dark against the green ground. A cheap trick, almost comical, but lesser eyes would have missed it. Instantly he knew who this guy was. The handyman. The guy who had been throwing spanners in the works.

Bradan waited for the right moment. The guy reached the wall by the main road, where he ducked down. When he popped back up, he had a satchel in his hand. Bradan was tempted to fire, but he paused.

When the man started to climb the wall by the main road, and was perched atop it, Braden saw the perfect moment and fired. But anger wavered his aim. A piece of the stone wall burst right by the man's hand. The shock caused him to slip and crash to the pavement. Bradan fired again, but too hastily, and this bullet went nowhere. In the next moment the man was up, running, satchel discarded on the pavement. Bradan cursed, aimed again, but by then the figure had darted past the bus stop, where Paul clearly lay dead, and vanished behind the van.

Emil reached the van and yanked the door open, and aimed his pistol inside. Two guards in black uniforms, the passenger a female.

'Where are my mum and dad?' the female yelled at him, her anger masking her fear and shock. Beside her, the driver was frozen with both, his radio to his face, trying to call for backup.

Emil did not recognise her, but he knew her name was Sara Everton. He knew it all, of course, thanks to Glendon's desire to try to stay alive.

He told them to pop the back door, and heard it hiss open as a mechanical lock was disengaged. He ran back there and, careful to stay out of sight of the manor house overlooking everything, pulled the door and poked his pistol inside. Two more guards, and a man in a suit. The infamous Mr Crossen, according to Glendon. He was small, dumpy, in his early sixties, and looked more like a solicitor than a criminal. He was smiling, until he saw Emil. He got up. His hands were cuffed before him.

'I do not recognise you,' he said, his Irish accent barely there.

'Let's go, sir. We don't have long,' Emil said.

The man got out, saluted his guards, and ran with Emil. 'Stay here if you want to live,' Emil told the guards.

He and Mr Crossen ran to the car blocking the road. Crossen got in the passenger side, and Emil jumped in the driver's seat.

And then, amazingly, the back door opened and the woman guard got in.

'Take me to my parents,' she said, sternly.

The prisoner put his hand out for Emil's gun, saying, 'Let me finish this one myself. It's been so long since I killed someone.'

'It's gonna be a bit longer,' Emil said, and swung the gun hard, cracking Crossen's temple, sending him out instantly. Then he started the engine.

17

Capucine jogged along the ridgeline at the top of the eastern hill, through the trees, alongside portions of the old defensive wall from way back when Barkelow Hall had been a promontory fort. To her left, further east, the land fell away in craggy slopes towards the River Wye, and she thought how correct Bradan had been in assuming they didn't need to fortify this side against police attack. Craggy rocks to contend with on both hillsides, and thick trees along the ridgelines, and no major villages or villages too close by. No way in for vehicles, unless there was a track Bradan's research had missed. And a scout right where Helen had been positioned, or atop Barkelow Hall, where Bradan and Denis would be now, would spot the approach of anyone on foot a mile out.

She reached the end of the trees. The edge of the promontory. Ten seconds before she had been aware of being perched upon a thin shelf of land high up, but now the land opened out flat ahead of her and the feeling of suddenly being on firm low ground was disorienting. She had to remind herself that she was still high above the world.

Ahead and to the right was the manor house. Dead ahead, the walled gardens. She ran across the open grass towards the main entrance of the house.

It was deathly silent inside. She went to the ballroom, where she found the townspeople sitting against two walls, silent, hands tie-wrapped. Fergal was sitting on the stage with his legs dangling, waving his rifle left and right, almost daring anyone to try to make a break for it. Surprisingly, everyone was silent.

'What are you doing here?' Fergal said as she burst in. Some of the people sat up, perhaps thinking she was here to rescue them. So far all the captors they'd seen had been wearing tuxedoes, not boiler suits. 'What's happening down there? Is it over?'

'Not by long way,' she said. Then, like a shopper perusing a shelf of books, she walked along the line of the people arranged on her left. Everyone watched her in fear, as if she was looking to select a victim.

'What's that mean?' asked Fergal. 'Have we got the boss?'

She stopped before an elderly couple squashed tightly together, holding hands. 'We will have, soon.'

'What's that mean? You heard about Cathal, then?'

'Yes. Of course.' She knelt before the couple, her gun in her hand. She put the barrel against the old man's chest, and her lips by the old lady's ear.

Fergal raised his voice a little. 'That piss you off, Cap? About Cathal? What you going to do about it?'

And now, in return, the woman whispered in Capucine's. Capucine stood and walked into the centre of the ballroom.

Fergal was determined to get an answer: 'You hear me? I asked if that pissed you off. What are you going to do about what happened to Cathal?'

She ran her eyes around the room, seeking a green shirt, and spotty cheeks, and wavy blond hair. And there he was. She walked towards him. He stared up with bright green eyes, exactly as described. She pointed her gun right between them.

'Eat a dish serving cold,' Capucine said.

'Eh?' Fergal barked.

Bradan was furious. That damned handyman. He had been unable to shoot the bastard because he was behind the van, nor when he rushed across the ground with Mr Crossen held on his right side, like a shield. He had thought the man was simply playing hero, saving the guards. Until the boss got taken. But now he suspected differently. This was bad news.

So, he had been unable to shoot the man, and had noticed too late one of the guards running to the car. The woman. The damn woman who'd been so compliant until this point. Had she called the handyman somehow, even though all communication lines were down? Was that how the bastard had learned of the mission? And what was their plan now? And then the car had vanished.

He turned his anger onto the other guards. One driver, two more escorts. A lull in the shooting had convinced them it was over, and once the car had roared away all fell silent. So out they got. And down they went. Three throat shots, just so The Reaper would have a wait. Bradan watched the three squirming in agony on the ground. And when their thrashing ceased, he put a bullet in each head.

He ordered Denis to restore the radios and put his own to his face. Keegan and Ó Caiside were clearly dead, because he could see so, and Whelan, Ahearne and Sheehy had also been put out of action. So he ignored those five. He tried the Nolan brothers, got nothing. The Guilloux mother and daughter: nothing. That left Luke Ó Ríagáin, the big brute with the low

IQ who had been in the southern farmhouse. And Luke answered.

Only it wasn't Luke.

'Hello, bad guy. Mighty fine plan you had, and well executed, by the way,' said a voice he didn't doubt was the handyman's. So Luke was out, too. 'You took down nearly a hundred people without word getting out. It's just a shame that the sole one who did escape turned out to be the ultimate thorn in the side. With all that planning, that near-perfect execution, it almost makes me feel guilty to now have to ruin it all. I'm the good guy, by the way. And I have your man, and that means things change.'

Denis was by his side, horrified. A hand on his arm. 'It's over, Bradan. Let's go.'

Bradan slapped the hand away. 'I hope that's jesting, Denis. I hope my old friend isn't serious about wanting to run like a coward because of one hitch in the plan.'

Denis waved a hand at the village. Angry. 'We lost him. We have to go.'

Bradan pushed him away. 'Just abandon him, when he's right here under our noses? Get back.'

'This man will call the police–'

'We prepared for the police, Denis.' But Bradan was beginning to think Denis was right.

'With fourteen trigger fingers, Bradan. Fourteen. Not three. He will give Mr Crossen to the police and we'll never get to him again, or we'll get him back and never get out of here because the police have surrounded the village.'

Bradan and Denis locked eyes. Denis was right: they were there stuck atop a hill, and the handyman was down below in a car. No way could they stop him driving beyond the range of the signal jammers and raising the alarm.

'Let's go,' Bradan said. He gave Denis the rifle, and pocketed his radio.

Denis slung the rifle over his shoulder. They headed for the exit. 'We should just be thankful we have this head start. We're lucky he didn't call the police from the next village the moment he escaped from us.'

And then something loose and hazy and floating clicked into place in Bradan's mind. He put a hand on Denis's arm to stop him. He pulled his radio again. Denis frowned, but Bradan was smiling.

In the ballroom, Bradan's voice came over Fergal's radio. 'Fergal, I want you to do something for me. Quickly.'

He explained. Fergal stood up and addressed the people. 'Listen up. The man who ran you all up the lift tonight. I need to know if he has a relative here. First to answer will be the first let go when this is over.'

Good friends of the handyman they were not, it seemed.

On the roof, Bradan listened as Fergal said, 'Seems the handyman has no friends in this dark hour. About half of them yelled out that he's got a son. And he was right here five minutes ago–'

The rest was smothered by Denis: 'What are you doing, Bradan? Let's go.'

Bradan ignored him. 'I didn't catch that last bit, Fergal. Say again? Capucine?'

'I said Capucine took him. She came in and picked a man and took him out. She said she needed some male company now Cathal was gone. I thought she was just going to get it on with some guy. But these people just said the guy she took was the handyman's son. You think she knew it was his son? How would she know that?'

Bradan couldn't get his head around it. Capucine was alive, and she'd somehow learned the handyman had a son, and she'd come for him. This had to be about Cathal, her dead–

Just then the roof door crashed open, and Bradan's confusion almost made him dizzy. There stood Capucine with a young man, her pistol jammed into his neck. She stepped out, and tripped him to the ground.

'Bradan. Young man here is reason handyman did not call police and will not. Handyman will not risk son killed in police shooting with us. He kidnap our man so he can try dare rescue mission.'

Bradan grinned. He flicked his radio to Luke's channel. 'Are you there, thorn in my side? Things do change, you are right. Because now more people have to die. I need you to think carefully about all the people I have as hostages. Picture their faces. Surely you know most of them, in a small, close-knit community like this. Your friends and colleagues. Let my man go, and I will not start killing them. All you'll hear is the gunshots, and you'll never know if I just erased a debt you owe someone... or if you just lost someone that means a little bit more to you.'

In the car, which was racing up the northern slope of the main road, Emil said, 'I'm off to release the hostages in the old hotel, and they're going to scatter and run and call the police. You don't have long, and I would advise you to not waste that time firing bullets. Best to get running yourself.'

On the turret of Barkelow Hall, Bradan said, 'No, my friend, no. You had all the chance in the world to go and fetch the police. You do not want them here any more than I do. Once the police arrive, we have a dangerous situation. They'll surround this place and send a negotiator in. I might get pizza out of it, but I won't get my man. And eventually they'll come in with guns blazing. And if that happens, many might die, and neither you nor I know who of the innocent will take a stray bullet. Maybe you lose that debt. Maybe you lose a lot more, and...'

Bradan sighed.

'Enough, handyman. No more allusive banter bullshit. I know you've got a son. You think your best chance to save him

was to take my man and threaten me into letting him go, anony-
mous amongst all the other hostages. Well, I've got him right
here on this roof. Spotty blond kid, right? If I don't see my man
alone, walking towards me, you nowhere in sight, I *will* let your
son go. Fifty metres straight down. You've got five minutes.'

18

––––––––––

The car passed through the battlement, hit the van and knocked it aside. He drove past the other car, and turned in the road to face the way he had come. This was the moment he had put all his chips on. If this went wrong, game over.

And he needed help. This woman's help, since she was the only one around.

'Sara, will you help me get my son back?'

'Your son? What about my parents? Where are they being held? Who has them? And how do you know my name?'

'Hang on a second.' Mr Crossen was coming round. Emil snaked an arm around his throat and put him out again. He continued as though there had been no interruption: 'I don't know where your parents are, but I'll help you rescue them. But more pressing is my son at the minute. They don't want to hurt your parents, but they do want to hurt my son. These are serious people.'

She was staring in shock between Emil and Mr Crossen. 'Who are they? Why do they want to break a murderer out of prison?'

'He's no murderer,' Emil said, still thinking. He patted the guy's cheek. 'At least not in the normal sense.'

She scoffed. 'What are you talking about? I saw the file. He's going to trial for murdering a drug dealer in London. That's where we were taking him. He even plans to plead guilty, from what I hear.'

Over the radio, Bradan said, 'Thirty seconds.'

'Look, do you think a lowly murderer would have the friends with resources to organise such a complex prison break?'

'What are you saying? Who is he, then? Who are these people?'

'Believe me, Sara, they are serious people. So I need your help. Will you help me?'

'Not until you tell me what's going on.'

'Remember they have your parents.'

Bradan's voice came over the radio. 'Ten seconds. I will throw this boy to his death.'

She gave him an angry look. 'You think I could forget?'

'You need to realise how determined and callous these people are. They won't be scared off by the threat of the police, and they won't stop until they get their way. But if they get their man back, they'll leave. Otherwise your parents will end up in a shallow grave with my son's body as a shroud. Believe that. So will you help?'

'I will kill this boy in five seconds. Four... three.'

No more time. No time to wait for her to agree. It had to be done anyway. Emil snatched up his radio. 'No you won't, Bradan. No you won't. You're a seasoned killer and I don't think you get that much pleasure out of it. Some, for sure, but not enough to keep you smiling for long. And when the smiling is done, when you've calmed down from the over-whelming joy at knowing you killed your enemy's son and ruined his life, your thoughts will turn to your man. Who will be dead on that road you were hoping to see him walking down.'

'You would risk your son's life? I will kill him right now. I'm sure a man's son means more to him than a business colleague, right?' There followed the unmistakable sound of a pistol cocking, as if Bradan felt he needed to fortify his threat.

Bradan was right, of course. Emil would give anything to get his son back. He would give his own life. But he reminded himself that his emotions weren't the only ones in the driving seat here.

And so with a heavy heart, and a shaking hand, he put the radio to his mouth and said, 'But does my son mean more to *you* than your so-called business colleague, Bradan?' He cocked his own pistol near the radio. 'Two men with guns to their heads. Both will live, or both will die, and it's your choice. Now *you* have sixty seconds.'

Ten seconds passed in silence, except for the sound of the wind across the roof of the manor house. 'A trade it is,' Bradan said. 'Might you have an idea where and how, or is that my choice too?'

He was aware of Capucine nearby, her jaw open, shock on her face. He winked at her.

'Sure I do,' the handyman said. 'I'll get back to you in ten minutes. Hang tight.'

Bradan saw Capucine mouth something at him, and he repeated it for the handyman: 'Thirty minutes. I need time to powder my nose.' Then he slotted away his radio.

'Why thirty minutes, Capucine?'

'Because I want part of this. He killed my Cathal, so I will kill him.'

Denis laughed. Capucine sneered at him. But to Bradan she said, 'You owe me. What is one more fired bullet to you? One more dead–'

Bradan held up his hand to stop her just as Denis started laughing again. 'Fine, fine,' Bradan said. 'Merry Christmas and happy birthday, Capucine. You can kill the man. But why thirty minutes? And don't give me crap about your nose powder.'

'Where is my Cathal?' she said, turning, heading for the door. He told her. At the door, she stopped with her hand on the handle, but did not look back when she said, 'You *are* plan to kill him? No trade?'

'I could hardly tell him the truth, could I? No, Capucine, I have no intention of doing a trade with that man. Yes, Capucine, I'm going to kill him.'

Mr Crossen said, 'The dead man in London was a local drug dealer who was killed by an associate of mine.'

Emil said, 'Explain how the police came to think that was down to you.'

'Evidence was planted that pointed to a hit authorised by me.'

'Where were you at that time?'

'Strangeways prison, held on remand for–'

'Shush. Don't give the spoilers away just yet. Your people planted the evidence. Why set you up?'

'So I would go on trial for murder in London.'

'And what was the plan when that happened?'

'To break me out en route.'

Here, Sara moaned, 'Oh my God, you mean this was all planned?'

Emil said, "Fraid so.'

Crossen and Sara had swapped places – at least, Sara had vacated the back seat and Emil had dragged Crossen in there. He had woken shortly afterwards, but was in no position to try to escape, and not just because Emil was leaning over the driver's backrest and pointing a pistol at him. Emil had put the seatbelt across, tied his ankles and handcuffed his wrists. His ankles were secured to Emil's seat mechanism and his wrists were under his legs. The cuffs were metal, tough, but wrapped in fluffy pink material. Don Hunter's private pairs, for use when his special lady guests visited for some fun. Emil had stolen them from Hunter's farmhouse, and he'd left the fluffy pink wrappings in place because he thought it made Crossen look more pathetic.

After that, he had woken the Irishman and given him a simple order. 'Answer my questions quickly, short sentences, don't elaborate unless I say so.' He had wanted Sara to learn the truth in increments, so the shock would not overwhelm her. And he had started with the less-shocking revelations for the same reason, although already she was appearing distraught. And there was worse to come. But he needed her to hear it all, and from the horse's mouth so she'd believe it, if he had any hope of getting her help in rescuing his son.

He continued: 'The men and women here today. They are all part of your organisation, right?'

'Yes.'

'And you hold the highest rank of them all. They do your bidding. What is your title?'

'My name is Sean Crossen. Rank: Quartermaster General of the Patriot IRA.'

He heard Sara let out a low moan.

Emil said, 'Tell her what that is.'

Crossen said, 'The PAIRA formed alongside the Real IRA in 1997 after the Provisional IRA split following a ceasefire.'

'Objectives?'

'We reject the Good Friday Agreement. We do not accept that the majority of Northern Ireland's people wish to remain part of the United Kingdom. We don't accept any government policy that challenges Irish independence.'

'What will your paramilitary organisation do once you are free?'

'Continue to fight the war until we achieve what we want.'

'With in-depth, intelligent conversation, or the use of wanton violence?'

Crossen paused here, as if not willing to say the next part. Emil urged him on by poking the gun into his forehead.

'We aim to achieve our objectives through the spread of terror and damage to economic infrastructure.'

'Well practised. You should get that tattooed somewhere. You've done well. You may now go back to sleep.'

A sharp blow on the temple put him out for a third time. Emil put his hand on Sara's shoulder. She had her head bowed, hands over her face. She looked at him when she felt his hand.

'This is all my fault,' she said. 'I brought him here. And they have my parents. They are going to kill them, aren't they? These are people who kill remorselessly.'

'It's not your fault,' he said as he started the car and turned it in the road. 'You were caught up in this. The Patriot IRA is a very secretive group, unlike the Real Irish Republican Army, which is out there bombing and shooting still. They don't acknowledge their crimes, and their leadership is shadowy. They've never appeared on anyone's radar, as if nothing more than a paper company. Maybe it's just a bunch of guys who refuse to give up their status now that the organisation they gave their lives to is no more. You only knew of him as a low-level murderer. There was no way you could have known his team were going to try to break–'

He stopped, because something in her face he was wrong. 'What happened?'

She started crying. And then she told him about something that had happened a few hours ago...

19

———

…'Mum, take your tablet.' Pause. 'Yes, and you're supposed to take another. The TV will know if you don't and it will go off.'

'What's all that about?' Sara said.

Dale Smith ignored her until after the van had taken a right turn off Southall Street and stopped at a pair of retractable bollards. He put his phone away and put his helmet back on. Past him, out his window, Sara saw a sign saying, 'Do not approach gate when lights are red'.

'My bloody mum,' he said. 'Cystitis. She's on some weird homeopathic remedy called Cantharis. Made from the guts of the Spanish fly, something like that. She has to take a tablet every thirty minutes. I have to remind her. I strapped her phone to her arm so she can't miss it. She thinks the burning sensations are pregnancy.'

'Sure they're not?' Sara said with a smile. Dale didn't get the joke. He told her his mum was seventy-one.

A minute later the bollards sank into the ground, and ahead of them the great grey gate in the red brick building rumbled open. Dale guided the van into Strangeways prison.

146

Twenty-six minutes later, Dale put his phone away following another call to his mother. 'What a palaver,' he said to Sara. 'Every thirty minutes: Mum, take your tablet.'

They both fell silent as their prisoner was brought into the reception area, flanked by two guards who would ride in the back with him. Rather than prison garb, the prisoner wore a grey suit. If not for his handcuffs, he might have passed for the governor.

'Why do they let some of these people wear what they want when being transported?' Dale grumbled. 'No one can see them inside the van. Just makes it easier for them to blend in if they escape. I don't get it.'

'Strange ways of doing things here, eh?' Sara said, expecting a laugh. But Dale just nodded.

'Flip you for the search.'

He flipped a coin and said 'heads', and heads it was. He took the clipboard off Sara, and she moved forward to search the prisoner.

'Mum, for Christ's sake, I'll put that TV in the skip!'

Sara tuned him out. She was glad that she wasn't in his shoes. Both her parents were still alive, and both had their faculties intact. She watched the gate rising.

'This is the first time I've had a single prisoner, and done a long journey. You?'

Dale ignored her. 'I reckon sixty is about the cut-off. After that, after your brain starts to go, you should be legally allowed to have euthanasia, or do euthanasia, or however you say it.'

'Think there's anything special about this guy? The suit, the fact that he's the only one we're transporting? And having two minders in back with him.'

'No. Maybe he's prone to trying to smash his own head open. You know, I reckon doctors should have a look at people once they hit sixty, and if you're a few cards short of a pack, it should be an option. The euthanasia thing. It's no way to live, when you get like my mum.'

Now she ignored him. 'Maybe he's famous in some way. Not just for murder.'

'Nah, just another scumbag killer,' Dale said.

'It's me, Mum, who else? Do you remember why I'm calling?'

Sara tuned him out. Out of the gate, they turned right onto the A56. And that was when Sara's phone rang. She pulled it, saw the name on the screen.

'My mum,' she said, and immediately regretted it. Dale was about to hear a decent conversation, and she feared it would make him sad given the strange back and forth he'd been having with his own parent. But he just stared forward, driving.

She answered it. 'Hello, Mum. What's up?'

'Sara, do not speak, and listen very carefully,' said her mother, her voice breaking. Immediately Sara thought she was ill, or her voice was coarse because Dad was ill. It was worse.

'We are being held hostage. The men holding us will kill us unless you do exactly as they say. Do not speak, only listen.'

'Mum? Is this a joke?' But she knew it was not.

Then there was another voice on the phone. A man. Irish accent. Nobody she knew, or even thought her parents knew.

'Listen carefully, Miss Everton. Say nothing that will alert your colleague to the shit that just entered your life. Do not even consider the mere possibility of even thinking about calling the police, because if you do they will arrive here to find two elderly corpses. You should be about to leave the prison now. Your route to London involves turning right onto the A6042 very soon. Make sure you turn left instead. Do that now while I listen.'

She looked at the phone. Looked at Dale. Fought the urge to tell him, to hang up and call the police. Said, 'Dale, at the A6042, turn left instead of right.'

He glanced at her, then at the satnav. 'Satellite says–'

'Go left. Trust me.' Said with no emotion, but sternly.

He didn't object. She was shift controller today.

'Good,' said the Irishman on the phone. 'Now you will call headquarters. You will tell your boss that your mother is ill and you need to drop off her tablets. She has a bad hip, of course, so say you have her medication. Tell him you really need to get them to her, so can you return to base to swap with another officer. Or can you change the route and drop by for ten minutes. The route to Barkelow is slightly east of your route south to London, and the detour will hardly add any time at all to your journey, and certainly will be quicker than returning to base. So your boss will allow you to go past your parents' house, despite the break in protocol and security and all that malarkey. Beats getting your prisoner to London late. Offer him an apologetic blow job if necessary. I will call you back in ten minutes. Meantime, instruct your colleague to turn right onto the A665 and follow the signs for the A62. Remember your task for the next hour or so is to keep your parents alive.'

The line went dead.

'I didn't know what to expect, you understand,' Sara said now to Emil. 'I thought they were thieves, just thieves. I thought they wanted the van. It's very expensive. I expected a hijack. I thought he was just some killer, please believe me. I was confused. A prison break never occurred to me.'

The tears came again. Driving, he touched her shoulder. 'It's okay. The trade was for my son. I will insist they release your parents, too.'

He did not expect what she said next. 'You're joking, right? You want to let a major terrorist criminal go free? You can't. The police will not let you.'

'There's no police.' He skidded on the brakes, and turned sharply left, seemingly right into the trees. But there was a track. It wasn't quite big enough for the car, and branches scraped against the sides of the vehicle as it rumbled and bounced through the blackness. Trees appeared ahead in an endless army of multi-limbed monsters swiping at the vehicle.

'What do you mean, no police? Of course there are police. What are you saying, you're not involving the police?'

She looked at him, and his eyes, even in the dark, gave the answer. Just as the terrorist on the radio had said: Emil did not want to bring about a siege situation in which people could die, including his son.

'Then you let me out here, whoever the hell you are, and I'll fetch the police myself. You say you don't want to risk your son's life, but this is risking everyone's. You can't trade with these people. It doesn't work like that. The rule is to never deal with terrorists. Do you know why?'

'You're talking about governments and major corporations, people who can be hit again and again. You think I'll make the trade and then next week they'll kidnap my son again–'

'You're a fool,' she cut in. 'Just what do you expect to achieve? A nice business deal, and a goodbye handshake? These people don't have morals. You think they'll just let you get away with killing their people? You can't do this. The IRA is a big organisation, and they will want revenge, and if you don't bring the police in, and you do this trade, then they will be out there, free, and they will come back and kill us all. They know where you live, and my parents. It's suicide. We'd all have to go on the run, maybe get new identities, or one day my mum's car explodes when she starts the engine.'

He stopped the car and faced her. 'Listen to me. This Patriot IRA, it's not what you think. The Troubles in Northern Ireland aren't the same any more since all the ceasefires. The Provisional IRA is no more. The Patriot IRA might have emerged from its ashes, but it's not the same beast. It is composed of just a few key members who were active way back, and a bunch of young, hot-headed volunteers they probably got just for this mission. There are no hardened killer crews waiting on backup. There are four-teen of them here today, and if those fourteen were to vanish off the face of the earth, that would be the end of it.'

'I want no part,' she said, and made to open the door.

'Wait, I need you,' Emil said, his voice pleading.

She paused. Not convinced, but curious. In the interior light, she saw his face, and the anger on it, barely contained.

'I know all about running, and I'm not running again. Ever. I'll tell you the truth, okay? This trade will get my son back, and your parents. It's the only way. But you're right, we can't risk letting these people loose out there in the world. It's not just us who won't be safe. I mentioned them vanishing off the face of the earth, right? Well, either *we* have to, or *they* have to. And, like I said, I'm not running again.'

He could tell she understood his hidden meaning perfectly, because her eyes now dripped wonder rather than fear. 'Who the hell *are* you?'

20

Capucine jogged between the garden mazes but slowed as she approached the hill lift. She stepped forwards carefully, like an acrophobic atop a cliff. But it was not fear of the drop. She was scared about what she expected to see.

The lift was halfway down the cliff, which meant she knew the black shape before it on the track was her lover, Cathal. Denis must have stopped the lift there to make things easy for him to check the body. She sat on the edge of the platform and twisted and lowered herself. Below the winch cable were wooden treads used as steps for maintenance personnel. Down she walked, slowly, but her caution was not due to fear of slipping. Indeed, she felt that a fall and a lethal tumble would at least end this misery.

The black shape near the lift was indeed Cathal. She saw his white face, smeared with blood. His body was twisted, arms and legs bent worse than they should have been even after a tumble down the slope.

She stopped. What had happened here? Maybe there had been a fight and somehow the handyman had gotten the better of her baby and pushed him off the lift. Or maybe the old man had killed him and thrown him over. It seemed hard to believe that her baby could have been bested by a single man, but the evidence was twisted and smashed before her.

The worst part was that he was no longer beautiful. Often, she had feared for his death, and often she had hoped it would come after hers, but if it should not, then he should exit the world at peace and intact, as if asleep. Not destroyed like this. Not contorted and battered and bloodied. She wanted to kill the man who had put him here, and everyone who had had a hand in putting that man here to do this thing. The people who gave him the lift job. The schoolteachers who hadn't educated him well enough so he could avoid a job like this. The midwives who delivered him into the world.

Then she realised something, and a new face entered her target zone.

Soon after, she bent before Cathal, and forced her hands under his cold body. Upon her shoulder, she carried him back up the cliff, apologising to him when she stumbled and dropped him. The adrenaline gave her strength she didn't know she had, and soon she was at the top, feeding him onto the platform, climbing up, lifting him again. She walked. Between the maze walls, then across the grass, and through the gate in the garden wall.

A rock-bordered little path wound down through the various tiers, past bushes shaped like squatting creatures; past water features; past little nooks and crannies where benches sat under ivy-laden arches. The black world was lit by fairy lights strung in trees and lanterns upon poles jammed into the earth.

She didn't know what she was looking for until she found it. A stone-based wishing well with no roof. She carefully laid Cathal on a bench nearby. The lip of the well was barred by a grille, but the padlock was tiny and she battered it away with two blows from a stone lifted from a rockery close by. She flipped the lid. Down in the blackness she could see a slight streak of moonlight reflecting off water. The rock took half a second to make a splash. She watched the light down there explode into a million pieces that danced and reformed into a single, wobbling mass. Ten feet, maybe.

The blood on Cathal's face was dried and she had to spit on her fingers to clean a spot on his forehead. She apologised to him. Said she wished she had time to bury him. Said she hoped his parents wouldn't mind that she couldn't get him back to them.

She lifted him in a bear-hug and carried him to the well and swung his legs over the wall and lowered him until his arms were on the edge, as if he were trying to climb out. She held him there by the shoulders, staring at his face. She kissed the clear spot on his forehead. And then let him go.

He vanished. His landing was more thud than splash, meaning the water was only inches deep, and that sound grated upon her soul. By the time of that thud-splash, she had already turned away, her face a contradiction: tears of sadness, a sneer of rage.

PART II

The unravelling of it all started with a request that came in to a man in a car in Tower Heights, London, who took his eyes off a prostitute's house to check the email. He called a woman: 'I need a fingerprint check.'

'I told you not to call me after working hours,' she snapped. Her tone softened a moment later. 'You only ever want me for my tits and for my computer.'

'That's all you've got,' the man replied. 'Besides, it's only because of your chest that the guy will do the check for you.'

After a little more banter, the call ended. The man continued to stake out the house, hoping for a certain wanted punter to approach the whore's pad. Twenty minutes later, his phone beeped. A return email. He forwarded it to another address, then casually read it as he waited. The name of the owner of the fingerprints didn't register at first. Not for another eight minutes, while he was leaned back in his seat, drumming his fingers on the steering wheel, waiting to see if tonight was the night that damned rapist would visit the prostitute so the guy could be shafted in a way he wasn't expecting.

He pulled out his phone again and used the internet to find a phone number. He asked for Elaine Van-Johnson, although he didn't expect to find her still there after so many years. But goddamn, the old bag still worked there. Jesus, what a bombshell her memoirs would be if she ever decided to publish them.

They started with small talk, which he hated and she was no good at, and then he got down to business.

Twenty-six minutes after that initial request to a mobile phone in Tower Heights, a phone rang in a public house called the Bladdered Goose, in Gravesend, Kent. It was karaoke night, and an aging rocker on the stage was displaying how loud he could shout Meatloaf's 'Bat Out of Hell'. The bar girl answered it and then pressed a button that rang a bell upstairs. The landlord barged through the door a minute later, wearing tracksuit bottoms and a sleeveless T-shirt, and stomped over with a limp. He moved the girl aside by pushing on her breast, like he always did. She never seemed to mind, but he had no idea she planned to press a sexual harassment charge when finally she finished university and could get a proper bloody job.

'Elaine?' he said when the caller introduced herself. God, Elaine, his old secretary. Still worked there after all this time. Must have seen five or six new bosses after so many years. And she remembered him.

'William Morse just resurfaced,' she said, and he nearly dropped the phone. Her information given, he told her he'd chat again soon, and with shaking fingers dialled another number. As it rang, he replayed that sentence of hers in his head. A statement he had never, ever imagined he would hear. He still didn't believe it.

Behind him, the karaoke song finished and everyone whooped and clapped. The landlord turned and screamed at them to shut up, and the room fell silent. The next guy up on stage chose a Stevie Wonder ballad, and it was probably so he wouldn't cause a racket.

The landlord listened to the phone ringing at the other end. And then: 'Who's this?' answered a voice.

'It's me,' the landlord said. 'I need some men, and a helicopter.'

He waited, and after eight seconds of silence, the voice said, 'This who I think it is?' He said the landlord's name, and when it was confirmed laughed aloud. 'Christ, how the hell are you? I heard you opened a bar in Spain. That right?'

'Half right. Look, I need men. Four or five.'

'Yeah, and a chopper. I heard. Where's that magic wand of mine again? Let me just–'

'William Morse just resurfaced,' the landlord cut in slowly. The same shocking sentence his old secretary had used.

More silence. Then: 'Jesus, you sure? In Spain?'

'I'm not in Spain. I'm in England. And the bastard just appeared up north. A planet this size, and he's right on my bloody doorstep.' He quickly explained. Years ago, he had fed Morse's fingerprints into the National Fingerprint Database and tasked a clerk at the Home Office with watching for a hit on them, in case the police ever arrested him here in England. Other agencies around the world also had a similar set-up. The clerk, now a police officer, was out of the loop, but thankfully he was still seeing that lady from the same department–

'She finally left her husband for him, then?' the man cut in.

'No. Listen.' He continued: the clerk contacted her after someone had, earlier today, requested a fingerprint search. Match: William Morse. 'And according–'

'What, so she's been, like, having a twenty-year affair?'

'Forget that.' According to the clerk-now-cop, the prints had been sent by someone who found them in a little village called Barkelow in the Peak District. 'So I want a chopper and some men with guns and I'm going up there to get the bastard. Got that?'

'Twenty years behind her husband's back. Good lord.'

'Listen. Chopper. Men.'

'I kind of thought all these years would have dulled your desire for revenge. So you're sure you want to do this?'

'I was already planning how I'd get to him in the next life. Chopper. Men.'

'Guess not, then. Okay, you got it. Send me your location and I'll send you some tough guys in a bird.'

The landlord hung up. No, nigh-on a quarter of a century had not dulled Alex Cavil's desire for revenge. Not in the least. Not when he was here, running a bloody pub, because of William Morse. Not when he still had this gunshot limp.

Bradan and Denis went back downstairs, into the ballroom. The hostages murmured when Bradan pulled his pistol and cocked it, and looked around at them. Now he had everyone's attention, he said, 'I bet you're all hungry. I need three volunteers to go out for fifty bags of fish and chips.'

He counted eight hands thrust into the air. Laughing, he approached Fergal. Denis sat at a table and started working on his laptop. Bradan asked Fergal to help him shift the crowd. 'We're going for a little tour of the house.' Fergal immediately stormed into the centre of the room, clapping his hands.

'Up! On your feet. We're taking a little trip. All of you. Now.'

'What about the chips?' someone said.

Bradan and Fergal were back in fifteen minutes, sans hostages, and Denis was proudly pointing at his laptop.

'Your ninja. His real name is William Morse.' Denis turned the screen towards Bradan. 'Or used to be.'

Bradan studied the screen. He saw a picture of the handyman as a younger man, clearly him even though he had glossy, dark hair and smooth skin, no beard, no wrinkles, no excess fat. But a thick neck, as if he worked out. Tough-looking, yet kind-faced at the same time. A passport photo as part of a file on: William Morse. 'How did you get this?'

'I've been doing this for years, Bradan, and all of a sudden you're surprised by my magnificence?'

'On this one, yes. Not the hacking part. How did you find out who to even search for? Meaning, if you know he has a real name, how did you even find out he has a false one?'

Denis looked smug. 'I took his prints off Cathal's knife, since it wasn't Cathal who put it in his own head. Bit of flour and oil from the kitchen, voila. Scanned it into the computer. Sent it to Carl. You remember Carl?'

'What, that copper? The guy with the...' Bradan pointed at his Adam's apple.

'Yeah, him. He's got an operation booked for that. Anyhows, he's still banging that Home Office woman, and he gave her a call and he's come back with some news you might find a bit intriguing.'

'Hasn't he been banging her for, like, fifteen years or something? Behind her husband's back?'

Denis tapped the screen. 'Check it out.'

'How's that guy not known for fifteen years?'

'Will you just look, and get ready to pat me on the back?'

Bradan looked at the screen. Denis had opened seven windows. From them he learned that William Morse attended Cambridge University, got a first-class honours degree in human, social and political science. Was a Royal Air Force Reserve for two years, then got recruited by the Secret Intelligence Service, MI6.

'A goddamned spy,' he said, looking up at Denis. 'Explains his skills. We might have been better off if he'd actually been a ninja.'

'How many times did we tell that goon Cathal that he'd one day pick a fight with the wrong man?'

Ignoring him, Bradan read more. In 1992 Morse became part of the Balkans Controllerate, working in Bosnia, and less than a year later was... dead.

'Dead?' he said. 'Looks good for it.'

Denis said, 'Officially he was listed as missing. He had a mother who wrote to a newspaper to complain. There was a little media coverage after that, but not much. He wasn't a celebrity or anything, just some guy. The Foreign Office barely admitted he worked for MI6, and certainly didn't give his mother details of what he was doing when he vanished. Intelligence gathering, that was the official line. But they did admit he was in Bosnia, probably because that place was a warzone back then and people die in warzones.'

'Well, much as I wish it, he's not dead. So what's going on?'

'There's a strange twist. At the time he went missing, Morse was suspected of a robbery. Nothing major, just a backstreet store robbery in Sarajevo, in Bosnia, where no one got hurt, not much money was stolen, and the story never got past the local news over there. I found no reference to it over here in Britain. No one here seems to know or care, and why would they? But apparently this robbery was a big enough deal that Morse's fingerprints and DNA are now on file in various countries. In a sense you could say he's wanted all over the world, as if he's a big-league arms dealer. But no one's heard anything of him in over quarter of a century. But as we now know, Morse didn't die. He relocated under a new name.'

'So something happened over there in Bosnia and MI6 had to cut short Morse's duty to them. Maybe something to do with that robbery. Maybe the robbed store was a front for something. Whatever. The government can't divulge mission details, so they make up a story about him going missing, and plant him here, in the middle of nowhere, with a new name. Maybe for protection, if he pissed off some terrorists. He's good at that, have you noticed? Or an ongoing mission to gather intel on cliff elevators.'

Denis didn't laugh. He seemed insulted. 'I looked deep into this, Bradan. Why such scorn?'

'No offence to your hacking skills, my friend. But it doesn't make sense. Why would MI6 invent a story about Morse being missing, presumed dead? There was no chance of an extradition to Bosnia because of some little robbery no one cared about. No one here knew the story, so there was no embarrassment to the government. Such a story would risk people asking questions, which his mother did. Much easier to let him return to his old life, cover up the robbery, and pretend he never worked for MI6. Instead, he now has a new name, and family and friends who still think he's dead, people he cannot ever contact again. Why would they do that? Why would Morse want to do that?'

Denis was smiling. 'I didn't say they relocated him. I said he relocated. As in, without their knowledge.'

'Explain.'

'This guy just stole a car. He's free, escaped. He could call the police, or his old buddies at MI6. There should be teams of good guys swarming on us, but there aren't. Morse hasn't called anyone. He took our man because he wants a trade for his son, but not because he fears his boy will get hurt in a police shootout.'

'I'm not following.'

'The government could have erased all knowledge of that old robbery in Sarajevo to protect their officer, like you said. But they didn't. I think MI6 didn't expunge that criminal file because they *created* it. Low-key, on the quiet, but worldwide, in the hope that Morse would be arrested, wherever he was. MI6 isn't helping him. They're hunting him.'

Bradan took a long look at the photo of a younger Morse, and told Denis to continue.

He was happy to show off his knowledge, gained via a few minutes with a keyboard. 'All this time he's been on the run, and it turns out he's living under their noses, not in a dark cave in a foreign country. I think that explains his son. Given the kid's age, he would have been born right around the time Morse went missing. Either the child was due, so he came back, or he didn't want to bring a baby up in a strange country. So he settled in the quiet Peak District with a new name. The kid probably has no idea about his dad's past as a spy, or even his real name. And the world doesn't know the truth about the kid. And Morse hopes to keep the secret forever. Which means he absolutely cannot have the police snooping around. That could undo everything.'

Bradan wasn't convinced. 'If he was that easy for you to find, then why can't a giant government agency find him? All it took for you was one little fingerprint.'

'But I got his fingerprint, didn't I? There's no law enforcement here to ink his fingers. Plus, MI6 is all new faces today, probably mostly fast-tracked university brains. Most of those who worked there back when Morse was around will be dead or retired now.'

'Not James Bond,' Bradan said. 'Still going strong. Maybe he knows Morse.'

Denis ignored the interruption to his spiel. 'Twenty-five years ago, Morse's face was probably on a wanted board and people were watching all his known haunts. Now he's old news, long gone, mostly forgotten, just a water cooler tale from the old days. Today, he's a free man, because today MI6 is a different beast and doesn't care about him.'

~

'Morse dies tonight,' Cavil said aloud as he watched a civilian helicopter coming towards the pub. He liked the taste of the words on his lips, so said them again.

The Bell 407 touched down in the garden behind the pub, where there was enough room to avoid a bad accident if a pilot was good. Cavil stepped out of the doorway and walked over, trying his best to hide his limp. He was now wearing a suit. It was old, used just once for his sister's wedding eight months ago, and it was a little tight around the chest. But he wasn't going to confront Morse in a tracksuit.

The pilot exited the chopper and barred him with a hand. 'Name?' he said.

'Alexander Cavil.' The pilot nodded and got back in the chopper. Cavil followed. He took the passenger seat and turned to face his fellow passengers.

Three brutes squashed in the back. They were young and had mean faces, as if they'd never learned of a smile. Any one of them could have crushed Cavil in seconds, being half his age and twice his size.

'Not a good first impression, fellas. That the extent of your security procedures? Asking my name? If I'd said it in a Russian accent, what would you have done?'

They seemed unnerved by that, as if they'd failed a test. 'Saw your photo,' one of them said.

'Maybe we were planning to interrogate you once in the air and you were beyond help,' said the pilot, giving a stern look.

Cavil laughed. 'Names?'

'Billy A,' said one guy.

'Billy B,' said the next.

'Billy–' the third started, and Cavil silenced him with a raised hand. 'Yeah, yeah, protocol, safety, a joke, some team-mate bull-shit. Whatever. Billy will do. Just make sure you stick with those names if we meet any of the locals where we're going. What have you been told about tonight?'

'Just to collect you and do what you need,' said another.

'Perfect answer. We're going after a man who was a pretty lethal operative twenty years ago, so don't underestimate him just because he's in his fifties now.'

Actually, they did know how to smile. Big grins, at his silly notion that an old guy could best them. Yeah, young and brash and full of ego, like many he'd known way back. The ones who didn't crash and burn early went far. 'Alive. Anyone kills him, then this time next week you'll be a doorman at a police station in Kirkuk. The location is 184 miles, at least two hours in this chopper. No farting, no small talk.' He slapped the pilot on the shoulder. The chopper rose into the air.

On the ground, some of his patrons came out, drawn by the roar of the flying machine. They seemed impressed. Some waved. Cavil didn't wave back.

He leaned back as the chopper cut through the air, thinking about that day all those years ago. About Morse. The only thing that stung as bad as the wound in his leg was the reason for it all. Why Morse had blown the mission like he had, and condemned himself to a life on the run. An answer that had long been denied him. He was determined to get that answer today.

His mind drifted back.

He'd first met Morse in early 1991 at the Foreign Secretary's residence in Carlton Gardens, where Morse had his panel interview in the MI6 selection process. Cavil had attended a few such interviews and was always appalled by nervous candidates, because those types struck him as desperate for the job and often had a rosy vision of life as an intelligence officer. They expected erotic women and exotic beaches and bad guys who were courteous to their enemies. Those bloody James Bond films were to blame. But Morse hadn't seemed that sort. He'd almost seemed like a guy forced into the interview, perhaps by a domineering father.

'The life of an intelligence agent isn't all cocktails and guns, Mr Morse,' Cavil had said, his first words to the man. 'There will be dark times as well as light. Can you accept that?'

'*Amor fati*, Mr Cavil,' Morse had said.

Cavil had been impressed by him, so had personally made himself the vetting officer for Morse's application. That meant interviewing his references, delving into his life, and conducting a final interview alone with him. Normally these things ended with a thanks and a handshake and a we'll-let-you-know, but Cavil had jumped the gun and, at the final interview a few months later in Cavil's home study, told him, 'If I pass you, you're in, and you'll owe me. Do you mind owing me?'

Morse shook his head.

'Then you're in. You were in the moment you stepped through the door. This interview isn't to see if you get the job. It's to see if you can snatch defeat from the jaws of victory.'

He expected Morse to suddenly clam up, fearful that he might do something to make Cavil change his mind. Or to try to bring a quick end to the interview. Instead, Morse seemed to go the opposite way with a risky move. He got up and helped himself to a glass of Cavil's brandy. Not a word uttered until he'd swallowed it, at which point he said, 'Do you mind?'

Cavil laughed and offered to get him another. He also got a book. It was called *Ecce Homo: How One Becomes What One Is*, by the philosopher Friedrich Nietzsche. '*Amor fati*, Mr Morse. You got me interested. The idea that all pain and anguish is to be accepted as part of a man's life because it cannot be changed. I wrote this on my wall: my formula for greatness is *amor fati*. Does it really work for you?'

'I don't sweat the small stuff,' Morse had said. 'Or the big.'

'Sounds good.' Cavil tapped the book. 'He did go insane not long after writing this, though.'

Four weeks later, Morse had arrived at Century House in Lambeth with a bag and two things MI6 had insisted he bring: a smooth face and his passport. Cavil had watched him approach the security desk and had tapped him on the shoulder and said, 'You owe me, remember.'

Morse had said, 'Yes, sir. What?'

'You'll find out six months from now, because you're on a learning course till then.'

Six months later, in early 1992, they met again, this time in Cavil's office. Morse strode in and took a seat immediately, as if to show he wasn't nervous about his first real day on the job. Cavil had planned to baby-step him through this, but that bold act made him toss away that plan. And the fact that Morse had beaten everybody on the new entrants' course. He got right down to it.

'My job is to send intelligence officers overseas to spy, and I'm the head of the Balkan Controllerate, so guess where you're going to be this time next week.'

The Balkan Peninsula, south-east Europe, quarter of a million square miles, was the focal point of the world's curious people at the moment because of a guy nicknamed Sloba in the Republic of Serbia. Here was a guy who, according to some, was a Tito-wannabe who yearned to hold Yugoslavia in his grasp, yet had done the equivalent of wrapping the country like a fist around a firecracker. Bang. Now that country was split like a heated shard of ice, and the separate fragments were warring.

He had tried to scare Morse, but the young man had wiped his forehead and said, 'Thank God. If bus conductors call the stop outside here Spies Corner, then for sure it won't be hard for terrorists to find, and it's made mostly of glass and it's got a ramp down into the basement. Give me my plane ticket.'

Even a high-ranker like Cavil couldn't work miracles with a probationer, so Morse got his plane ticket two months later, not one week. By that time he was fully versed on the republics that made up the former Yugoslavia. It was April 19, 1992, and the wars were halfway through. The War in Slovenia was over, the Croatian War of Independence was into its second year, and the Bosnian War was just a few weeks old. Nine more years, three more wars. Much murder and mayhem already, and it was Morse's job to go to over there and dive into the thick of it.

22

————

E mil looked at Sara, sitting just feet from him in the car. He did not know her, but for some reason he felt like unloading. He had lived a fake life for so many years now, and part of him just wanted to tell the truth. If only to remember, to not have to play a role. If only to hear it from his own lips, even.

Already he had told her about joining MI6, and so far she hadn't looked at him with scorn. Told over a pint in a pub, maybe his spy story would have gotten a wry smile. But it was harder to doubt tales of espionage after what she had witnessed so far this evening.

But that had been the easy part. Now, facing what was ahead, he searched for the correct way to begin. But it was a terrible tale and no opening gloss would change that. So he just started to speak.

'I was sent to Bosnia. My job was intelligence gathering, but my boss, a man called Cavil, had other plans. MI6 is not into murder, understand that, but lethal force is sometimes authorised, and Cavil liked to flout the law a bit. He sent me after a guy called Zdravko Brena. Brena was a local businessman from Bijeljina, who just happened to be out of that city in April 1992 when Serbian forces were sent in. Non-Serbs were tortured and killed, and various paramilitary groups were involved, including the Black Tigers. MI6 suspected that The Black Tigers were headed by Brena. He hid while his own vicious men helped ransack his own city.

'The Black Tigers had ties to other Serbian paramilitary groups that were involved in massacres at Zvornik, Glogova other places in both Croatia and Bosnia. But Brena, although previously photographed atop a tank with a rifle at the head of his group, was never witnessed anywhere near these kill sites.

'I was to get close to him, find out who his main people were, find out what his next targets were. He owned a restaurant in Bijeljina that he lived above with his wife. I got a job there as a gardener, not long after the massacre in Bijeljina. For six weeks I was there, reporting on what I found out. Sometimes there were snippets of conversations between people in the restaurant, army-types that Brena met and was respectful of, but mostly I got nothing. They weren't suspicious types, they just never gave anything away. I got bored. It was very mundane. Hell, I felt like a real gardener after a while. To spice things up, I started sleeping with Brena's wife, Joanne. That gave me a bit of a thrill, I hate to say now. Knowing I'd probably be killed if he found out.'

She was captivated by this tale, like a child. The world outside didn't exist at the moment. Nobody was dead, nobody was kidnapped, there was no danger.

A week after they first slept together, they repeated the act at another house, a small one Brena owned that not many, and certainly not MI6, knew about. It was a treasure trove. Here, after they had sex and Joanne rushed into the shower, Emil, still called William Morse back then, had a look around the house. He hadn't expected to need his mini-camera – in fact he'd never gotten chance to use it – so had had to write notes on his arm, same as he'd today written the names and radio channel numbers of the terrorists. He'd seen plans scrawled on notepads, stuck to the fridge by magnets, even something written on a Scrabble board in tiles. This was a place just for Brena and, his wife claimed, his girlfriends, and there was no need for security or care. There should have been.

Later, he'd called Cavil and relayed the news of his discovery.

A sudden jerk of the helicopter whacked Cavil from a half-sleep, dragging him out of an old memory and into a world of noise. The roar of the rotor blades. The three Billys bickering over some combat fitness test they'd taken.

'Shut your faces,' he yelled at the arguing trio, who did just that. And the pilot got an unfair order to hit no more damn turbulence. Cavil grabbed a pair of ear defenders hanging near his head and allowed his mind to rewind the years again. Back to Bosnia, and Morse, the real source of his annoyance.

Morse had learned that Brena's paramilitary group was distancing itself from the forefront of the action while Brena built up his legitimate business portfolio, instead concentrating on supplying weapons and explosives to other groups, and helping to train them. A plan was formed, but it involved forcing his new officer to overstep a line.

There was evidence that bomb construction was taking place in the rooms above the restaurant in the city centre. Bombs were dangerous things to mess around with, because one mistake could bring the whole building down. If such a freak accident occurred, Brena and his inner circle would be wiped out, The Black Tigers would topple, and a chain of other paramilitary groups would find themselves suddenly handicapped.

Now all Cavil had to do was wait for a freak accident. Or help it along.

Morse, still new to the job, did not know that Cavil had received no permission for a hit. He also didn't know he could refuse to take such a job. So he turned up for work on June 3, 1992, in his coveralls, driving his old Volkswagen, carrying his bag of garden tools. At a final briefing with three overseers in a room above a shop a hundred metres down the road, Morse was shocked to see Cavil. He had flown over just to observe, because despite his being the Balkan Controllerate boss, he'd never been to Bosnia before. And he'd never seen a real-life explosion.

With his overseers watching from above the nearby shop, Morse entered the restaurant as Amel Kulenovic, gardener, and forty-seven minutes later the sign came. Dead simple. There was an alleyway leading round back, to the garden, with some bins at the mouth. Morse carried a plastic sack of garden detritus out to the bins and dropped one of the lids on the pavement. The bomb was ready.

Cavil started the countdown. Morse had ten minutes to get clear. He was supposed to claim to Brena that he had a supply to fetch, and then scarper. The mission could not be aborted. Any one of Brena's men, investigating the remains of the bomb that exploded, would recognise an anomaly amongst their devices, and that could come back to haunt MI6. So it had to be detonated. Even if Morse wasn't out.

Six minutes later, though, someone knocked on the door of the room above the shop. All four men jerked. Nobody was supposed to know they were here. It was an empty upstairs room. Cavil sent a minion to the door.

'Shopkeeper from downstairs,' the minion said, peering through the spyhole.

She must have heard him, because she shouted through the door:

'*Imam poruku za vas. Abort. Razumete li to, gospodine?*'

The guy turned. 'Says she has a message. We must abort. What the bejesus is going on?'

'She said what the bejesus is going on?' another guy said.

'Be quiet,' Cavil hissed. He'd heard the shop phone ring downstairs just thirty seconds earlier. 'Morse must have called her. Tell her to get lost.' He checked out the window again. Amazingly, he saw Morse was at the end of the alleyway, just standing there, staring, making no effort not to look suspicious. Cavil yanked up the blinds and the window and leaned out. Morse started dragging his finger across his throat, the sign to terminate. He was very agitated.

It was all signwork. Cavil shook his head. Held up the detonator, stuck a single finger in the air, jerked his thumb like a hitchhiker. Message: no, I'm blowing it, you have one minute to clear the hell out.

Morse vanished. Thirty seconds later, Cavil heard a gunshot from the vicinity of the restaurant, and the front window blew out.

'Bastard,' he screamed, loud enough that people on the street who were facing the sound of the busted window now whirled and looked up at him.

'You'll miss the best bit staring at me,' he yelled down at them, and pushed the button.

23

———

Emil stared out of the driver's side window, forehead against the glass. 'That day I was supposed to fabricate a reason to not have to use the outside toilet, so I could get upstairs. But even before I could sabotage that outside toilet, Brena did me a favour. He was with three of his men and his wife in the restaurant, which had a window facing the back garden, and it was open, and he called me in as I went past, told me to go fetch him a medicine box from the bathroom upstairs. I went up. I'd already gotten a copy of the key for the spare room, and that room was right across from the bathroom, so I quickly went in. The room was just bare walls and floor, and on fold-away tables was all the bomb-making equipment, right there, no curtains on the window, although there was no building directly across with line of sight inside. Still, it was bold to just leave all that equipment sitting there, even if the door was locked.'

Emil checked his watch. Sara was still watching him intently. Before continuing his story, he checked out of all the windows, although the darkness would have easily hidden anyone approaching.

'I put my device right there on a table, next to the others. I didn't know much about bombs, so I didn't know what it was or how it worked. And I wasn't sure of the effect of so many devices clumped together like that. But Cavil had assured me that the detonation would ruin the entire top floor and start a fire powerful enough to weaken the structure and cause a collapse, and that only the people inside would die, although flying debris might hurt passers-by. So I relocked the door and got the medicine box from the bathroom and went downstairs.

'It was awkward to be near Joanne, Brena's wife. We weren't close. I knew she'd cheated on him in the past, and she clearly loved him. She just liked men. But although I didn't love her, or her me, when you've been intimate with someone like that, there's always a strange kind of bond. So I found it hard. I was wracked with guilt, knowing she was going to die. By my hand. But I had a mission. I passed over the medicine box and headed for the backyard. I took a bag of garden trash to the bins out front and dropped the bin lid on the ground, our pre-arranged sign that the bomb was ready. All I had to do was tell Brena I needed to fetch some supplies, and get out of there.

'But on the way in, I heard clapping. I saw Brena's men shaking his hand, and congratulating Joanne. I had no idea what was going on, and I didn't care to stop and find out. But I did find out. I saw Brena lean down and kiss his wife's belly.'

Sara waited, but Emil said nothing further for a time. She prompted him. 'Brena's wife was pregnant.'

Emil nodded. 'I knew he'd shown off a pregnancy test that was in the in the medicine box. I also knew it wasn't his. I just knew. That baby was mine.'

'My god. What did you do?'

'It was like a switch had been thrown. In the next instant, bombs didn't matter, murderous paramilitary groups didn't matter – the whole Bosnian War didn't matter to me. What mattered was that baby. I was going to be a father. For the next few minutes, that was.'

She repeated her question: *what did you do?*

'The only thing I could do,' Emil said, and then told it.

He had rushed to the bins again and stared up the street, at the blind-covered window set in grimy stone above a bookshop a hundred metres down, hoping Cavil would see him. And cursing the fact that, because Brena often randomly searched his employees, Emil had not been permitted a radio.

He had tried to order an abort, but Cavil was having none of it. When Cavil held up his finger to indicate one minute remaining, Emil panicked. One minute offered no time for a plan. In that instant he saw only one way to save his child – force.

He went inside the restaurant, straight over to Brena's group. His wild eyes, maybe, or his forceful stomp, or some negative aura emanating off him – whatever, something gave away his intent, and a moment after the group turned their eyes to watch his approach, one of Brena's goons stood up and whipped out his pistol. Emil let the arm arc all the way towards him, then grabbed the wrist and twisted, and yanked the gun away, but not before the goon pulled the trigger, sending a bullet into the big front window, shattering it.

He pushed the goon away with a front kick and grabbed Joanne's hand, yanked her into his arms. By this time, Brena and the other two goons had pulled their weapons, and it should have been game over. But Emil knew Cavil, and what would happen when Cavil saw the window blow out.

Emil dove onto the floor, pulling Joanne on top of him, then rolling on top of her, and that was when the entire world trembled.

Cavil looked out at the black world whizzing by underneath the chopper and had a sudden urge for coffee. 'Anyone brought coffee? Even tea?'

The men shook their heads.

'Dickheads,' Cavil muttered, and closed his eyes to sink back into the long-ago.

The explosion had been tremendous, perfect, a work of art. The thick walls of the building held quite well, but the old roof allowed the explosion to rise upwards into the sky like an erupting volcano. Ten seconds later he heard the heavy rain of debris all around, including on his own roof. Fire was eating the entire upper floor of Brena's building. Every window was gone, even in the downstairs rooms. Stone and glass coated the street, cars and roofs were smashed, and pedestrians cowered and screamed – this literal warzone had been given a Hollywood-like tint.

'Cajun on the menu tonight,' Cavil said with a laugh. Then he got serious. He screamed at his men to get the hell out. Down the stairs they went, through the lady's shop, out into the street, towards their car, ready to escape.

Then, amazingly, Morse rushed out of the alleyway down by Brena's burning restaurant, and he was dragging a woman by the hand. Brena's wife. Cavil's jaw dropped. *Some kind of double-cross, this?*

He ordered his men to pursue on foot, while he jumped in the car and tore off in the other direction.

He circled the block and came from the south, and there was Morse with his new friend, running across the road, headed for a gate in a stone wall that led to a park. Cavil's men were behind and closing because the woman couldn't run that well. As he watched, Morse let her go and hung back and grabbed one of the guys barrelling at him. The second joined the action, while the third side-stepped and raced past, pursuing the woman. She reached the gate and threw the handle and it swung open, but she got no further as big arms encircled her. But two seconds later she was running again, once more with Morse's hand in hers.

Cavil raced past his two men, flat out on the ground, put there in five seconds by Morse's bare hands. His car skidded to a stop near the gates and he leaped out with his pistol. He jumped over his third minion, put down in two seconds, and raced into the park. He saw Morse and the woman to his left, thundering along a dim concrete path between high hedges.

'Game over,' he yelled, and fired a bullet into the sky. At the gunshot, or the shout, Morse stopped, but didn't turn. The woman ran on and out of sight around a corner, and only when she was gone did Morse turn to his boss.

Thirty feet between them. He saw a pistol in Morse's hand. Cavil cursed. A weapon taken from one of his men. Where the hell had Morse learned such high-level skills so quickly? Not from one six-month intelligence officers' new entrants' course, that was for damned sure.

'You chose a rotten path, Morse, and there's no turning back,' Cavil yelled.

'I think I'd like to hand in my resignation, Mr Cavil,' Morse replied.

Cavil laughed. 'If you think today's foolishness means nothing more than a verbal warning, Morse, then surprises are coming. If you're lucky, your death by torture in Čelebići prison camp will happen before you can see the guards rape your new girlfriend.'

The wild threat didn't change Morse's stony face. He simply shrugged '*Amor fati.*'

The insubordination, the rescue of the woman, his own anger at knowing he'd put his trust in a traitor – those things had pissed Cavil off, yet he'd retained his cool. But that final pair of words from Morse, and his deadpan delivery, caused an instant combustion. Rage grabbed the wheel and, before he could stop himself, Cavil jerked up his gun and fired.

Morse raised his weapon a fraction of a second later, and that he was able to do so caused Cavil to freeze. He had missed. Emotion had skipped his round right past his target.

But only just. He saw Morse jerk slightly as he fired, and the bullet meant for Cavil's chest or head instead found his upper thigh. The leg was swept out from under him and he went down hard onto the cold concrete. His gun went flying from his grasp, and he knew then he was a dead man. His threat of prison and torture had forced Morse upon this rotten path.

But when he looked up, Morse had vanished.

24

───────

S ara felt a chill, but it wasn't the cold. 'What happened to Brena's wife?'

Emil said, 'When the bomb went off, the entire ceiling suffered, but the portion below the room containing the explosives burst downwards like a meteor shower, throwing stone hard into the floor, which then bounced everywhere like fireballs. Brena and his men were cut down like bowling pins, but only smaller pieces of masonry and brick hit me. I grabbed Joanne as a fire started and we got out of there before the rest of the ceiling came down.

'I dragged her down the alley. She was yelping about her husband, but I convinced her that she would be fine if she stayed with me. She thought the government was coming after Brena, and I let her think that.

'Outside the alley, I saw Cavil and his men up the street, so we ran the other way. I knew Cavil would have me arrested or framed for the bombing, but I didn't care about that at the time. So we ran. We ran to a park. I had to take out his three men when they came at me. Ever since I had been approached by MI6 and the thought of working for them had taken me, I had started teaching myself martial arts, knives, lockpicking, all the things that I thought spies would need. Based on what I thought spies got up to, of course. Action books and films. Cavil, too, I had to take him out. I knew he might have to kill me. An illegal op of his had been compromised, and his new golden boy, a few months in the job, was trying to escape with his target's wife. It would end him if word got out. Better, I assumed he thought, if he could kill us both and invent a story. I had to shoot him, but I couldn't kill him. I blew out his leg. I'm sure he thinks I aimed for his face or his heart.'

Emil jerked as the night beyond the car was shifted by a noise, a movement, but it was an animal running by. But he didn't relax. He clutched his weapon tightly. He no longer seemed to have the desire for storytelling.

'That's it, really. We crossed the water to Italy, thinking that Cavil would expect me to flee to Bulgaria or Romania or one of the other countries sharing a border with the former Yugoslavia. From there took a series of trains and buses and finally a plane when we got to France, where I found a man who could give us fake passports. Mr and Mrs Torrance, Emil and Louise, British citizens. We went to Scotland, but I was still undecided about where we should try to start a new life. But it had to be Britain. I wanted my child to be raised in a country I knew. Right outside the airport, on the rain-soaked pavement, was a pamphlet about the Peak District, and right then I knew the future.'

'I get it,' Sara said. 'You set up a new life here. Your son, he would be close to twenty-five now. Does he know?'

'Halfway to the Peak District, Joanne said she didn't want to leave Bosnia. We'd travelled so far already, and now this bomb-shell. I said she couldn't go back. We stayed a night in a hotel in Newcastle and talked about it. In the morning she was gone. I stayed in Newcastle and hid low, taking cash-in-hand jobs. I hate to say that sometimes I had to mug people and do other things to raise cash. I built up contacts and did research, and eight months later, with a month to spare, I went and confronted her. I had learned where she'd gone and had had someone watching her. I had given it eight months so I could return into her life when my baby was nearly ready to be born. But when I got there, she'd already had him – a boy.

'Five weeks premature, small, but not ill. But being cared for by a house full of crack addicts while she went out to prostitute herself. I took the baby. I called him Peter, after my own father. In the month it took me to secure a place to live and a job here, in Barkelow, I put Pete in the care of the sister of a man I did leg-breaking work for. She was great. And I put a man on watching the crack house, to tell me how many police cars turned up ten minutes after Joanne returned to find her baby gone.'

He looked right into Sara's eyes, the only things he could see in the dark.

'No police cars. Nobody called them. Here's the funny thing. The baby had enough clothing and food and was clean. He was treated well, as if by a caring family. But when he vanished one day, his mother didn't care. Think of that what you will.'

Sara said nothing, unwilling to break Emil's flow.

'I took my son away from a possible life in Bosnia where there were no drugs, there was money, and there was a loving mother and father. I put him in a life where his mother was gone, his father was a wanted man, and there was no close family. So did I really save that baby from anything? I asked myself this many times. War raged for three more years in Bosnia, and Brena and his wife would have been serious targets out there. But still I wondered. When my son was nine months old and healthy again, I brought him here. Today he's alive and happy and we have a good life. But something I still wonder: did I save him?'

Her eyes met his. 'I should say yes. Because he's alive and

happy, as you say. But the truth is it's impossible to judge such a thing. We can't know how other paths in life would have worked out. It's best not to ask yourself such questions. But I have a question. Your son. Pete. Does he know any of this? Does he know where his mother is?'

'I checked up on her a couple of times a year, and eight years ago I got the news that she'd died. I told my son the truth, except for a few things. I said I met his mother in France, not Bosnia. Bosnia back then was a warzone, so how could I explain to anyone why I was there? And talk of Bosnia might spread, and get to Cavil's ears. So I used France. But I told another, far more horrible lie. I told Pete his mother died when he was two. Out there, overseas. I told him his parents had no family, so he wouldn't seek out aunties and grandparents. And my hope was that France was too far for him to try to visit her burial place. He's never insisted on a visit, but if the day comes when he does, I will do what I have to. Either I will tell the whole truth, or I will have a fake gravestone made and slotted into a French cemetery and then I will sneak us across the water in a boat. If I have to. I don't like to think about that day coming, though. Selfishly, I hope it never does.

'So that's my story. I am now Emil Torrance, an unskilled worker my whole life, and I've never travelled anywhere abroad but France. And my son is Pete Torrance, born in Newcastle to a French mother. And for over two decades we have lived here in this little village. And no one will ever know different, if I can help it.'

Sara rubbed her eyes, as if trying to wake from a dream. 'This is... shocking. So, you're on the run from the government. You said Cavil would invent a story about that night...'

'I died. That's the story. William Morse went to Bosnia and became a casualty of war.'

'What about your family? Mother? Brothers? Do they still think you're dead?'

'No brothers or sisters. My mother died about ten years ago. She died thinking her son's body lay undiscovered or destroyed in another country.'

'Didn't you ever think about contact–'

'No,' Emil cut in. But he apologised for it. 'Cavil would have found me. He set me up for a robbery, in part to aid my capture and to fortify his story to his bosses that I went AWOL. And I shot a superior officer. I have no doubt I would have been arrested the moment I contacted my family, and probably for a whole host of invented crimes far worse than robbery. And if I tried to tell the truth, the government would produce an array of evidence that I was lying. Then, when the media interest in the rogue MI6 agent waned, I would have been shipped overseas to some hellhole prison, where an inmate would have put a knife in me. I couldn't ever risk that. Even now, so long after, I daren't even leave this village in case I have an accident or get mugged or something else that warrants police taking an interest in me. If Emil Torrance's photo or DNA or fingerprints ever goes into an official file...'

'But your mother would know you were alive, so–'

'Again I must interrupt. She would have watched her son carted off to prison, where he would be killed. This way, at least she could have hope. I was missing, not dead. And I had a son to think about, Sara. That was the most important thing to me. I couldn't have Cavil take him away, perhaps back to Bosnia. I couldn't have my son grow up fatherless, and knowing that father was a convicted criminal.' He paused. 'But the truth is something I owe Pete one day. Today, hopefully.'

She nodded, understanding. 'And Cavil? What happened to him?'

'I know that eight months after the Bosnia thing he was

transferred, but soon I stopped caring. The first couple of years were tricky. This is a tourist spot, remember, so strangers were common, and strangers scared the hell out of me. I looked over my shoulder a lot. There was a tourist who took a photo of me once, and I very nearly had to... get rid of him. But it turned out to be nothing. And then, as time went on, I managed to stop worrying. It's been over twenty years. I can't forget the threat, of course, but now it's at the back of my mind. And as for Cavil? I would like to think he's retired now, living in Spain like he always wanted, and no longer even remembers William Morse, the employee who gave him a headache.'

Cavil wondered if Morse still thought about him.

Cavil had arranged a robbery in the Bosnian village of Tuzla and planted Morse's fingerprints, in the hope that the man somehow had decided to stay in the country. He had also done the same in four of the nearby countries, and here in England, in case the man fled home. Not something he had expected, that latter one, but now look.

Cavil had managed to hide his involvement in the Bosnian thing, but had been unable to explain Morse's disappearance. So he convinced MI6 the man had gone rogue and fled during a routine intelligence mission. Although he had gotten away with that, it had planted destructive seeds that had eroded Cavil's career quickly. He was a handler who'd lost a man. Never good. Six months afterwards, following local newspaper and MP pressure arranged by Morse's mother, the brass had ousted him. He was offered a sideways move in the organisation, effectively a demotion, and, as they damned well knew he would, he refused it and instead quit. His experience got him a high post in a securities company, and his pension got him the public house he now ran. In a way he was glad, because now he was his own boss. But still, Morse had messed him over and cost him dearly, and he had never given up the hope of getting revenge on the man, something his long-time secretary had known when she called him earlier.

Now, he had the chance to kill Morse and put to rest those bad memories.

'Faster,' he told the pilot. 'Keep the noise down and wake me when we're ten minutes out. Someone brought me a gun, right?'

A pistol appeared under his nose, like a move from a cartoon. He took it and felt the weight. God, it had been so long since he'd held one. He put it aside and closed his eyes.

Morse, surely, had forgotten all about Cavil and would not be expecting a comeback now, after all these years. He would be an old man, no skills, rusty, and about to have a very bad day.

25

Emil checked his watch. 'Four minutes.'

He started the engine, drove with the lights off, bumping over the track. Two minutes later, Sara saw the land open up to their left as the trees ended. *Some clearing*, she realised. And a building of some kind. Small, with a chimney, but in the dark she couldn't make out if it was wood or stone or anything. Emil turned into the clearing with a crunch of gravel beneath the tyres.

'You get a free hot drink for finding this place,' Emil said.

'What is it? Where are we?'

He ignored her. Pulled the radio. Said into it, 'Thirty minutes down, Bradan. Time for action. You ready?'

'Born ready, Mr Morse.'

Sara felt the shiver run through Emil at the mention of his real name. She turned on the interior light to see his face, which was ashen. He made no move to turn it off. He sat frozen.

'Don't think you have the upper hand here, Mr Morse. As you can tell, I know more than you think.'

Emil didn't move. Sara snatched the radio, and said to Emil, 'What's the plan?'

Bradan said, 'That got your attention, right? So now we do things my way, unless you want the police here after all? I could certainly arrange that. They'll want to talk to everyone, and check them out for criminal records. Something surprising might turn up.'

Sara grabbed his chin, turned him to face her. 'Plan?' she hissed.

He whispered it, his voice cracking. But his mind was on Bradan's veiled threat – what did he know about the past?

'You there?' Bradan said.

'We're here,' Sara said into the radio. 'With your man, who won't be going on trial for murder in London after all. He might end up doing life for terrorism, that Shard thing and all.'

Silence. Emil felt Sara staring at him, but he didn't look at her. She would see the new worry in his eyes.

Except for the thump of her heart, which seemed to make her whole body vibrate. But once more she injected false bravado into her voice. 'See, Bradan, you're not the only one who can uncover deep secrets. So this won't be your way at all. It's ours. And it happens like this. You'll wait and watch the hills for a pair of car headlights coming on, somewhere out here, so stay high so you can see. Your man will be in that car, tied up. One driver will bring the son and my mother and father in another car and park next to it. He'll have no weapons and the interior light will be on, so we can see everyone. If the son and my parents aren't sitting up and waving their hands with their eyes wide open so we can see everyone's okay, then a rifle bullet will kill your driver. Then we will take all four hostages, and guess which one of them will be headed to prison?

'But if all looks good down that high-powered rifle scope, your driver will swap cars. He drives away with your man. We drive away with our people. Everyone's happy.'

More silence. Then Bradan said, 'Okay, that's a deal. Hide

and seek. Go hide and I'll count to 300. That's how long you have. Five minutes. If I don't see headlights out there in five minutes, the deal changes to something you really won't like. Now that you've involved Mr and Mrs Everton in this, I have a significant advantage over you. Three versus one. I don't even need that many, so you're lucky I don't kill one of them right now. Let's just do this. Go hide. The count begins. 300... 299...'

Bradan stopped counting, put his radio down. 'I'm going to the roof. Get hold of Fergal and tell him to get the son and the parents off this rock and into a car on the ground and wait for my call.'

Denis said, 'How do you want to do this?'

'I was about to tell you. You don't have to ask. Fergal will drive up as they say. We'll do the deal. You'll go out after Fergal, and after he's driven away with Mr Crossen kill Morse and the girl from the shadows.'

Denis nodded. Right then his own radio crackled.

Capucine: 'Denis, what is a Ukitti?'

Denis looked at Bradan, and answered: 'Why?'

'One is in this wishing well.'

'What?'

'I do not know. It is here, halfway down, stuck on wall. A small box. Says Ukitti on it.'

Bradan looked at him. Denis's jaw had dropped. 'Is that a problem?'

Denis said to him, 'Ukitti's a Japanese firm, and they make listening devices. Surveillance. Long-range. But why would one of those be in a wishing well in a garden?'

'You're asking me? Who could have planted that? Our irritating ninja, Morse? Is this bad?'

Denis shrugged. 'A well is a strange place to put one. Middle of a garden. But a surveillance device near us while we're doing this could be a bad sign.'

'Shit,' Bradan said. He looked worried now. 'Tell her to bring it here. Can you take it apart, maybe find out what it's recorded?'

'Maybe.' Denis told Capucine to retrieve the box and bring it to them.

She said she couldn't. Fixed to the wall too far down and she didn't dare touch it because it was buzzing.

'Denis, go get that damned thing,' Bradan said. 'You've got about ten minutes, since Fergal will take time getting the hostages out of here and onto the ground. Tell him the plan as you go.'

A few minutes later, following her directions over the radio, Denis came down the steps to the area where Capucine was waiting for him in the dark. He'd just finished outlining the plan for Fergal, who was not happy that he was the guy stepping into the firing line. Denis stopped before her, looking at the stone wall of the well.

'The listening device is in the well? What are you doing out here?'

'Fresh air. Time to think. My boyfriend just die, remember. And my mother.'

Embarrassed, unsure what to say, Denis just shrugged.

She pointed at the well. 'Not sure you should touch it. What if a trap?'

He laughed. He moved past her, put his hands on the edge and peered in. 'I can't see anything.'

'Take a closer look,' she said from behind him. She grabbed his radio off his belt and pushed him, hard.

He fell forwards, but the well was only three feet wide and he stopped himself from tumbling in, propped there in some weird pose like a guy playing *Twister*. She raised her pistol and struck an arm braced against the stone, and with that prop gone he vanished. Splash-thud, and a scream as she heard the snap of bone. He began shouting.

She looked down. His white face was there, like an apparition. She could vaguely see him sitting up, staring up, clutching his arm to his chest. Lower still, there was the outline of her Cathal, with one outstretched arm disappearing beneath Denis.

'Apologise to him. And get off him.'

Denis was already shouting, but the tempo increased when he realised what lumpiness his legs lay upon. Soon he calmed. 'What the hell's going on? Help me.'

'My last look at my Cathal was bloody, battered mess, and it was your fault,' she said.

He looked annoyed. 'Silly bitch. What are you saying? That handyman killed Cathal. You think it was me? You'll pay for this.'

'It was not you who kill him. I know that. But you make him unbeautiful. You ride lift so you can get to my Cathal, and he is dragged. You bend, tear, twist my Cathal. My last look at him is disfigure and bloody. You give me that memory for all time.'

He said nothing. Which said to her he did not deny this fact.

Then he started shouting for help. She grabbed a rock the size of her fist and lobbed it into the well. Heard him grunt. She grabbed two more, launched them one at a time, heard the splash. One made no noise other than a grunt from Denis.

He started screaming for aid.

She picked up a larger rock, two hands needed. Clutched it to her chest and stood so close to the well that Denis couldn't fail to see what she carried.

'No,' he yelled up at her. 'Help! Bradan!'

She dropped the rock. Vaguely caught sight of him trying to shift aside. Heard a meaty thump, and a scream. His next cry of 'help' was wet and weak.

She went back for a bigger rock.

Cavil stared at his phone until it rang.

The voice said, 'Okay, here we go. Police files. The guy your copper mentioned, Denis Mulrennan. Fifty-eight years old. Born in Belfast. Joined the Provisional IRA in the late seventies, as a teenager, and at the age of twenty became a company leader in the Ballymurphy district...'

Intriguing. Cavil listened intently. The call lasted eight minutes, and for that entire time he didn't say a word. At the end, he said just one: 'Thanks.' And hung up.

The three Billys were watching, waiting. He didn't feel the need to tell hired guns anything, but felt like talking aloud, just to get the facts straight in his end.

So he told them what his guy had found out for him in just fifteen minutes.

Morse's file had been sought by a guy called Denis Mulrennan. A teenager at the time, Mulrennan, an electronics expert, was loosely suspected of involvement in the death of Lord Mountbatten in 1979. His name appeared again in August 1981 in relation to a bombing at the Sunrise Bar in Belfast, where the targets were members of the Ulster Volunteer Force.

'Irish Republican Army?' one of the Billys said. 'Why are they interested in Morse?'

Cavil ignored the question. Mulrennan's many known associates were names that had featured in myriad crimes during The Troubles in Northern Ireland. One guy Mulrennan was thick as thieves with was Bradan Brogan, who was right-hand man and bodyguard to a guy called Sean Crossen. Crossen, once an officer commanding in the Belfast Brigade's Second Battalion, had been part of a peace talks delegation that met a British group that included William Whitelaw, then Secretary of State for Northern Ireland. So, a pretty high-ranking guy in the IRA. Mulrennan, Brogan and Crossen had all seemingly vanished off the face of the earth after the 1998 Good Friday Agreement.

A different Billy said, 'And now they're in Barkelow. And Morse is hooked up with them?'

Then, nine months ago their main man, Crossen, got arrested for drunken conduct in Manchester, England, and a night in the cells turns into a spell in Strangeways when the government realised who he was and decided they better try to hold on to him for a bit. Just in case. Nine months down the line they got a stroke of luck, because he was suddenly in the frame for some London murder, and now they could stop dallying because they had something concrete to pin on him.

Cavil paused before delivering the twist: 'Today Crossen's due a transfer to London to appear at the Old Bailey for trial. Prison to prison, probably by van. A nice little period when his security won't be rock-solid.'

The two Billys who'd had a say actually looked at their partner, as if by some unwritten agreement they knew it was his turn. And this one said, 'Crossen's old Provo pals are going to break him out of prison, up in this Barkelow place, and your old pal Morse has been recruited to help them.'

Cavil tutted and wagged a finger – no, no, no. 'Morse will be in Barkelow way under anyone's radar, probably living life as a farmer. Ingrained there, part of the furniture, causing not an ounce of suspicion. In such a small village, his false ID won't come under much scrutiny. I doubt he's ever had to show his fake driver's licence to join a bowls club, and why would they doubt a single thing he tells them about his past? He's a maestro at playing a ghost, and if I couldn't find him, no one could. And he certainly wouldn't tell the IRA about his past. So, if these people are researching him, it's not to make sure he's a trustworthy candidate for a job. It's because at the last minute he's crawled out from under his rock to try to ruin their nicely laid plans. And I love it.'

26

Fergal went to the dining room on the north side of the great ballroom and unlocked the door. As he barged inside, everyone shied away against the back windows, which looked out onto the tennis court. They were locked, but nobody had dared to try to break the glass and escape. There was also a doorless entry into a corridor running alongside the north side of the house and a door that led to a pantry with an exit on the other side, but he did a quick head count and found nobody missing. The last hero who'd tried to escape had provided a lasting memory.

He ordered the Everton couple to step out and took them to the security room, where he had earlier escorted the young man they now knew was Morse's son. He was on his arse against an old radiator, tie-wrapped to it. He cut him loose, told all three to stand against the wall, facing him.

Bradan called him. 'Has Denis come back?'

Fergal, holding his gun on all three captives as they awaited his next move, said, 'I haven't seen him. Call him. Or ask Capucine.'

'She's right here. Left him at the well. I've got his radio. She said she found it in the tennis court, so he must have dropped it on his way outside. Are you about ready?'

'Just tying them up now. Five minutes, we'll be on the ground. Five more, we'll be in a vehicle.'

Fergal slotted away his radio. 'Now don't move,' he told his captives. Morse's son was whispering to the old couple, telling them to be calm, it would soon all be over.

'It'll be over quicker than you think if you don't shut up,' Fergal said. He jabbed the boy in the throat with his pistol to prove a point. Morse's son offered a sneer, but made no other move.

'Now this bit's tricky,' Fergal said. 'The portion of our journey where bullets are most likely to fly, as your brain realises it's the single best chance for escape. I'm going to tie you all together, and for a half-second here and there I won't have the use of my gun.'

He stepped close to the old guy, put his face close, pointed the gun at his eyes.

'The War Cabinet is in session in your bodies right now. Prime Minister Pituitary has ordered General Adrenocorticotropic to mobilise his men for action. The body prepares. Here, look, the pupils are dilating so they can absorb more light, making sure they can see better than ever during this momentous time. You could take my gun right now, old man, and save the world.'

He stepped to the side, in front of the old lady, who was shaking.

'General Adrenocorticotropic sends out thirty or so of his best, including Colonel Epinephrine and Sergeant Norepinephrine. That shaking isn't fear. That's you tensing up for the fight, hairs standing up, more blood making its way to the major muscles as the brain shifts attention from simple things to take care of the bigger picture, and the blood pressure's up. God, right about now your entire being is telling you you could take me down.'

He stepped in front of Morse's son. 'The warrior hormones are ready. The whole body's on red alert, eh, boy?' Put a palm on the boy's chest. 'Heart rate is up, blood pressure's up. You probably all feel invincible at the minute, knowing this could be it, this is where we escape.' He stepped back. 'Just remember that people all get this reaction, and they still die by the thousands every day. So don't try anything or I'll blow some kneecaps. Your legs will come right off and you'll be too short to ride anything decent at Alton Towers.'

They didn't try anything. He tied Morse's son's hands behind his back and Mr Everton's in front of him, then one of Mrs Everton's hands to each of their bonds, creating a three-person chain with the boy at the front.

'Looks good enough,' Fergal said. 'But maybe you're all three-legged-race champions and could still run away from me. What to do?'

Quickly, he stamped on Morse's son's ankle to hobble him. He fell with a scream and dragged Mrs Everton down with him.

They moved out of the house and between the garden mazes, and stopped at the lift. Fergal pressed the button to call it up.

'Where are you taking us?' Mr Everton asked.

'Don't worry, and this time I'm serious. You're being traded, so if you don't do anything daft, ten minutes from now you'll be safe and free. And you two can have relief-at-being-alive sex.'

Down they went. The wind was cold. The captives huddled on one side and Fergal leaned against the railing on the other.

'Your father's quite the man,' he said to Pete.

'I know,' Pete said.

'You know, do you? What else do you know about him? Did you know his original name was William Morse? He changed it.'

'I'm sure he didn't have that beard or the same car when he was younger, either.'

Fergal laughed. 'Funny kid. No, those were different, too. Smooth face, different car, different job. Know what his job used to be? Know what job he held when you were conceived?'

'Male escort?'

'Let's just say travel. He had an overseas job. Eastern Europe.'

'Okay, let's just say that, and no more. He worked in Eastern Europe. Good for him.'

Fergal decided to leave it there, but he gave the boy a grin that he hoped would fire his curiosity.

They got off the lift and wound their way across the courtyard and out into the market square, where Fergal got his first look at what had happened. Where they all did. He noted the shock on their faces.

'Looks like we all missed a party,' he said to them. 'Move. That way.'

There was a car parked partway down an alleyway between two shops. Fergal peered through a busted window and saw a shape inside, sprawled on the floor and missing the top of its head. Kane. So Morse really had taken them out. Jesus. He tried to hide his anger and shock.

He failed.

'My dad's never liked parties,' the son said with a grin.

Fergal cracked him on the chin with the gun.

He forced them into the back of the car, which took time. If they worked together, with good choreography, they could take him out as he drove. But he was sure he would have time to react accordingly. So he jammed his pistol between his legs, and started the car. Put his radio on the dashboard.

'Now we wait.'

The call came just ninety seconds later, two seconds after Fergal spotted a pair of red pinpricks appear in the darkness far ahead and slightly above him. 'I have it,' Bradan said over the radio. 'Headlights, Fergal. On the eastern hill.'

'I see them. Between two of the farmhouses. Here we go.'

He started the car.

~

Sara took her foot off the accelerator and turned the wheel, cutting a curve in the grass. When the vehicle was facing the village, she stopped and opened the door and turned off the engine, but left the ignition on.

God, this had better not go wrong. She was half expecting the bad guys to know their targets would use the hill, and to be out here already, ready to pounce the moment she made her next move.

She turned on the headlights. Their beams cut the night in half and lit nothing ahead but grass. And then she ran.

She ran fast and hard, and she did not look back, fearful of seeing men hot on her tail.

It took ten minutes to get back to the cabin in the clearing.

It was made of stone with an exoskeleton of timber, and timber window frames, and a Dutch door of timber. As she got close, the security light came on, as it had when Emil had approached. She ducked her head, as if that would help her avoid being seen while all lit up like a rock star on a stage. She slapped the handle and shouldered the door and went sprawling on the tiled floor within. Tried to kick the door shut, realised she was facing the wrong way. The Dutch doors – not locked together. She had rammed open the top half and gone tumbling over the lower section.

Over to her right, in the dark, something moved. As she lay there, she laughed. Something? Mr Crossen, tied up near a table of jars of locals' jams and a big tea urn, where tourists could pour their own. That was the deal here: the place was out of the way and not on maps or otherwise advertised, and if you found it you were owed a free hot drink. It had once been tea and cake, Emil had said, back before the introduction of social media sites.

She got up and slammed the door half and bolted it and moved backwards until her bum hit the serving counter, and then she sat down on the floor.

'Let me go now and there will be no comeback,' said Mr Crossen. 'I promise.'

'Let me just think about that for two seconds.'

He moved. Getting comfortable or trying to break his bonds, she couldn't tell. But she watched him closely. He shifted and stopped. She relaxed.

'Bear in mind, please, madam, that my people know who you are, and no matter how lucky you are today, all it takes is one. Are you sure that I do not have at least one more man out there somewhere, who needs only a blade and a plane ticket and a pair of ears to hear a call to action?'

She shivered. A threat. Sometime in the future, someone might come for her.

'I cannot control my fate that day, but I can today,' she said, deliberately cryptic, deliberately forming a Hollywood-style soundbite to match his own. It seemed like the best way to respond, for how could such a line convey either anger or fear? 'So you will remain tied up and praying that your men care for you enough to do the right thing.' The words felt strange on her tongue. But not the act of saying them, because she had made a career out of telling criminals what to do, of showing them she was in control.

She got up, though. If he did suddenly free himself and make a run at her, she wanted to be on her feet for the best chance of defending herself. As she reached up to the counter to pull herself up, her hand caught the old-style rotary phone on the counter and knocked it, causing a loud ding.

Phone. She snatched up the receiver at her first blind snake-like grab and jammed it to her ear and heard a dial tone. Emil had said these people had mobile phone jammers and had compromised the landlines, but this one was fine. She could call the cops and be done with this mess.

But Emil had warned her not to. The police would not allow the terrorists to leave, and the terrorists would not allow themselves to be captured, and they would collide like a pair of juggernauts with the innocent people trapped between them. His way might let bad men free, but at least everybody would walk away alive.

She hung up the phone and stared past the counter, towards the curtained doorway at the back, and wondered exactly where he was and what he was doing, and why the hell she was defying her instincts and logic by trusting him.

27

———

Emil was a man very much interested in his surroundings, but not their history. Early on into his arrival at Barkelow, even before he had begun to look for a job, he had made a point of learning the geography of the village and who everyone was. He was a stranger from strange lands, but with a tale about a dead wife and an urge to relocate and a baby son in tow, people warmed to him. The last portion of the village to learn had been Barkelow Hall, but luckily that was where he got a job. That was how he found out about the secret passage. But all he knew of its history was that it had been some kind of escape route. If the outer wall around most of the village got breached, the owners could flee half a mile underground and emerge in the forest and be gone. He wondered if they'd ever considered that a chance finding of the entrance would allow an enemy of those holding the fort to slip inside and wreak havoc, as he was planning now.

The passage cut south-east, under the main road, forty feet below the surface, and under the market square, where there was a stone section of tunnel because of a cave-in back in the 1950s, and then ran up the hill, parallel to the lift. Here there were stone steps and a railing. It levelled out at the top, now only eighteen feet below the surface.

He moved in the dark, but soon the passage levelled out again and he saw a flicker of light ahead. He reached a junction. The path continued ahead to the house, but a fork sloped down to the left. On the wedge of wall between the two passageways was a lightbulb in a case that was lit whenever the garden lamps were turned on. He went ahead.

The tunnel ended abruptly at a wall with a metal ladder attached. In the ceiling was a trapdoor that led into the library at the front right corner of the house. The bolt was stiff, but soon worked loose. He lowered it. Another lay two feet above, but this had no bolt. This one had a simple piece of half-moon metal protruding. He waited, listening, but heard nothing and grabbed the handle and pushed.

It didn't move. He pressed at all four corners, but only one had any give.

Damn. There were sunken bolts in all four corners of the trapdoor topside, he knew, and it seemed three of them were in place. He could probably manoeuvre himself into a position to use his feet against the door, but there would be noise, and he had no idea if anyone was in the nearby rooms, or even in the library itself. Bradan, Fergal, Denis and the young girl Capucine were still alive. One could be chilling in a chair right above him.

He cursed. He had told Sara that he planned to rescue the other hostages as well, claiming that he believed the terrorists might try to kill some before they escaped, but that wasn't really the reason he had decided to sneak into the house. He expected to be tricked, and it would go down one of two ways.

If his son was still in the house, Emil would perform the rescue from within.

But if Bradan had sent his son out with one of his men to try some trickery during the trade, Emil wanted Bradan in his hands before that happened, so that he could force the leader to give up whatever trap they had planned and let Pete go.

Both depended upon Emil getting to Bradan before Bradan's man got to the trade site and realised Mr Crossen wasn't there. The moment Bradan got word of that, he might do something lethal.

And both required this trapdoor to be open.

Time was wasting. Panicking, he went back to the fork and took the other path.

Capucine stepped out onto the roof, and Bradan didn't turn. He heard her approach, she knew, because he held up a hand. He was sighting down the rifle's scope, into the hills. She stood by his side, buffeted by the cold wind. She put Denis's radio on the parapet. 'I found Denis's radio downstairs. He must have dropped it.'

He looked away from the scope, down at the radio, then up at her, then put his eye back to the scope. 'How do you know it is his?'

She gulped. If he'd been staring at her, she feared, he would have seen the guilt smeared right across her face. She said, 'I do not know. I did not see one on his belt. I left him try to get listening device from wall. What is happening?'

Still without looking away from the scope, he pointed into the dark. 'You see the headlights?'

She did. There were a million pinpricks of light in the distance, from faraway villages and villages, but closer, on the hill, two bright balls burned.

'What is that?'

'Hopefully, the car containing Mr Crossen. Fergal's gone there with the man's son and our prison officer's parents. When

Fergal tells me Mr Crossen is safe, I'm going to pull this trigger and end it all.'

She slapped his arm like an upset child and finally he looked at her again.

'I thought I will get to kill him?' She pulled a sour face, made sure she did a good job of it.

It made him smile. 'Hey, calm down, I meant you. You can kill him. Now stand back and relax. I'll call you over when it's time. Did you see Cathal?'

'Yes. What will happen to him when this over?'

'Well, the authorities will doubtless want to remember his brazen brilliance, so probably they'll erect a statue outside number ten to commemorate him.'

'What?'

He got serious. 'Capucine, what do you expect? They'll crack open his skull, and chop up his brain to see what made him tick so badly, and pieces will go to university laboratories so hungover students can prod at them. The rest of him will be buried and forgotten.'

'I know, and I do not want that. I do not want my Cathal brain in a jar on shelf. I have hide his body–'

'Excuse me?'

'–so we can come back and take him home. Real burial. Proper. We deserve to be together forever.'

'You will. You'll be in a jar next to his. Look, let's just concentrate–'

She stamped a foot in anger. 'You joke, always joke. I will not lose my Cathal. I want proper burial for him. Will you help?'

He stared at her for a long time, then put his eye back on the scope. 'Yes, Capucine, yes, yes, yes. Whatever you want. Your wish is my command. But can we just concentrate on the problem at hand for the moment?'

She stared out into the dark, at the headlights, and something hit her. Something about that car out there.

'You are doing trade, Bradan. That is your plan. You are going to let bastard who kill my Cathal go free.'

He looked at her again. This time stood up and faced her. 'No, I told you–'

'You do not have shot. At this distance, in dark, you only make that shot with night vision, and he is park with headlights facing us. Can not use night vision in bright light. You are letting him free.'

His silence told her everything.

Emil reached a circular grate at the end of the tunnel and slid it out and dropped it away, and it landed with a thud a few feet below – and a yelp. He looked out and down and there were two bodies – Cathal, the first guy he had killed, and another one, both sprawled amongst rocks littering the flooded floor of the well. He aimed his pistol, but the guy was no threat. Bloody and battered, yet staring up at him. Emil saw this in the meagre moonlight soaking the insides of the well.

He climbed out carefully, one-handed because his pistol never left the man watching him.

'You're supposed to be waiting for your son,' the battered man said. This must be Fergal or Denis. 'Unless I have the wrong ninja.'

'Where are the hostages?'

'Your son is being taken to the trade. We were doing the trade, so there was no need for you to sneak here. He's out there somewhere.'

Emil didn't answer him. He turned to the wall, to start the climb. He knew exactly where he was. Two paths led off from the well, one to a gateway in the garden wall, and the other to the side of the house, where he planned to make his way inside. From well to house if he ran – fifteen seconds.

He was a few feet off the ground when he felt hands on him. He spun and knocked the man away, and aimed his weapon, but the guy just lay back amongst the rocks, half-submerged in the grimy water.

Emil stuck his fingers in the gaps between the rocks, and found spaces for his toes, and started the climb. Eleven feet. He was two feet from the top when he heard the crackle of a radio. Instinctively his hand went to his waist, but his radio was gone – snatched when Denis or Fergal grabbed at him. Too late now to do anything, he turned his head and looked down and saw the man with the radio to his lips. About to give away Emil's location and end it all. There was no time to even drop and prevent it.

'Bradan,' the man said, and he was smiling.

28

B radan snatched up the radio. His eye did not leave the rifle's scope.

'Denis?' he said. Behind him, he heard a gasp from Capucine.

'Good luck with your life, Bradan, and I'll see you on the other side.'

'Denis, where are you? How did you get a radio?'

'Bradan, know this and act decisively. It was Capucine, she's bad and evil and she's not going to let you let Morse go, and she tried to kill me.'

Bradan laughed derisively. 'Denis, don't be stupid. Capucine is–'

But that was all he said, all he'd planned to say. A distraction for her, a few words to lull her anxiety a jot as she concentrated on what he was saying, so he might get a half-second's advantage. Even as he said that final word, *is*, he was rising, spinning, pulling his pistol.

But too late. Far too late. The moment she had heard Denis's voice, he knew, she had pulled her own pistol, and there it was, aimed right at his chest, as it had been even before his brain formulated an escape plan.

He thought he was quick, and perhaps he was, but he was playing catch-up. Maybe the bullet had already been fired, in the air and speeding towards him before he'd moved away from the rifle. Or maybe he was slow in his old age after all. Regardless: there was the bullet, hitting him in the chest, and here was the darkness, smothering him, pulling him into its embrace.

~

'Fergal? What is happening?'

It was Capucine's voice, but on Bradan's radio. Fergal lifted his own device to reply.

'Where's Bradan? Put him on.'

'Busy. He has told me to watch. What is happening?'

What was happening was hell. Fergal had found a gap in the stone wall on the far side of the road, but the car's wheels had churned the soggy ground and bogged down, and he had had to drag his captives out to make a trek. And here they were, climbing the hill towards the headlights, still a hundred metres out. The old lady kept stumbling and falling, and pulling the others down with her. He suspected a trick and kept his distance, kept the gun on them, ordered them to their feet, to continue. The old couple were muttering under their breaths, the old guy chanting some kind of prayer, Fergal thought.

'We're nearly there,' he told Capucine. 'Mr Crossen needs to be mobile, because we're on foot.'

'Yes, I see you. Keep going.'

'That was the plan,' he spat. He didn't like this girl. The Guilloux mother, she was okay, pretty good with a gun, loyal to the cause, but most of the crew hadn't wanted her wild tomboy daughter to come along, and she probably wouldn't have if she hadn't started sleeping with Cathal, the other lunatic who got in only because of a family member's involvement.

'Turn off headlight when you get there, okay? Now tell me what plan is. Show you do not have bad memory, Fergal.'

What? Bitch. 'I know what to do, okay. Put Bradan back on.'

'Busy, I say. He is ready to leave when this all over. Just make sure you turn off headlight. Out.'

He slotted his radio away.

'Are you, like, bottom of the food chain here?' said Morse's son.

Fergal looked at him, but the boy had his eyes dead ahead. 'Hey, shithead, did you know your dad was an MI6 agent?'

Now he looked. And stopped.

'Yeah,' said Fergal, 'and he killed people, and now they want him. Your dad's a murdering fugitive from justice and he's hiding here under a false name. His real name was William Morse. Murdering criminal bastard.'

The kid was trying not to appear shocked. 'MI6? That shows why he's been able to run rings round your people.'

Fergal decided not to respond. He'd let the boy dwell on his revelations for a bit.

They were now just thirty metres out, off to the left side, and Fergal told them to stop and sit on the ground, and after a few protests they did. He stared at the car past the barrel of his gun, but could see no shapes inside. He moved closer, gun aimed, eyes seeking out movement in the surrounding land. Nothing. He got closer. Nobody inside. The driver's door was open. He reached in quickly and twisted a stalk on the steering column, and cursed when the wipers kicked on.

When he yanked out the key, the car started beeping because the lights were still on. Again he whirled around, ready to blast anyone charging him. Nothing doing. Finally he ducked right inside and twisted the other stalk and the lights went off. The encroaching darkness suddenly made him feel better.

'That is good, Fergal,' said Capucine on the radio. 'Is Mr Crossen there?'

'Is he hell,' Fergal said. He popped the boot and ran to it. Empty. But there was a bottle of water that he quickly glugged from.

'What clues are there where he is? A letter? Anything?'

'Nothing.'

'Shit! Where is bastard?'

'Mr Crossen?'

'Bastard who kill my Cathal.'

Something jarred about her lack of care that Mr Crossen was not here. 'Put Bradan on, Capucine. Right now.'

He sensed a lack of movement. Thirty metres away down the hill, the three squirming people became two squirming people, the boy and the woman. The old man lay in the damp grass, far too still given the temperature. As Fergal stared, the woman turned towards her husband, and shouted something in distress, and then fell over backwards, onto the boy, pinning him face-down because his hands were behind his back.

As he watched, her head exploded.

'Are you shooting?' he roared into the radio.

Clothing fluttered on her back as more silent bullets from hundreds of metres away pounded into her, and Fergal knew she was trying to shoot through her to hit the boy, who was cowering beneath his human shield and bellowing for help. Help Fergal wasn't going to give him.

Fergal ducked behind the open door, because her line of sight meant a wild miss might hit him. And he told her so. And yelled for Bradan again.

'Get the boy,' she said, laughing. 'I stop shooting.'

'You're a bloody lunatic,' he yelled as he raced towards the boy. 'Bradan's going to kick you out for this.'

'No he will not,' she said, calmly. Too calm. No concern at all, and that told Fergal everything. He stopped, and stared at the spotlighted manor house across the valley, at his level. Thought he even saw the flash of a gunshot. A spark of tiny white in the moments before the world went black forever.

At each back corner of the house, just before the garden wall, was a loggia with wooden pillars and modern furniture. There was a sign planted in the earth before it that warned visitors not to touch. There was a door in one of the walls. Emil entered a small room with a door ahead and an arch barred by a retractable metal gate, which was open. Beyond, a corridor hung with old paintings on the left, between spacious windows, and alcoves on the right, and it was here that he found the hostages. As he stepped into view of the first, he saw them. The alcoves were curved at the back and here sat four people, squashed together, mouths taped, hands behind their backs and secured to the bench with cable ties. Their eyes widened as they recognised him. He knew three of the terrified-looking people, but not the fourth. Some out-of-towner wishing she'd stayed in bed that day.

'Oh God, where are the men with guns,' Emil blurted, his terrified eyes darting everywhere.

Their own eyes were pleading, mouths making noise against the tape across their lips, but he shook his head frantically. 'I can't, they're coming, they'll kill me.'

He heard their murmurs of distress as he left them. Moaning, he staggered past the other alcoves quickly, not even looking but sensing the different colours of clothing and shapes, and as other voices joined the murmuring the volume increased. He left the corridor amid a chorus of noises like the muffled wailings of a haunted house. Once he was free of scrutiny, he stood up straight and retrieved his pistol from a pocket.

Just then, his radio crackled. Denis had tossed it back to him after making the call to Bradan. After Bradan had suddenly ceased talking. Both men had been thinking the same thing, given what Denis had said to Emil right afterwards: 'You end this only after you kill that bitch.' Bradan, they agreed, was probably already dead.

Now, the voice he heard was not one he expected. Ever. Not Bradan, not Capucine, not some terrorist he's failed to kill.

Pete, his son.

'Dad, are you there?'

Emil froze. He hardly believed it. A trick of the mind, or maybe someone playing a trick on him. He put the radio slowly to his face.

'Where are you, boyo?' Boyo was what he called his son when Pete was scared as a child. Said in a stern voice, to let him know he was being a wimp. Not a tactic Supernanny would ever advise, but Emil had found it always worked. Mollycoddling, no. Now, he hoped that it would help Pete past any fear he was feeling. He wanted to tell the boy he loved him, and laugh and joke with him – just in case he never again got the chance. But time was pressing, and they could spare none for that.

'Dad, it's good to hear you. Jesus, what's going on here?'

'Bad things, boyo. But don't you worry. Your old man's going to sort it all out. Where are you?'

Pete explained. Western field, near the farmhouses, where the trade would take place. Him and an old couple. But someone with a gun had shot them. And one of the bad guys. One of their own had done the shooting, based on what he'd heard the man saying to that person on the radio. 'What the hell's going on, Dad?'

Enemy-on-enemy kills? Capucine for sure. So Bradan was dead, and that insane young woman had taken his firing position on the roof. And she had killed Sara's parents. But that had been a few minutes ago. Why hadn't she shot at Pete?

'Listen, boyo, are you able to run? Take that car and get the hell away. Or run into the woods. Is anyone around?'

'I'm trying.' He broke down now, despite Emil's efforts to avoid it. With a quivering voice, he told his dad that he was tied to the dead couple, unable to break his bond, but had dragged them a few metres to get to the radio the shot bad guy had dropped. 'Can we call the police on the radios? Have you called them already?'

The police. He thought about that. To avoid a siege situation that might get his son, and others, needlessly shot, he had planned to end this all himself. And, as he'd intimated to Sara, he was going to kill all the bad guys so he'd never again have to keep looking over his shoulder, just in case one of the bad guys or a bad guy's daughter's second cousin twice removed woke up one day with a desire for revenge. But was that necessary now? Pete was free – sort of – and there was only one terrorist left in any position to do damage. He could call the police and take the risk that they wouldn't delve deep into his past–

'There's someone coming, Dad. Up the hill. I can't see who. Running. Who is it? What do I do?'

Without answering, Emil ran on. The rest of the house was quiet. He moved through a dining room, a breakfast room, then into the great ballroom. He took door after door, not wanting to exit the ballroom into the entrance hall, and soon found a small spiral staircase. The more he progressed without meeting an enemy, the quicker he moved, and the bolder he got, until he was sprinting almost blindly, taking corners without looking, gun hung down by his side. Moving ever upwards.

Capucine ran across the road and into the field, pounding hard, clutching her pistol hard in both hands as if fearful that the wind might whip it away from her. Soon she saw the shapes upon the dark hill, one of them moving. The boy, trying to free himself. He was facing her, his hands now in front of him because he must have threaded his legs through somehow, but he did not see her. He was staring at his bonds, bent over, trying to bite through them.

Finally he saw her approach. She came at him with the gun and a grin. He tried to stand, thinking he might run, but of course he couldn't do that with two corpses in tow.

Fergal lay beyond him. She patted the boy's head as she walked past. 'Back for you in a second.'

Fergal was on his back, breathing slowly, staring up at the sky. He had not moved since he'd fallen. Maybe he couldn't. The bullet had taken him in his gut, and maybe it had passed through and shattered his spine.

His eyes watched her as she went past and looked in the car. There was a can of some fizzy drink in a holder and she took it. Cracked it and took a sip and went back to Fergal. She looked around down the hill, at the village splayed below. Very beautiful. Again, she thought how much she would have liked such a place for her and Cathal. No crowding high buildings. No mass of people.

But there was no Cathal.

'You are all to blame,' she said, looking down at Fergal. His eyes were bright, as if they alone survived in a dead body, like a lightbulb in a wasteland. She put her pistol to his forehead, but looked away as she pulled the trigger. She put a thumb over the lip of her drink. The splatter of blood across her hands and neck said that had been a good idea.

She walked away without looking at him. Fergal, of all of them, had been the only one never to check out her breasts or her legs. Maybe he was gay, maybe not. Either way, it accorded him a tiny mark of respect. Of course, in the end it got him nothing. Except to avoid the eyes of his killer in his final moments.

The boy was watching her. On his knees, he had stopped fighting his bonds. He watched her approach, and his face said he knew there was nothing he could do now but wait and see what the future brought.

'Do not move.' She put down her can and put away the gun and took out her blade and snapped his bonds, and then pushed him onto his back. She put a knee hard into his chest and pressed the knife against his neck. With her free hand she hauled Denis's radio and called *him*.

'Hey, handyman, it is time for change. Please guess what I have got?'

And he was there. 'Coke all over you,' he said. And then she jerked as liquid splattered her. Shocked, she rubbed her face, and saw her Coke can laying nearby, now rent apart.

She looked across the valley, to the manor house, where she had stood twenty minutes ago and stared at this spot through a rifle scope. Just as her enemy was doing now.

~

Emil put the crosshairs on Capucine's face.

'Step away from him. Move back. Till I tell you to stop. And throw your gun and knife.'

But she didn't. As he watched, she hauled Pete into a sitting position and held him in front of her. Now Pete's face filled the sights, and Emil moved his finger away from the trigger in case of a freak accident. Her arm raised the radio again and seemed to clamp it to Pete's face, so well hidden behind his head was hers. The knife went to his throat.

'You love son too much to risk shot. All you will get is flesh wound, and I will have time to cut his throat, and you will watch him die in zoom. It will feel like close enough to reach out and help, but you can not help. This is why you have not already take kill shot.'

Exactly the reason – he hoped. He had snatched up the rifle, sighted, zeroed on her head, and he should have blown her away. Or a chest shot. Balanced on Pete's chest like that, even a flesh wound would have knocked her away, and for sure he could have fired again before she got a chance to kill Pete.

But he hadn't. Nerves. He cursed himself for it. The blasted Coke can proved the scary event hadn't affected his aim.

'Maybe it is my pretty face. You do not want to destroy my face. We pretty girls wrap men around fingers, is that not right?'

Not that, for sure. Her looks were simply packaging, like a bomb wrapped in glittery paper. A shot of roughly 300 metres – easy for a guy who had practised for many hours with a long-range rifle in his past. Why hadn't he risked the kill shot immediately?

He saw her face briefly as she turned her head. Then Pete turned his. And then he heard it. A helicopter. He did not take his eye from the scope as the sound grew louder. Until it was so loud he knew this was not some chopper just flying over. It was coming here.

He looked away, up, and there it was over the hill, and then a spotlight searched the ground and lit on Capucine and his son.

He looked down the scope again. Capucine had released her grip on his son, and was holding her hands up. And then she ran, leaving his son there.

The police?

Emil recognised the machine as a Bell 407, which was a multipurpose helicopter, but it was bland red, no law enforcement markings. Despite the spotlight and what appeared to be a man with a rifle, he knew the new arrivals weren't police. And then he saw a familiar face through the cabin window, and nearly dropped the gun. It was older, but unmistakable, although it couldn't be, couldn't be. But it was.

Alexander Cavil.

30

'You get after her,' Cavil said. 'You, get that man.'

One of his guys ran in pursuit of the woman, a big grin on his face as he set off. Cavil thought his joy was more to do with her status as a young woman than as an enemy. He wondered about just what kind of people he'd been sent.

Another Billy got the young man to his feet, while the third strolled over to have a nosey at the three dead bodies lying nearby. Throughout, the kid talked ten to the dozen: something about terrorists, and a mass kidnapping, and a sniper. In his haste to get the story out, the kid fumbled half his words and barely made sense, but Cavil wasn't listening anyway. He stood ten feet away, staring, not believing what he was seeing. The resemblance was uncanny. But surely that was just Cavil seeing Morse everywhere.

'You got parents?' Cavil asked him.

'Just a dad. He's the hero here today. I don't know where he is, but I think he's been giving the terrorists a bloody nose. You guys SWAT or something?'

'Or something,' Cavil said. He saw a radio laying by an abandoned car and picked it up. 'What's your dad's name?'

'Emil. Emil Torrance. You got, like, the cavalry coming, then? There's people held in an old hotel on the north road, and loads more in Barkelow Hall.'

Cavil could see a manor house lit up on a hill, which he assumed was Barkelow Hall.

'Where's your dad?'

'I don't know,' the boy said. 'Must be around, but – ow!'

One of the goons had grabbed him by the hair and yanked his head back. He kicked out his knees and pulled a blade, which went to the throat. Cavil stood before him.

'Don't mess with me, boy. I'll have your throat cut. Right now, where's your father?'

'I don't know!'

'Not the legs because we need him to walk,' he told the goon, 'but start breaking bones until he remembers.'

Right then, a puff of dirt from nearby. Nobody saw it but Cavil, who ordered his man to stop. The goon had the boy's arm held as if he were going to snap it with his bare hands like a twig. He stopped.

Cavil turned and stared at the manor house, and remembered the way the young girl had shielded herself behind the boy, facing the village.

He put the radio to his mouth, on the channel it was on.

'*Amor fati*,' he said, remembering the last thing he'd said to Morse, almost a quarter of a century ago.

'Your man is one second away from a colostomy bag for the rest of his days, Cavil,' returned a voice that sent a shiver through him.

Capucine had run as far as the trees, not looking back, and then stopped and fell to her knees, exhausted. She looked back, but the figures were just pinpricks at that distance. As she watched, the car's headlights came on again, but not the engine, which puzzled her. Who the hell were they? She pulled out her radio and turned it to Bradan's channel, ready to speak to her enemy, but instead found herself listening to two men chatting on that channel already.

So they were enemies, Morse and the other MI6 man. Cavil, who hunted Morse. So, now Cavil was threatening Morse with his son. He wanted Morse to wait for his arrival. And Hidden Gem? That place she had seen on photos of the village that Bradan had had taken last month? She knew where it was, and headed that way. This was not over yet.

'Hey, sweetpants, where are you?'

One of the men, not far back, coming after her. She knew she had left a trail of wet grass. If he was any good, he could also follow her progress through the trees. She needed to get to The Hidden Gem. There, she stood her best chance of killing her stalker.

'I'm coming for you, my lovely.'

'Go to hell,' she shouted. Not because she wanted him to, or thought it might work, or even because he was annoying her. It was simply to help him out, just in case he'd lost her scent.

Emil re-sighted down the scope, right on Cavil's face. The guy wore a suit, so maybe he was still MI6. Emil had Googled his name a few times over the years, but never found anything. No news of a promotion, no obituary, nothing sinister. He wondered how far up the ladder the man had gotten. And he wondered how on Earth Cavil had found him here tonight. A blind fluke, or did it have something to do with tonight's events?

He should have kept quiet, he knew, but he hadn't. He had

made that joke threat about the leg, and now there was no going back: Cavil knew for sure that Emil was alive and close.

'I have your son, Morse. Or Torrance, as you're now known. You see this, don't you?'

'I do,' he said. 'I see a lot with what I have in my hands.'

'How much do you see now?' Cavil said, and bent into the car, and the scope turned white. Emil flicked off the night vision and returned his eye to the scope. The car's headlights were on and he could barely see anything behind the vehicle. It was the same trick Emil had planned to use.

'What's your plan here, Cavil? Kill that boy? I should let you do it. It'll punish the little shit for getting caught.'

Cavil looked at the boy. He saw the shock on his face. 'You, Morse. I came for you. And if you want to talk to your son again, you'll come out with your tail between your legs and beg my forgiveness. Don't think I'm falling for your little trick to pretend you aren't that bothered about him.'

Beyond the headlights, he could see nothing of the people congregated there. He knew he could not stop Cavil from hurting his son now.

'How about a trade? The Patriot IRA, heard of them? This is all about an escape attempt by their leader, Sean Crossen. He's north-east of your position at a place called The Hidden Gem. He's a much better capture than me. There's also a bunch of hostages in the old hotel on the main road, just a few hundred metres from your position. You can have the credit for their rescue.'

As he watched, Cavil waved at two of his men, the ones who had been ready to chase Capucine across the land. They ran. North-east. Going in search of Mr Crossen, no doubt.

Cavil got back on the radio. 'I like it,' he said. 'But only as a DVD bonus featurette, Morse. I came here for my old nemesis, and he's going down. Your escape set me on a sideways path at

MI6, Morse. I ended up nowhere, working a bullshit desk job. I wanted to be chief. I ended up running a bar. So no, there will be no deal along those lines. You will come in, and I'll allow you to say goodbye to your son. I'll even help arrange visitation for you. Otherwise, you gotta run again. And you'll never see him again.'

Emil didn't answer.

Cavil said. 'We're bringing the chopper to you. Stay or run, your choice. If you're not outside that building waiting for us when we arrive, then we leave with your son and that's that.'

And he watched the remaining men rush back to the chopper. As it rose, he thought of his options. But his mind turned to Sara, out there alone and oblivious to what had happened. He could not bring himself to lay the scope upon her parents' bodies – how on earth would he find the resolve to tell her they had been murdered?

Then he heard a gun cocking behind him, and turned to see Bradan, not dead at all, and sitting up against the wall, holding that gun.

31

Sara had set the urn going and made tea, and lit a gas lamp on the wall so they could see what they were doing. She helped Mr Crossen sit up against the wall, but didn't untie him from a thick boiler pipe on the wall. Now she gave him tea, holding it so he could sip.

'I'm sorry you got ensnared in this,' he said. 'I understand you can't let me go, and I don't hold that against you. You've shown how nice you are, by giving me tea. If your plan goes wrong and I do get free, I will make sure you are unhurt.'

She didn't meet his eyes as she lifted the cup so he could drink again. It sounded like a bit of an indirect way of asking to be freed.

'Perhaps you don't know much about events back in my country when... things weren't going so well. People like me... the actions we undertook... it was all political. We weren't monsters. My world back then isn't my world now. You're not my enemy, despite your actions today.'

Sara said nothing. She lifted the cup. Crossen drank. After a short silence, he either decided his trick – if it was one – wasn't going to work, or needed a new angle. 'Tell me, please, why did you become a prison escort officer?'

But before she could answer, she heard the crunch of footsteps outside. She got up, peered through the window, and saw a young girl with a gun and a knife approaching. Another terrorist.

~

Bradan did not fire. He put the gun to his own eye. Suicide.

'What are you planning, Bradan? Your young lackeys don't know the details. But you've got something in the works. One of those bombing things that does nothing but hurt innocent people. I know you're IRA.' Emil moved closer, aiming the rifle from his hip. Too close to use the scope. He didn't mind if Bradan took his own life. He didn't trust the man not to decide to take someone to hell with him.

'What am I, some James Bond baddie? You want me to spill my guts in the final act? You think I want to waste the last moments of my life explaining things to you?'

'At the minute you're just insane idiots to me. That's the story I'll tell. You were weirdos. The newspapers will mock you, not make you out to be heroic fighters for your cause.'

Bradan nodded as if agreeing. 'Good plan. You could say we all wore frilly pink wigs and googly eye glasses.'

'I know you brought bombs and grenades. One of your team was very talkative. Is your target this manor house? Are you planning to kill all the hostages?'

Bradan laughed. It hurt to do so. 'Forget what you were told by whichever of my team folded when you whipped off his shoes and socks and brandished a feather, Morse. They know nothing. And anything the police believed based on the fact that Mr Crossen was arrested here in England – pure presumption.

His cause died with mine many years ago. He worked in a restaurant. I was a plumber. We drifted apart years ago to live normal lives. But that doesn't mean I want to see him rot in jail, cause or no cause. They held him without charge while they tried to find something to pin on him. I came here to rescue an old friend, Morse. That is all. Plain and simple. A nice little rescue story.'

'Bullshit. You're more likely to lie to me than some young punk facing pain.'

'Maybe, Morse, maybe. Of course, a man can only tell you what he knows. And maybe he knew only what I told him.'

He seemed to perk up as doubt entered Emil's mind – must have showed on his face. 'Forget what my so-called lackeys told you, Morse. They needed an incentive, and I gave them one with promises of renewed killings and political talks and a host of other bullshit. The cause, the cause, the cause. This was nothing but one guy helping out an old friend, that is all. The guns, the killings – just proof of my determination.'

'Bullshit again. If you wanted to get your man freed, you could have ambushed the prison van out on a dark road in the middle of the woods. Why pick here? Why have hostages?'

'This whole rescue mission took months to plan, Morse. And its success rested on one scared woman and whether she would call the police. What if she had? Picture our chances out on that dark road you mention, with cops swinging down out of the trees. I chose this place because we could see everything. I chose hostages because I'm not going into a jail cell. This way, we had a chance if the prison woman brought cops with her. There, you turned me into a James Bond baddie.'

'Two sets of hostages. Double the trouble for the police? Stretch them thin, or delay them while backup arrives.'

Bradan laughed. 'I never thought of that. Cops would have to mount two infiltrations at the same time. Good idea. I wanted the other hostages in the hotel only because it was close to the housing estate, that's all. Didn't want them being marched up a mountain to get here. We had enough already. Shit, Morse, you're a thinker, should have been on my team.'

'But then I'd die with the others in the explosion, right?'

Bradan looked at him.

Emil said, 'The plan was for all the team to meet back here after it was done. When I heard that, it made no sense. The rescue takes place down on the main road. Why have your people bring Crossen all the way up to the manor house, just to go back down? Surely the people here would instead head down to meet the others. Then I realised when I saw something in the wilderness east of here. A hidden Jeep, lost in all the shrubbery not far past the gardens of this house. A big vehicle, capable of traversing the land out there. But it didn't have fifteen seats, which was what you'd need if every single one of your team was getting out of here.'

Bradan said, 'We were splitting up. We've brought cars and quad bikes, and someone needs to take them all away.'

'Glendon said you could hold the manor house for days.'

'Only if necessary. If the prison woman tricked us.'

'I think the getaway was planned for you and your closest, and to hell with the others. I think your team of young men and women thought this was all about a siege, with the police surrounding the place, and demands for the release of prisoners and all that stuff. But long before the police get wind of anything happening here, you and your closest slip away, over the wall, into the wilderness and the Jeep and away. Then bombs go off. A right mess. When the authorities come in, they don't know which leg belongs to who, whose nose this is. Terrorists and innocent townsfolk all messed up like jigsaw pieces. And since they don't know how many bad guys were here, they assume they all died. Nobody's seen anyone get out, have they? So you and your closest are free, and maybe you like the idea that the Barkelow carnage will go down as a final parting blow against the system by the PAIRA. Or maybe, once you're back in Ireland, you and Crossen take up where you left off, and the manor house deaths are a springboard for renewed hostilities.'

'Very Hollywood, Morse. But sorry, it was just a rescue mission.'

'I don't believe you.'

'Well, that's your version. I told you mine. I guess you'll never know, will you?'

'No, I won't. Know why? Because the whole thing failed anyway. You probably won't live the night through, and Crossen's going back to jail, and your team of scapegoats is gone.'

Bradan nodded like someone accepting the truth. But then he grinned. 'All but one, of course. Young Capucine. Very volatile. The cause probably kept her away from being a plain old serial killer. You killed her boyfriend. She's quite mad about that. And just plain quite mad. Shame for someone like that to remain free, isn't it?'

'It's not over yet, though.'

'She took grenades. Be careful.'

'You want me to succeed?'

'No, the hell with you both. But dog shit tastes better than cat shit. She killed one of my best friends. That's why I didn't put a bullet in your back two minutes ago. You're the only one who can stop her now. Cut her head off for me. Feel free to catch a bullet in the face in the process. I'll die a happy man.'

'You'll never know, will you?'

Bradan gave him a sincere look. 'Maybe I'll wait. I don't imagine you'll come back and tell me it's done, or bring her here and do it in front of me?'

'For you to then shoot me?'

Bradan smiled. But his eyes started to close. It was a chore to keep them open.

Emil, though, did not want this man to have his way, even slightly, even on his deathbed. So he said, 'She's done nothing to me, so I'm going to let her go, Bradan. Go free. Going to let her walk right on out of here and live to be an old woman.'

If he expected anger, or despair, he was left lacking. 'I doubt it, Morse.'

Emil walked past him. Gave him his back. He did not expect a bullet, and none came. Bradan knew him well, it seemed. Knew he was not the forgiving kind.

With no time to spare, Capucine pushed open the door and entered the shack, and shut it behind her. Even before she looked around to see who was here, she rushed to the window and peered out. She wanted the man to find her here, but not for him to know for sure she was inside. That way, he would formulate a plan of attack. If he wasn't certain, there would be less caution and more haste, because an error would allow her to get further away if she was not here.

She saw him emerge from behind the trees, look over. Even in the dark, she could see his eyes light up. An assumption. He started running over.

'There's a girl in the back,' said a voice. 'She's the enemy, but she's nice, so please don't hurt her.' He was in a corner, sitting against the wall, hands tied behind his back, feet bound, too. 'I know you. I saw pictures. Bradan showed me the people he'd gotten to help break me out. Good people for our cause.'

So he was here after all. Mr Crossen. The man Bradan and the other old ones talked about with such respect. He didn't look like much, especially not tied up like that. She didn't care about his cause. She had come here because Cathal had come. Bullets and pain were fine and well, but the cause meant nothing to her. The Troubles had been way before her time. The famous Good Friday Agreement – also before her time. She had grown up in a more peaceful world.

'You're Maryse's daughter. Maryse is a good lady.'

'Was,' Capucine said. 'Dead now.'

'I'm sorry. Please, untie me and we'll get out of here. Where are the others?'

'Dead. Now shut up. Someone is coming.'

Mr Crossen was smart. He shut the hell up right away, just as they both heard the creak of a floorboard. The man was on the porch outside.

She told him what she wanted him to do. He said yes, like a loyal servant. She knew he needed her. It only reinforced her opinion that Bradan and his ilk were just old men now without an army, which meant 'powerless'.

The door handle turned slowly, but then the door itself burst open, and there he was, still with his foot in the air, momentum shifting him forward. His gun was ahead of him. In he came, fast, low. Silent. No more crude lines.

Mr Crossen, on cue, said, 'Hey, thank God, here I am,' and it worked. The man jerked his head and his gun that way. Capucine popped up from behind the counter and fired. Two bullets. One missed and gouged a chunk from the wall behind him. The second painted that wall with blood as it powered through his neck. He dropped hard onto his butt, gun gone, hands around his own throat as if trying to strangle himself.

Writhing, gurgling, he seemed almost not to object as she took him by both feet and dragged him outside. When she returned, panting with the effort, Mr Crossen said, 'You are very good. The cause needs you.' She scowled at him. She did not need his cheap compliments.

She went past him, ignoring his pleas to be released. Just before she'd hidden behind the counter, she had peeked into the back room, but seen nobody there. She hadn't expected to. She had heard about a secret passage in The Hidden Gem. Now, she tried to find it.

She found it quickly. A hidden door, not fully closed by the last person to flee that way. The woman from the prison van. And before her, Morse. Surely the route he had taken in order to get to the manor house.

There was even a map on the wall with the underground passage highlighted.

The man on the radio had said he was going to the manor house to get Morse. Morse would surely stay there because the man had his son. Two enemies of the man, both wanting him. She would get there first.

She entered the passageway and dragged shut the door, and started the long trek through the dark in order to surprise her enemy. The chopper might already be there, but there was still a chance for her to exact revenge.

32

———

Amazingly, they ganged up on him.

First the damned pilot, telling him it was their duty as upholders of the law. Then the other three Billys chimed in. Same shit: we need to go release the hostages in the hotel. It's on the way. Morse is going nowhere because you have his son. It will take only a few minutes. The damned hotel was right there in view, sitting all dark and forlorn, as if pleading with them.

'On your heads if he escapes,' Cavil snapped. 'Dickheads. Okay, go to the hotel. You dickheads just want your story in the papers. If he gets away because of it, I'll put you in *Islamic State are Pussies* T-shirts and drop you in Baghdad city centre.'

The chopper hovered low over the car park out front, its downdraft exciting the weeds poking between the paving slabs.

'Jump,' Cavil ordered. 'Any Billy will do.'

Billy B got up. 'I'll do it.' And with that he leaped out, landed, rolled, and was running towards the old hotel. Cavil checked the street left and right. No one around. Ghost village? He should have checked this place on the internet. He knew nothing about it.

'Go, he can catch us up.'

'We wait,' the other three chimed, like robots on the same program. The pilot added: 'Sir.'

'Just think T-shirts and Baghdad,' Cavil snapped.

Inside the house, Billy B rushed into the main room with his gun drawn, and made a TV FBI guy show of rolling through the doorway and coming up on his knees and sweeping his gun left and right. Everyone screamed, or cheered.

'You're all safe now, help is here,' he yelled. 'My name is Daniel Blake, and I am here to rescue you.'

They started getting to their feet. Hands tied, feet tied in some cases. But otherwise not bound. Not secured to anything. Maybe they had been warned not to try to leave, told a gunman was outside the door.

'Daniel Blake, that's me,' Billy B yelled again, then rushed back out through the door, leaving it open.

The chopper had moved towards the edge of the car park, where there was a rotting fence. Billy B used it to gain height, jumping, grabbing the skids, hauling himself up. He sat down hard in his seat, panting and grinning.

'Done. Safe,' he said. His comrades high-fived him as the chopper turned towards the big house on the hill, all lit up like something atop a Christmas tree.

Cavil wasn't grinning. 'What size T-shirts are you bozos?'

Sara stumbled in the dark and landed hard on her knees, but the fire came from her ankle.

Her scream of pain raced away down the tunnel in both directions. She sat on the cold, rough ground and rubbed her foot. And cursed that she'd ever gotten up today. A routine prisoner transfer, and now look. Bart, her boyfriend, had rolled those stupid fortune-telling dice of his for her, his insistence, and when one had landed on top of the other, he'd claimed she had a special gift coming her way. Was this it? The gift of abject misery and fear beyond comprehension? The busted foot, maybe.

'Bart, you dick,' she shouted into the tunnel. She reached around in the dark for what might have tripped her and found it. Right in the centre of the tunnel, as if planted by some sadistic tourist way back. A big, square rock. She jammed it against the wall, out of harm's way, and struggled to her feet. For a moment she panicked, unable to remember which way she had been facing, but then she remembered that the tunnel had started to climb. She stood sideways and straightened both legs and felt herself start to tip to the left. So, to the right.

Her movements were now a limp. Not that she wanted to go running, anyway.

On she went. Thirty seconds later, she heard a yelp from behind her. The blonde woman, coming fast!

Capucine threw caution to the wind and moved fast. She hugged the left wall, left hand running along it, right hand, holding the gun, out before her like a cop stopping a car, and jogged down the tunnel. She knew the woman Mr Crossen had mentioned would also be moving quickly, but not this quickly. She began to smile. And that was when she fell.

The floor was stony but free of obstacles, except here was a rock pressed against the wall, probably placed there to be out of harm's way. She kicked it and fell forward, dropping her gun, and sharp stones dug into her palms. She unleashed a roar that was more rage than pain. She picked up the rock and tossed it behind her, got off her knees and continued along the tunnel, but now at a safer pace.

Eyes on the ground so she could see sudden chasms opening up, shoulder scraping against the left wall, moving quicker now, her feet hit something hard and she fell, and put out her arms to break the fall, and the fall was over quicker than it should have been. Sharp stone, digging into her at various places. She realised she was laying on steps. Stone steps, heading up. She scrambled up them.

At the top she saw light up ahead. Closer, she saw a lamp on the wall and two black holes where the tunnel branched into two, either one of which could lead to a trap. That was her thought, based on her only experience of underground tunnels: damned video games she used to play when she was rotting in a university bedsit without money. Left: the way out. Right: a chamber filled with snake pits across which fiery-bladed scythes swung. Or the other way round.

A bullet decided things for her. She heard the bang, and sensed a flash behind her, and heard the round hit the wall ahead of her, blasting away a cloud of dust. She screamed and took a dive.

Capucine ran ahead and reached the junction and stopped. Two ways. She cursed. She had rushed the shot. The moment she had reached the top of the stone staircase, she had seen the woman at the junction, silhouetted against the lamplight, and she had fired too quickly, worried that the woman would run and be lost again in the dark. The shot had missed, the flash from the gun lighting up the tunnel before her for a half-second. And when her eyes had adjusted again to the dark, the woman had gone. And now she didn't know which fork the bitch had taken.

'End of road, bitch,' she screamed, her voice racing away down both tunnels. She aimed left, and aimed right, knowing her enemy might be watching her as she stood in the light. Hoping the bitch made a rush, and thus a noise that would give her away.

Nothing.

She turned the gun in her hand and smashed the lamp. Blackness again. She scraped her foot across the ground, hoping to give the impression that she was moving in the dark. Hoping that it would force the woman into faster movement, movement Capucine would hear.

Nothing.

'I will shoot up your pussy,' she yelled now. 'Here I come.'

Nothing.

But there were only two tunnels to pick between, and one went downhill, and the woman was probably a prissy bitch who wouldn't like the idea of travelling deeper into the earth.

33

———

The chopper flew high over the manor house, and Cavil searched the area through his binoculars. On the roof he saw a dead man in a black suit. He ordered the chopper lower for a better look, but already he knew it wasn't Morse. And was glad. He wanted Morse dead, but not by the hand of another.

There was no one else on the roof, and no movement in the gardens, although there were sheds and other outbuildings where anyone could hide. He could cover those later. The house first. He ordered the pilot to land.

A second before the 407 touched down on the gravel pathway where it widened in front of the manor house, the two Billys jumped out and ran for the front door, weapons drawn. They went in quick, eager, and Cavil shook his head. Fooled by their own sense of magnificence. Believing there was no threat against their brilliance, they just ran in.

He got on the radio. 'Morse, I am here, and so better you be, or I'll take this bird up to 63,360 inches and let your boy out, and guess how long you'll have to panic and regret ever messing with me?'

No reply.

'Eighteen seconds, Morse. One mile.' He did so love his useless facts.

No reply.

'So be it. Pilot, one mile up.'

They got ten feet in the air and the pilot jerked as something hit his windscreen. There was a hole right at the top, and spiderweb cracks running across the plexiglass.

'What the hell was that?' the pilot moaned as he steadied the chopper.

'A reply,' Cavil said. He got back on the radio. 'Let's do this, Morse. Out you come. No more chances.'

Capucine made her way to the corridor where the hostages were held. At each end there was a retractable gate. She pulled the first closed behind her. She ran past the alcoves, peering in. People moaned when they saw her gun. She stopped at one in which she saw just women, all elegantly dressed, their faces a mess because of running make-up.

She stepped inside and lifted her knife. The woman she chose started to scream.

'Stop, I am here to help.' She leaned over the woman and slit the cable tie binding her tiny wrists, and yanked her to her feet. 'What is your name?'

Others in nearby alcoves had heard her, and now they too yelled for help.

'Joanne,' said the woman in the dress.

Capucine led her into the corridor, and then stuck the gun against the side of her head and pulled the trigger. She landed hard, with a thump. Everyone started screaming. Capucine pulled off the woman's shoes.

∽

Finally, light.

Faint, and coming from just around a corner. But a glow that pulled her like a traction beam. Of course there was a way out – no skeletons down here.

She turned the corner and found the tunnel closing to an aperture no wider than two feet, waist-height. She dropped to her knees before it. The light, just a smear of sunlight bouncing off the moon, came from above. It showed her tube-like stone walls.

She peered out and knew instantly she was in a well. The exit was eight or nine feet above her. All she had to do was drop a few feet into the water at the bottom and try to climb, and this looked easy enough because there were great rents and cavities between the stones. However, she froze, and knew she might be unable to climb out of the tunnel. Because of the zombie below.

They were not zombies, of course. Just a pair of dead men in tuxedos, half-submerged in the dark water. There was enough light for her to see both were bloody and battered and dead. Emil's doing, she figured.

Zombies or not, they would not stop her. She had come too far, been through too much, and the events back at the junction had surely been a sign that she was not destined to die down here in the black.

Shockingly, the blonde woman had stood at the fork, barely ten feet from where Sara lay a short distance down the left passage. Close enough that Sara could hear her angry, ragged breathing, and see the rage on her pretty, boyish face in the lamplight. And she knew the woman could not see her. But what she could see or not didn't matter. Two passages, two choices, and if she came left, it was all over.

She had lain there in the dark, knowing the next few

seconds would determine the rest of her life, and how quickly it might be over. There was the gun that would do it, hanging down by the woman's leg, shivering with the woman's volcanic emotions.

'I see you, you bitch,' she had screamed. Sara stayed still, knowing the woman couldn't see a damned thing. The passages became black voids three feet down. She aimed the gun down the left passage.

Then the right.

Then, amazingly, the woman had stomped off to the right.

Now, she dropped into the water, trying to avoid looking at the dead men or imagining them grabbing her legs, and started to climb the wall.

Cavil got out, dragging the boy with him. He stood with his back to the open door, the boy used as a shield before him. The pilot was aiming a handgun at the boy also.

Into his radio, Cavil said, 'Morse, there are two guns on your boy. If my head explodes, his pistol fires. If his head explodes, mine fires. You're quick, but you aren't that quick. Now out you come.'

He was staring up at the roof, where he wished they could have landed, although the pilot said no way. He expected to see Morse's head poke out up there.

'Show yourself.'

Morse's crackly reply was immediate: 'Let my son go. Let him run away. As you saw when you flew in, there's no way out for me except down a cliff or over the marshland, and you could pick me off either way. Let him run.'

'Let me see you first.'

'On your ten.'

So not on the roof. Ten o'clock. Cavil turned to his left slightly, and there he was. At an iron gate in a wall running away from the side of the house, fifty metres away, and aiming a rifle at them from behind one of the gateposts.

'I could have already put you all down. I didn't, so that means I'm legit. Let him run away.'

'But then you won't get to say goodbye, Morse. I'll let him go. How could I keep him? Innocent young man. He won't be arrested or jailed. So he'll just be a burden to me. So come get him. Come to me, hands up. Toss the gun first.'

34

B illy B turned immediately left while Billy C went ahead. Through a cloakroom, then a men's room, and into a larger room. There was a door to the right, and it led him into a summer loggia. He continued north, kicking open doors, pointing his gun ahead as he stepped through. Soon he found himself in an anteroom with just one other exit, a room leading into a corridor.

The doorway was barred by a retractable lattice gate. Beyond it, Billy B could see alcoves arranged down the left side of the corridor and another gate at the far end. Halfway down lay a woman in just her underwear, half her head gone, painted across the floor and one wall. People were shouting.

He rushed to the gate, shouting. 'Hey, listen up, my name is Daniel Blake, can you hear me?'

Amid the moaning, he heard people say yes. 'Help us, please. We're in here.'

'My name is Daniel Blake. Remember that. I'm the guy who rescued you all. Daniel Blake.'

He grabbed the gate and yanked it open. Unlocked. He did not notice the item that fell from its place in the lattice.

He reached the first alcove. Two men and a woman sitting together like people at a bus stop, except they looked terrified and had their hands behind their backs.

'My name is Daniel Blake. Say it.'

No one said anything, and Daniel Blake, Billy B, said nothing ever again. Three seconds after the gate yanked it away from its pin, the grenade exploded. Four feet from him.

Emil knew Cavil was right. He was out of plans. He could only hope that, after so long, MI6 would have no issue with him. Just Cavil. Maybe Cavil would try to get him jailed, or maybe he had something more lethal in mind. But even if Emil avoided both, he didn't fancy his chances of seeing Pete again. And he had to hold him one last time. If he ran now, he would regret that for the rest of his life, and the pain would eat at him, and being eaten alive for years was no kind of life at all.

So, against better judgement, he stepped out from behind the gatepost. Out into the open, dragging the gate shut behind him. The lock clicked closed and he tossed the gun through the bars. Tossed it out of the equation, just to finalise things, to make sure his brain didn't have some macho plan brewing in its subconscious.

Cavil snapped his fingers and the pilot started running. That was when they heard the explosion from inside the house. It was a muffled boom and Emil didn't know where it came from. But he could hear the faint sounds of screams. God, the hostages. Capucine had grenades.

'Cavil, you need to get in there. There's another terrorist and she's got grenades. The hostages, she's probably killing them all.'

Cavil was staring at the house. Then his eyes were right back on Emil. 'We'll get to her later. Get him,' he told the pilot.

Emil couldn't believe what he was hearing. But he thought he understood. Cavil had wanted revenge for many years, and now it was just seconds from his grasp.

'Get after the hostages, Cavil. I'm not going anywhere.'

The pilot had a pistol on him. His pleas were falling on deaf ears.

He put his hands behind his head and dropped to his knees and let fate take him.

Billy C took a staircase up, and turned a corner to find a woman in the hallway, sitting against the wall. She was in a low-cut dress and had her hands over her face. A loose hostage. She was moaning like someone injured.

'Hey, it's okay.'

She looked up at him, and stood.

'Oh, thank God. There are murderers in here.' She ran to him, and out went his arms, and she fell into them. He felt wetness, on the hand that he laid on the shoulder of her dress. It came away bloody.

'Are you hurt?'

'Not my blood,' she whimpered.

'Let's get you out of here. How many terrorists are there? Do you know where they are?'

She shivered in his arms. 'Yes, I– oh, God, behind you.'

Billy C yanked his pistol as he pushed her away, turning, raising, ready to put lead in a head.

Eight feet out, Cavil told the pilot to step away. Emil knelt there, two guns on him. Cavil stopped three feet away. He had a big grin on his face.

Emil tensed himself for something bad. He now knew Cavil had no plans to put him in a courtroom. Probably a box.

'Know how long I've waited for this moment?'

'Worth it? You said I could see my son.'

Pete was in the back of the chopper, straining against the grip of a hulk pressed against him. His hands were behind his back, probably tied.

Cavil didn't move. Emil could see him thinking. It would be good, he knew, to deny his long-time enemy a final piece of joy. But he had given his word, and breaking that might sting more. Seconds ticked by. He thought Cavil was probably enjoying the tension Emil felt.

'Let my son out.'

'Get in instead. Do your goodbyes. I'll let him go afterwards.'

Emil had no choice. He got on the chopper, and hugged his son, who said, 'One of them said you were an MI6 agent, Dad. That true?'

'Yes, Pete, it's true. We'll talk about that another time.'

'And these guys are MI6 as well? Are you going to jail?'

'I don't think so, Pete,' he said, throwing a glance at Cavil, who was now in the front of the chopper and watching.

'Smart man, your dad,' Cavil said. 'Best tell it here and now, Morse. There'll be no time later.'

'What's he mean by that, Dad?'

'Ignore him, Pete.'

Cavil laughed. 'Morse, why don't you start your story by telling the kid his mother was married to a war criminal when you knocked her up?'

Pete looked at both men, back and forth. 'What's he talking about, Dad?'

The other guy got in the back with them and shut the door.

The engine started. Emil leaned forward to whisper to his distraught son. The other guy, who had a gun jammed in Emil's flank, grabbed his shoulder, but Emil twisted the hand away as if it were no more than a fly that had landed there. The man yelled in pain and looked ready to react with violence, but Cavil warned him to stand down.

'Now let my son out, Cavil. You got everything you ever dreamed of in the last twenty years,' Emil said, just for Cavil's ears.

'I don't think so,' Cavil said. 'Pilot, go.'

35

The moment he saw no one behind him, he knew it was a trick, but part of his brain said no, it couldn't be. A woman in a dress? No.

That pause, maybe that did it. Or maybe he had no chance anyway. But he started to turn back, stepping away at the same time to give himself the range to fire. That step became a stumble. Down he went, hard onto the carpet.

The woman in the dress kicked at his arm and his gun went flying. She stood over him, holding a bloody knife. Now he felt the pain. Upper back, neck. He couldn't move. He felt the wetness under him, as if he'd fallen in a puddle. Warm.

He heard the whine of the chopper. For a moment he forgot his wound, his enemy in front of him, and thought about how he would get home if they left him here.

The woman ran to the window, and slapped the glass, and cursed, and his final thought was that she also seemed quite annoyed about being left behind.

〜

'I can't just let him go now, Morse. He aided and abetted a fugitive. A traitor to the country.'

'Piss off, Cavil. He knew nothing. He found out today.'

Cavil shrugged. 'He'll have a hard time proving that. Now sit tight.'

The goon jammed the gun harder into Emil's side.

The chopper rose, began to turn. In the light cast by the instrument panel, Emil and Cavil watched each other in the windscreen, and beyond their glass faces the pattern of the house washed by.

'Guess you should have killed me, Morse.'

The chopper rose towards the top of the house, and the glass of windows flashed by, and the brickworks flickered by, top to bottom, and the dark sky came into view like a black blind rolling down, and their faces were defined in the glass of the windscreen even more clearly, eyes locked, but knitted into that black sheet was a humanoid shape on the roof, clad in red, staring at them, pointing something at them, but they saw it only for a half-second before the glass fragmented.

Capucine fired hard and fast with her pistol, three, four times, each bullet jerking the pilot in his seat, until the last split his helmet and rocked his head back. He toppled left, and the chopper jerked that way like a boxer's head rolling with a punch. Like a pair of images in a slideshow, the sky skipped aside and grassy ground filled the windscreen.

At the last moment, Emil had pulled Pete into him and turned his own back towards the front of the chopper, and it had saved them both. But the impact of two bodies fired at him hadn't done the goon sitting opposite them any favours. His bleeding head hung forward at a bizarre angle, one ear against his collarbone. The neck had gone, and with it all communication between brain and other organs. Luckily he would sleep through his final few minutes.

The crash had twisted and ruptured the carbon fibre body panels, shrinking and warping the interior of the chopper. The door was hanging open and Emil pushed his dazed son towards it. Pete stumbled and fell out, but the drop was short because the chopper's skids had collapsed upon impact with the ground.

Once Emil was also clear, he hauled Pete upright. 'Get going, Boyo. Run and don't stop.'

But Pete refused to move, or couldn't, and needed a heavy shove to get his rubbery legs working. He staggered about fifteen feet beyond the end of the chopper's tail boom, which had snapped and was angled down to the ground, but stopped when he realised his father wasn't following.

'Dad, come on.'

But Emil wasn't ready to flee just yet. He yanked open Cavil's door. Having taken the facedown smash worse, the former MI6 handler was suffering. His nose was busted, one lip torn, both leaking blood, and his left leg had been crushed against his seat when the entire nose of the chopper had crumpled inwards. But the majority of the instrument panel had been shunted towards the pilot, so Cavil had been lucky to avoid becoming fatality number three.

Cavil was breathing fast, clearly disoriented and in pain, although his eyes were clear enough to display anger directed at Emil. But Emil's own eyes didn't catch this, because they flicked up and over his former boss's head. Through cracked plexiglass in the misshapen side window he saw a woman in a red dress exit the manor house at a run. With a handgun. Capucine.

Bullets started to ping off the chopper. Emil again yelled for Pete to run, then he grabbed Cavil's arm. He drove a hard boot hard into the instrument panel, jerking it momentarily away from Cavil's trapped leg enough to allow movement. After four mighty kicks, Cavil was free, and both men collapsed to the grass. Cavil screamed as his bad leg twisted.

Emil bent down to hoist him up, like a groom carrying a bride, but upon his first step his own legs failed him. Again both men hit the ground. Emil scrambled to his feet. Cavil moaned for help, but Emil didn't move. It was too late.

Capucine walked into view around the chopper's angled tail boom, cutting off his view of Pete, who had his hands up. One of her hands tried to spin the tail rotor, but it was frozen. The other aimed a pistol. The barrel pointed at one man in particular.

'Handyman,' she said. 'I dream this moment. Why did you think you will escape me?'

Beyond her, Pete lowered his hands.

'No,' Emil yelled. But not at Capucine. Beyond her, Pete ignored his father's order and took another step towards the armed woman.

'No indeed,' she said. 'At last I get to kill you. But first I show you what is like to see a loved one unbeautiful.'

She spun to face Pete just as he started to run at her, her pistol pointed right at him. Before Emil got chance to move, there was a gunshot.

Capucine jerked around, eyes and mouth wide in shock. A hole in her lower throat immediately leaked a sheet of blood that matched her dress, as if she'd added a modesty panel. She dropped the gun and fell to her knees, and beyond her, beyond Pete, Emil saw Sara leaning over a wall forty metres away. She must have exited the well and followed the path that didn't lead to the house.

And she'd reached the wall right where he'd dumped his rifle.

Capucine dropped her gun and collapsed onto her back, staring into the night sky. She was still alive, spitting blood, and her eyes watched as he approached. But he ignored her and rushed towards Pete. Beyond them, Sara dropped the rifle and clambered over the wall. Soon all three were hugging.

Emil softly pushed Sara away, so he could look into her eyes when he delivered the words that would rip her world apart. But he didn't get chance to speak. She saw something in his eyes and it caused her own to drop.

'I knew,' she said, her voice cracking. 'I just knew they were dead, somehow. Where are they?'

But again Emil didn't get chance to speak. Because there was another gunshot.

Emil turned, but he'd already realised he'd made a critical error. Cavil had crawled to Capucine and taken her gun. Now, that gun turned away from Capucine's blasted head and towards Emil.

36

———

'What are you doing?' Pete yelled. 'My dad just saved your life.'

Cavil ignored the boy. He spat out blood from his ruined upper lip. It mixed with Capucine's blood on the gun he still pointed at Emil. 'Aren't you curious how I found you, Morse?'

'Not really.'

'Someone here ran your prints to a police officer they had on their side. By a fluke of luck, he happened to be a guy I had on my side all those years ago, and he remembered, and he did the right thing.'

'Right thing? A police officer in league with Irish terrorists? Maybe someone should have a word with him about that.'

Cavil tried to stand, but his twice-injured leg refused. Masking the pain with a grin, he said, 'See, Morse? People's actions come back to bite them, even years later. Did you ever really believe you would get away from me forever? Really? Or were you always looking over your shoulder? I think I'd like the latter a lot.'

'I didn't care, Cavil. Don't you remember? *Amor fati.*'

Cavil laughed. 'Even now you accept your life as it is? After all the years of running and hiding, and standing here now with a gun pointed at you, you would change nothing? Surely you would have seen me dead as a baby boy to avoid this.'

'Maybe, in an alternate future, I would now have untold riches and limitless power. But I would not have my son. My boy is healthy and by my side and it's only because I did everything I did the way I did, when I did. So I accept everything. I accept Bosnia, and the shot I put in your leg, and I accept you and the gun you point, and whatever happens next.'

'Noble, Morse, very noble. I suspect you hope that I'll have the same outlook. Today, right now, I have my chance for revenge. Perhaps, in an alternate timeline where I killed you way back, I might have met a gruesome death by lion mauling or meteor strike. I think you hope that holding this gun on you now, *knowing* I won in the end, will be enough of a sweet-sailing ending to satisfy me. Well, we're about to find out.'

'Leave my dad alone!' Pete yelled. He tried to get between the two enemies, but Emil yanked him back.

'It's okay, Pete, Mr Cavil's not going to kill me. He's going to call the authorities in and co-ordinate the rescue of the hostages in the manor house, and the others in the hotel, and oversee the capture of a wanted man from The Hidden Gem up north. After he tells his story of getting a tip about a prison break and coming here to save the day, he'll be a hero. And why would he do anything to change that? *Amor fati.*'

The gun was still aimed at him. But it did not fire.

'She knows the truth,' Cavil said, indicating Sara. 'And your son. And you.'

'We'll say nothing. Too much to lose. You would come back for me. We'd have this conversation again, only the next time you wouldn't fall for it.'

Still the gun did not fire. Emil took Sara's hand. And like

that, holding his son and the prisoner escort officer, Emil started to back up.

They got one step, and then Cavil said, 'You're missing some logic. The nosey media will invade this place and dig into people's pasts, and they'll learn that one of the residents is a former MI6 agent who worked for the hero. Nothing I can do about that.'

'The local handyman of twenty years, a man worthy of such intense research? No one will be interested in me when they have you and your people and the terrorists to write about. And only DNA or fingerprints could tie Emil Torrance to a man called Morse, who died in Bosnia a quarter of a century ago – which is something you can definitely do something about. Oh, by the way, there's a satchel in the field, just over the wall by the main road, that might cause problems if found. You should send a man to dispose of that.'

Cavil shook his head, slowly, as if Morse had said something stupid. 'Won't work, Morse. The hostages. They will recall that their saviour looked more like you than me. Am I supposed to convince them that their fear and panic made them confused?'

'I was seen by friends, you're right. They saw a terrified old man running for his life. I'll be branded the village coward for some time.'

Emil took another step backwards. Cavil continued to aim the gun, but for a few seconds he said nothing. Emil's vision of a glorious path ahead of his former MI6 handler was proving stubborn to eject, clearly.

'So what do you want, Morse? A miraculous discovery that you were alive and well in Bosnia all along, perhaps working in an orphanage or something else mighty and noble? To get your name back, your life back? A medal? Newspaper headlines, maybe a Netflix documentary about your life? A bestselling autobiography?'

'My name is not Morse, it's Emil Torrance. Emil Torrance is just an invisible handyman who's never left Derbyshire, and never will. All he wants is for things to go back the way they were when he woke up this morning.' He looked at Pete, who was staring back. 'And he wants time with his boy, to tell a long story.'

He took another step with his son and Sara. And another. But the gun tracked them. It continued to do so until the darkness had taken them.

THE END

ACKNOWLEDGEMENTS

As always, thanks to all at Bloodhound team, especially Betsy, Fred, Tara, Clare and Heather. And all their authors, for the advice and the great reads. Although it's probably those great reads that caused the waistline issue.